THE GI

by I

*To my Dad.*
*"Don't make me get the spoon."*

*First edition in English 2021*

Cover Design by Coco Merwild
www.cjmerwild.com

Formatting and Book Design by Franziska Stern
www.coverdungeon.com
www.instagram.com/coverdungeonrabbit

Editing by Sarah Grace Liu
www.threefatesediting.com

Map Design by Brittany Czarnecki

Printed in the United States Of America.

ISBN: 9781662920752

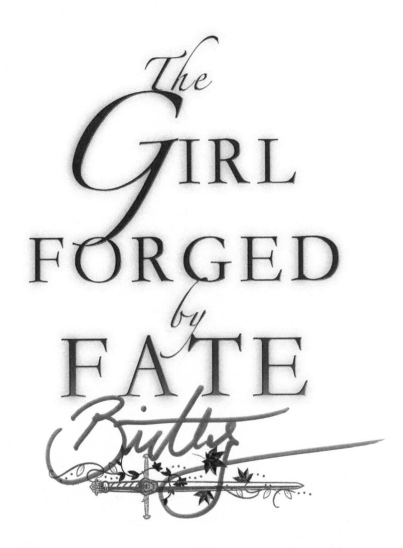

# The GIRL FORGED by FATE

BRITTANY CZARNECKI

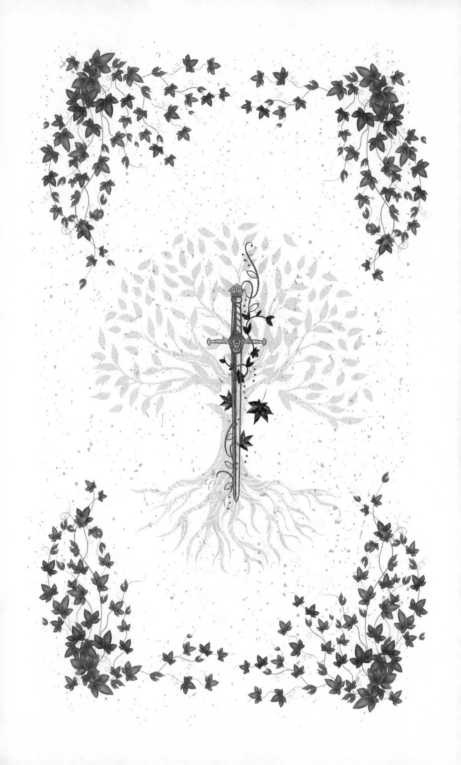

# PROLOGUE

Magnus wanted to go home.

The air was clouded with smoke and falling ash that obscured the cobalt blue of the autumn sky. Smoke seared the king's lungs as he breathed in the destruction that lay before him. Magnus imagined for one second that it might be snow—that this was all just a bad dream. As he held out a gloved hand to catch a flake in his palm, it didn't melt, and Magnus snapped back to reality. And then he heard it—the thunder of hooves. The raiders were coming back.

"Magnus-" a familiar voice called to him.

He kept his eyes on the horizon, waiting for the dreaded moment he'd spot their flag.

"Magnus," the voice called again. "Are you alright?"

Magnus finally turned to see his oldest friend, Helvarr, atop his stark white stallion. "Ah, there's our trusted king. Your orders?"

Helvarr had always been one for combat ever since they trained together as kids. Looking at his friend now, Magnus felt a shudder go through him. Helvarr's black hair looked even darker now, with the blood crusting at the tips of his beard and down the braid that hung over his armored back. His copper eyes were warm as if war and bloodshed gave him life; as if it set a fire within him. Helvarr patted his horse on the head and grinned. "I think Hella likes her new look." As if on cue, the horse whinnied and shook her now pink mane, sending a fine mist of blood into the air.

Magnus ignored him and turned back to the horizon, where the thundering hooves boomed even louder.

"They're coming back," Helvarr sing-songed.

"I know." Magnus sighed, running a hand through his wavy auburn hair.

"We've lost a lot of men," Helvarr pressed.

"I'm aware of that."

Helvarr narrowed his eyes. "Should we just stand here and let them run us down?" Magnus didn't answer. "They're getting closer—."

"Dammit, Helvarr, I know!"

His friend held up a hand in surrender and waited for orders.

Magnus sighed and spoke quietly. "Form up the remaining men and get a wall of archers at their backs."

Helvarr's lips curled into a crooked smile with the promise of more blood. As kids, Magnus had been more focused on becoming king of Godstone one day, but Helvarr always dreamed of being a knight. Though, he wasn't always good at taking orders. Magnus suspected that Helvarr was jealous, but Magnus never asked to be king. The Blackbourne's had been kings of Godstone for hundreds of years, and Magnus had been the only son of his father.

Now, Magnus watched as Helvarr shouted commands at the men to form up as the raiders started coming over the hill. "Archers!" Helvarr yelled. "Nock your arrows!" Magnus could see the shine of the raiders' armor, the knights in the front-line gleaming like new coins in the sun.

"Draw!" Helvarr commanded. "Hold!"

The raiders were closing in. The thunder of their horses' hooves was so loud it shook the very ground his men stood on.

Helvarr was practically shaking with anticipation as he shouted. "Loose!"

An enormous flock of arrows flew toward the sky, slicing through the smoky air like an eagle diving for fish. Some raiders fell from their horses, and the final thud of the dropping bodies was drowned by their cries of fury.

"Again!" Helvarr bellowed.

The archers stood their ground as the raiders closed in, taking aim and firing. Some of the horses didn't seem to realize they had a dead man in the saddle and continued to charge into battle alongside the others.

Magnus flexed his fingers, curling them around the hilt of his sword. It hung heavily at his side. Just thinking of lifting his sword again today physically drained Magnus, but he'd do what he had to for his kingdom. Taking a deep breath, Magnus lifted his sword in the air and held it.

Time seemed to slow as the raiders charged toward them, but all noise of the battle faded away until all Magnus could hear was his own rapid breathing and his wife's last words before he left: "Come back to us." He locked away that memory, then brought down his sword and watched his men burst to life. The chaos of the battle came tearing into that quiet place, but he let himself feel it as he kicked his horse and followed his men into the slaughter.

The two armies crashed into one another, sending men flying

over their horses or off the back as spears pierced clean through their armor. Magnus spotted Helvarr and followed his path, but was quickly cut off as his horse picked up speed.

Blocking the king was a knight clad in shadow and black armor, mounted on a stallion even darker. Muscle memory kicked in, and Magnus didn't hesitate to raise his sword. It crashed down just as the knight lifted his shield. The black knight swung his blade, forcing Magnus to throw himself down on his horse's back. He heard the whoosh of the sword as it sailed just above his face. Sitting up, Magnus raised his sword barely in time to block the knight's downward swing. Their blades kissed, sending sparks flying as Magnus struggled to keep the knight's sword from coming down.

They were close enough that Magnus could see the murder of crow's feet framing the knight's empty grey eyes. Just when the king thought his arms would fail him, a mist of hot blood burst from the knight's lips, covering Magnus. The raider dropped his sword, then swayed in his saddle before slumping over to reveal a spear buried in his back. Breathing heavily and wiping his face, Magnus searched the crowd just beyond the dead raider and saw Helvarr riding toward him.

"I had him," Magnus proclaimed, anger rising in his throat.

"Did you?" he mocked. "What sort of friend would I be if I let you return to your new wife with a scar?" He cocked his head and smiled, observing the king with mirth in his eyes.

"Though it may be an improvement," he winked before smacking Magnus with the side of his sword and riding off again. Magnus growled and let his narrowed eyes follow his friend into battle.

Helvarr always considered himself a better fighter because he slew more men, but the real difference was that he enjoyed it too much. Magnus was king. How would it look to his men if his best friend did all his killing for him on the battlefield? He shoved the thought from his head and charged on, thinking of all the men they had lost thus far and all the families he'd have to face when they returned to Godstone. *If* they returned.

The whizz of a flying arrow sliced through his thoughts, and Magnus felt the quick brush of the feathers against his cheek before the arrow embedded itself into a man's skull. Turning his horse, the king scanned the crowd to find the archer, then another arrow flew past just as Magnus's eyes locked on. He hissed as the arrowhead grazed his cheek. *So much for not going back with a scar.* Magnus tightened his grip on the reins and kicked his stallion, which charged straight to where the archer stood, nocking back another arrow. The rhythm of his heart matched his horse's steady gallop, but it slammed to a stop when the archer pulled back and fired again.

The bolt struck his horse in the neck, forcing a scream that tore up its throat as the horse reared back, throwing Magnus from the saddle. He hit the ground hard, the air knocked from his lungs as he scrambled to find his sword in the grass. Magnus looked up to the archer pulling another arrow from his quiver. Adrenaline fueled his muscles, coursing through his veins like a flash flood. He should've worn a helm or carried a shield, but Magnus had wanted his men to see him; he wanted the raiders to look in the eye of the king they fought against when he killed them.

Spotting his sword, Magnus crawled for it, staying low to the ground. As he grabbed the hilt, he wondered how something that had become an extension of himself could also weigh him down. The king rose to see the archer drawing his arrow, but it was too late to move. The snap of the bowstring was so final that Magnus closed his eyes, picturing the son he had yet to meet. He wondered whether he'd have Magnus's dark auburn hair or his mother's golden curls-if his eyes would be the signature Blackbourne purple.

When Magnus felt no pain, he opened his eyes to see that one of his men had run in the path of the arrow, who now lay writhing in pain. A few men came to his aid, snapping the head of the arrow off from where it protruded on his thigh. Magnus took off in a sprint toward the archer, who tried to draw an arrow from his quiver in a panic—but his hands wouldn't obey him. Instead, he threw down his bow and drew a dagger from his belt, but he wasn't quick enough; Magnus was on him, grabbing the man's wrist with a grip that made the archer shriek and drop his knife. Magnus thrusted his sword up through the archer's stomach, watched his eyes go wide, then flutter. Magnus ripped his sword free, and the archer fell dead.

Magnus sat atop a hill, observing the aftermath of the battle. The small town of Ashton was lost along with many of its residents. Most of the raiders had been killed, though his men did manage to capture a few knights who tried to flee. It was no comfort to Magnus. He knew that there would be more. There was always more.

They claimed to be fighting for the one Supreme God. Although Magnus didn't know who led them, he did know their leader was of flesh and blood. The North had a long, violent history with the South, with countless wars going back hundreds of years. Magnus's ancestors had been refugees that escaped the South during a time of civil war. Those refugees decided to settle on the black beaches of Godstone.

"Your Grace," Ser Osmund called, guiding his horse toward Magnus.

Ser Osmund was one of the best knights in the kingdom. He was older than Magnus and many of the other knights, and he had many battles under his belt.

As he drew near, Magnus saw that he was injured. A blood-soaked rag was wound tight around his left shoulder.

"Your Grace," Ser Osmund repeated as he drew his horse to a halt.

"Helvarr is—"

"What happened to your shoulder?" Magnus interrupted. Ser Osmund looked down as though he'd forgotten the injury. "Ah." He waved a dismissive hand. "It's nothing. It will take a lot more than this to take me down."

Magnus opened his mouth to speak again, but Ser Osmund interrupted. "Pardon, Your Grace," he urged, "but Helvarr is beating one of the captured knights down by the stables."

"What?" Magnus growled. "He knows we need those men for questioning."

Ser Osmund looked irritated as well. "I tried to tell him, but... you know him better than any. That boy will listen to no one."

Ser Osmund had been a young knight when Magnus and Helvarr were just boys, and he'd often been present during their training. Magnus could still remember Ser Osmund's words to their trainer: *"A boy shouldn't fight with so much anger when he lacks the discipline to control it."*

Magnus kicked his horse as he rode down the hill in a fury toward the burnt village. He didn't want to discipline Helvarr in front of the other knights, but Magnus was left with no choice. Many times, their friendship had saved Helvarr from punishable offenses.

Too many.

He could see a crowd gathered around the captives, with Helvarr in the middle, hovering over a knight who was on his hands and knees. Magnus swung down from his horse and stormed across the muddy street to where the crowd stood. He shoved his men aside to get through, and others moved out of his path when they saw their king.

"Helvarr!" he shouted. His friend turned, wearing a smile. His knuckles were bright with fresh blood, and the sight of him made Magnus stop in his tracks. "What do you think you're doing?"

"I was questioning our captives as you wished," Helvarr replied with a grin and a mocking bow. Magnus looked to the knight on the ground. The man had a broken nose and a gash above his right brow where blood trickled down into his swollen eye.

He snapped his eyes back to Helvarr. "I said to question them, not beat them," he spoke through gritted teeth. "How will they talk if they're unconscious?" His anger was rising, and his next words came out sharply. "You never think before you act, Helvarr!" Helvarr almost looked sorry.

Almost.

"I apologize if I've displeased you... *Your Grace.*" He was a great actor; that much was certain. He frequently made Magnus out to be the bad guy, and though Magnus knew he was being manipulated, he was still filled with guilt at the thought of punishing his oldest friend.

"He's had enough," Magnus insisted.

"My friend," Helvarr started, "I was just starting to—"

"I am your king!" Magnus exploded. "And you will not question me in front of my own men." Helvarr took a step back; his eyes grew wide. Magnus had never yelled at him in front of the other knights before, but he'd tried Magnus's patience for the last time.

Magnus turned to the bloody raider. "What's your name, Ser?" he asked. The knight stood to look the king in the eye.

"Ser William... *Your Grace,*" he added with as much sarcasm as he could muster.

"And who gives your orders?"

He lifted his chin. "Ser Cumber leads this army."

Magnus leaned in. "And who does Ser Cumber take orders from?" The knight didn't answer. He stood there smirking, then shot a look to Helvarr, which only enraged Helvarr even more.

"He's toying with us!" Helvarr snapped as he stepped toward the knight.

Magnus placed a restraining hand on Helvarr's chest. "Bring the others," the king commanded.

Two men from the crowd hurried to bring the other four captured knights forward. They still had their helms on, their hand bound behind their backs. Magnus went down the line and started to remove their helms one by one. As he removed the last helm, long auburn hair fell loose. It was a girl.

"What's your name, my lady?" Magnus asked curiously.

"Roeana," she answered coldly, "but you may call me Roe."

"Lady Roe, can you tell me who commands Ser Cumber?"

Magnus studied her. She had hair the color of copper that fell past her shoulders. Her eyes were forest green, and her lips a soft pink. She was beautiful, but she couldn't be more than fifteen years old.

Magnus knew other kingdoms had female knights, but it was rare, especially for one so young. Not many girls were lining up to become knights. Most would rather be married and swept off to a castle than go to war. Magnus had been king for only two years, and he inherited his father's knights. They mostly consisted of grown men, some twice his age. Perhaps he would seek to recruit some female warriors when he returned home.

Magnus was so consumed by this girl that he didn't notice Helvarr storming up to them.

He cracked Lady Roe across the cheek hard, sending blood flying from her mouth. Helvarr came at her again, but Magnus shoved his friend aside.

"They won't give us answers willingly, Magnus!" Helvarr yelled. "Don't treat her differently because of what she has between her legs!"

"Stand down, Helvarr!"

Magnus moved to start untying the ropes that bound the other knights.

"What are you doing?" Helvarr exclaimed.

Magnus ignored him, working at the ropes with shaky hands, surging with anger. "Ser Osmund," he called over his shoulder. The knight came through the crowd to stand before his king, gray beard blowing in the breeze. "You'll gather ten men of your choice and escort these knights as far as you see fit. You'll return their weapons to them and make sure they continue on their path south, is that understood?" Without question, Ser Osmund moved to obey.

"What?" Helvarr snarled. "You're letting them go?"

Helvarr was fuming, but Magnus knew if the knights were kept for questioning, they'd only be slaughtered. He'd had enough bloodshed for one day. He turned back to Ser William. "You'll go back from where you came and tell your leader that you were defeated. You will preach to him of how merciful I was, allowing his knights to return home safely."

Ser William considered, saying nothing. Finally, his lips curled into a sneer, and he half bowed toward the king.

"No." Helvarr drew his sword. "I won't allow you to set them free without getting the answers we need." Magnus turned to face his friend, furrowing his brow.

"You won't *allow* me?" Magnus cocked his head to one side. "Have you forgotten your place?"

"If you don't have the guts to do what needs to be done, then stand aside...*my king*."

Magnus was taken aback. Helvarr had never spoken to Magnus with such disrespect before, especially not in front of his own men. Helvarr lowered his voice to a growl and bared his teeth. "I said, stand aside Magnus, or I'll cut you down." The words echoed in Magnus's head, growing louder every time.

Magnus looked to his men, who watched with wide eyes, waiting. What other choice did Magnus have? If he let this pass, his men wouldn't respect him. Rumors would spread of a weak king. His reign had just begun, and he needed to earn the respect his father had commanded.

Despite the chilly autumn weather, Magnus felt sweat running down his back. With a heavy heart, he drew his sword on the only brother he ever knew. The captured knights backed away into the circle of men, looking shocked at the event unfolding.

"I'll give you one last chance, Helvarr." Magnus's face remained stern, but he begged with his eyes for Helvarr to see that he was forcing his hand. "Stand down."

But Magnus knew the answer before he finished speaking. Helvarr would never yield. He couldn't go back on what he said, not without injuring his pride. "And are you going to stop me?" Helvarr mocked.

"You've left me with no other choice."

Helvarr glanced toward where Lady Roe stood in the crowd and lunged at her. He was as quick as a viper striking its prey. Magnus shifted on the balls of his feet to block his path, but Helvarr threw up his sword and sent it sweeping just overhead, the king ducking only in time.

It was a warning.

Magnus lifted his sword to block the violent attacks; Helvarr was coming at him with everything. It was how he always fought, fueled with anger and adrenaline.

The crash of steel rang in his ears as he blocked blow after blow. Helvarr's sword came down as Magnus sidestepped out of its path, swinging with his free hand to land a punch to the jaw. Staggering back, Helvarr spun and whirled his blade, just missing the king's throat. They came together in a crash, sending sparks flying as their blades slid over one another. Helvarr head-butted him through their crossed swords, and as Magnus stumbled back, Helvarr threw down his sword and came charging.

He plowed into Magnus, knocking them both to the ground and sending the king's sword flying. Magnus grunted and gasped for air as his back slammed into the ground. A few knights started to go to their king's rescue, but Ser Osmund gave them a stern look, and they backed off.

Helvarr had Magnus pinned to the ground and landed a punch that filled his eyes with stars. He reared back for another blow, but Magnus moved his head just in time and Helvarr's fist pounded the muddy earth beside his ear. Magnus returned the headbutt and kneed Helvarr in the ribs, then threw him to one side and watched him spit out a bloody tooth before pulling a dagger from his boot. Magnus was ready for him this time. Helvarr staggered to his feet and charged, but one of his boots got stuck in the mud giving Magnus an opening.

He charged forward, nearly losing an ear on the blade as he grabbed the hand that tried to slice him. He twisted until Helvarr cried out in pain and dropped the dagger. Kicking it away, Magnus threw his arm back and elbowed Helvarr in the nose, breaking it. Helvarr dropped to one knee, clutching his broken nose while Magnus paced, trying to catch his breath. His head was a raging storm of thoughts, and his heart pounded so loudly in his chest he thought it might explode. Magnus couldn't let this go unpunished; he knew that, but it did little to ease the pain of what he was about to do. The king stopped before his friend, fists balled at his sides to keep them from shaking.

"Enough of this," he breathed, defeat hanging in his voice. "You've had too many chances." Magnus felt a knot form in his throat, but he forced himself to continue, all too aware of the eyes on him. Swallowing the knot, he said, "Saddle your horse and leave."

Helvarr stood, his cold copper eyes showing signs of concern, a rare sight. "I don't understand...Magnus...I-."

"Save your apologies," Magnus snapped. "I've heard enough of them to last a lifetime. You've disobeyed me for the last time. You've insulted me for the last time." Magnus drew in a shaky breath, trying yet failing to compose himself. He felt sick to his stomach, and his next words tasted like ash on his tongue. "Helvarr Rassman, you are hereby banished from Godstone and all my allied lands."

His heart dropped to his stomach as he watched Helvarr sink back down into the mud. He'd never seen Helvarr look so defeated.

"No," Helvarr muttered. "Magnus...brother, please don't do this—"

"You did this!" Magnus exploded. "You've never treated me as your king, and you've abused our friendship more than I should've allowed because of my love for you!" Tears threatened to fall, but he snapped his eyes shut, shaking his head. "But no more," he continued. "You've forced my hand; this is your own doing." Magnus forced himself to look into Helvarr's eyes, making his face as stern as he could as the lie he spoke next slipped between his lips. "And you are not my brother. Mount your horse and leave."

Helvarr rose to his feet to stand face-to-face with Magnus. If there was any sadness within Helvarr, it quickly vanished, replaced with a wave of burning rage. His crooked smirk was already returning to his lips, and Magnus fought to keep a stern look as he watched his friend's mask slip back into place. Helvarr cocked his head, taking a half bow. "As my king commands." Helvarr snatched up his sword and stormed off toward the stables, men shuffling from his path as he passed.

Magnus felt a pain so deep in his heart, he feared it would stop working altogether. He'd cast out the only brother he'd ever had. Already, Magnus knew it was the wrong choice. His men seemed hesitant to look at their king. They turned to leave the circle, suddenly finding their muddy boots to be interesting. Magnus hung his head as well, making his way toward the raiders who were to be set free. He could still do something right. He believed in sparing lives where it could be afforded, and he wouldn't allow the raiders to be slaughtered after being captured. He looked up to see Lady Roe standing with her fellow knights when something moved behind them.

Helvarr sat mounted in the distance on his horse behind the captives, clutching a bow in his hand. Everything happened so fast. The king felt his stomach churn as Helvarr drew back the bowstring and let go. Before Magnus could even open his mouth to yell, the arrow ripped through Lady Roe's throat, jerking her whole body forward. He ran to catch her as she fell, both of them collapsing to the ground as blood spurted from her lips. Those beautiful green eyes of hers faded, swallowed up by the blackness of death.

When Magnus looked back up, Helvarr was gone. Ser Osmund rushed to the king's side, but Magnus couldn't hear anything the knight was saying. A dull ringing sounded in his ears as he looked at the dead girl in his arms. It was his fault, and her blood would forever stain his hands. What if this had been his daughter?

Laying her gently on the ground, Magnus stood and vowed to himself never to have female knights in his kingdom, not after he led this one to an early grave.

"Your Grace," Ser Osmund said gently. "Should we go after him?" Magnus thought for a moment, staring out to the barren hill.

"No," he answered. "We've fed the ravens enough today."

Magnus turned around, looking at the carnage of the battlefield. Ravens and vultures were already circling above, choosing which body they wished to feast on. Focusing on the sound of the leaves whispering in the wind, Magnus took in a steady breath and turned to face Ser Osmund. "Rally our men. We're leaving."

"What about the raiders?"

"Let them go. They're on their own."

"Of course, Your Grace. Where shall I tell the men we're going?"

Magnus's gaze drifted north, though his broken heart was being pulled south where Helvarr was riding farther from him, from everything he'd ever known. He started walking to his horse, fearing he'd stand trapped in that moment forever if he didn't move.

"Home, Ser Osmund," he said over his shoulder. "We're going home."

# CHAPTER ONE

# IVY

**Nineteen years later**

The wind picked up, blowing dead leaves across the thin layer of snow that dusted the frozen ground. It was too loud to walk on, so Ivy stayed up in the trees using the snow-filled branches as cover. She maneuvered through the trees, using the larger limbs, careful not to knock any snow from the smaller branches. Ivy could hear him coming; the crunching of leaves underfoot gave away his position. Tightening the grip around the hilt of her sword, she spotted the knight just as he came into view.

Ivy smiled as he swept his eyes over the ground, looking for her tracks. His long white beard was braided as usual and swung gently over his breastplate. Tucked in the knight's belt next to his sword was the golden silk scarf that Ivy's father had given her. The knight was getting closer, and Ivy knew she only had one chance. She slowed her breathing, crouched down on the branch, and let go.

Ivy landed silently behind the knight, jabbing her sword forward and landing it in the middle of his back. He grunted as he turned, swinging his blade just above Ivy's head. The metal whistled through the cold, still winter air. She twirled around him and sliced at the back of his ankles, her sword screeching against his armor. Locking her eyes on the scarf, Ivy lunged for it, staying low. The knight brought his sword down, forcing Ivy to throw hers up to block. She reached for the scarf again with her right hand, but he shoved her away, forcing her to stumble back. The knight swung his sword in a flurry, yet Ivy ducked and slid out of its path with ease, the blade never touching her.

The knight was breathing heavily by now, yet he continued to pursue her. Ivy took a step back with every blow that came her way, leading him farther into the trees. The knight's sword came down on her left side, but Ivy stepped out of its path, reached up, and tugged on a branch. A dense wall of snow came crashing down on the knight, giving Ivy an opening. She quickly stepped toward him, ducking under his swinging arms, and snatched her scarf from his belt. The knight shook off the snow and turned to see Ivy's sword at his throat, her free hand holding the golden scarf. The knight stared at her for a moment, then cracked a smile and started to chuckle.

"Well done, my lady!" Ser Osmund exclaimed. "You're getting better."

Ivy had been training with Ser Osmund since she was nine years old, and it had been a long eight years since. Her father didn't approve of it at first, but Ivy had fought with her brother so many times that her mother finally convinced him. "*She's going to do it anyway. She might as well learn to wield a sword properly,*" her mother had argued. Though he was still hesitant, her father finally gave his consent and asked Ser Osmund to train her.

"We should be getting back, my lady. We don't want to miss supper," Ser Osmund said. Ivy tucked the scarf into her belt, and they began their walk back to the castle. The scarf was part of a game they played to help Ivy with her training. Every day Ser Osmund would walk around with it tucked in his belt, and her goal was to get it from him without being touched by his sword.

"When can I have a real sword?" Ivy asked as she looked over the practice blade in her hands. "That would be up to your father," Ser Osmund answered. "Perhaps you should talk to him when he returns."

"But Rayner has a sword already, and he's only two years older than me," Ivy argued. "I'm ready, and I'm not a child anymore."

Ser Osmund stopped and turned to her. "Lady Ivy, you don't need to convince me of your skills. Rayner has a sword because he's your father's heir and almost a man grown. Did you think he would accompany your father south with a practice sword? I would speak to your father on your behalf, but you know the king's rules about female knights. You should count yourself lucky that you're allowed to train at all."

Ivy scrunched up her nose, "That's a bullshit rule, and you know it."

Ser Osmund sighed, "Ivy—"

"Do you think I could be a knight?" she interrupted, hope shining in her purple eyes. Ser Osmund smiled, placing a hand on her shoulder. "I would sooner see you knighted than many of the young men in Godstone."

She smirked. "Even Rayner?"

"Now, Ivy," Ser Osmund warned. "You know I can't choose favorites between you and your brother." Ivy crossed her arms over her chest, raising a brow at the lie. Ser Osmund chuckled and winked, then nodded in the direction of the castle. "Come on, it's getting dark."

Ivy fell in step with the knight as her mind drifted. She'd always wanted to become a knight and fight alongside her father and brother, but the kingdom's rules kept her from doing so.

Whenever Ivy asked her father about the rules, he would brush her off or offer reasons that didn't make sense to her. As a child, Ivy would devour any book that mentioned female warriors and dream of her name scrolled across that page next to theirs.

Ivy could see the silhouette of the castle rising over the hill, its black walls heavy against the orange sunset. Godstone sat in the middle of what seemed like four worlds to Ivy. To the east was the Shadow Sea surrounded by black cliffs, the beach covered with even darker sand. To the north lay snow-capped mountains going all the way to the edge of the world. West of Godstone was the Blackwood Forest, where Ivy liked to train with Ser Osmund. To the south lay miles and miles of grasslands, as far as the eye could see.

Ivy had only traveled as far as Grey Raven Castle, which lay about forty-five leagues northwest. Grey Raven was home to House Reiburn, her father's longtime bannermen and allies, ruled by Lady Oharra Reiburn, who inherited the seat after her brother died. The woman was a warrior, ruler, archer, hunter, and the most beautiful in her kingdom. Ivy envied her. Ivy would never be any of those things if she stayed in Godstone her whole life.

They were almost back at the castle walls when Ivy heard the pounding of hooves behind her. They both turned to look at the coming horsemen, and Ivy could see banners, but they were too far away to make out. Her father had only left a week ago and shouldn't be back for another few days. The sky was growing dark, but Ivy spotted something light soaring above. The bird came lower, its long white tail trailing behind it like a banner.

It was Luna, her father's bird.

Ivy took off in a sprint toward the gates. "Ivy! Wait!" Ser Osmund yelled, but she kept going. As she ran closer, she could make out her father's banner, a Blackwood tree encircled by its own roots set against a white field. She could also see her father's bannermen flying their house flags. House Reiburn flew two ravens circling a sword on a black field, and House Daemont flew the Twisted Tower on a field of red.

The gates flew open as the riders raced for the castle. Ivy reached the gate, out of breath, and started scanning the incoming knights for her father and brother. She could see that many of the knights had bandages wrapped around bloody wounds, and some had to be towed in wagons, while others looked as though they might fall off their horses. Her father had gone south with his bannermen to help the village of Ashton build defenses against the southern raiders, who had completely destroyed it nineteen years ago. Ivy knew the North had been fighting with southern cities since long before she was born, though there had been periods of peace as well, but this looked like war.

The central square inside the gates was a sea of knights. The commotion brought citizens to their balconies, and vendors from the market to see what was happening. Ivy snaked her way through the mounted horsemen, feeling nervous though she didn't know why. She spotted Magister Ivann and began frantically pushing men aside. "Move!" she shouted.

"What the—" One knight said, then bit his tongue and stepped aside when he realized who he was talking to. Ivy could hear yelling from where the magister stood, and as she drew near, Ivy saw that he was wrapping a cloth around a man's head. The last of the knights shouted at others to make way as Ivy stepped through the crowd, but her heart dropped to her stomach when she saw who the magister was tending to. It was her older brother Rayner lying on the ground, bleeding from a wound on his head.

Panic rushed through her veins. "Rayner!" Ivy cried as she ran forward, but she didn't get two steps before a strong hand grabbed hold of her arm "Ivy, no!" King Magnus stepped in front of her, trying to block the view of her brother. "You don't need to see this. He'll be alright," he said, though even he didn't sound convinced. Magnus let go, and Ivy looked into his eyes, trying to find the truth of what had happened, but her eyes drifted to the blood crusting in his auburn hair, and the lines of worry streaked across his brow. He looked tired and beaten, and that's when Ivy noticed the spray of blood covering his armor. "Father," she reached up a hand to touch his chest plate. "Are you—"

"It's not my blood." Magnus cut her off, taking her hand in his. "Ivy, I need you to find your mother and bring her to Magister Ivann's room." She hesitated, peering around her father's shoulder, but Rayner was already being carried away.

"Please," Magnus urged. Ivy nodded, and her father forced a smile as he bent down and kissed her temple. "It's going to be alright, sweetling," he whispered. Ivy nodded, and Magnus stood up tall, taking on the role of the king once more and shouting orders to his men.

Though he stood tall and strong, Ivy could see the weight that role put on his shoulders. She just wished she could take some of it for him.

# CHAPTER TWO

# THE KING'S COUNCIL

L ater that night, after Rayner and the other wounded had been cared for, Ivy's father held a meeting in the Great Hall with all his bannermen. The Great Hall was where King Magnus held feasts most nights and special gatherings for holidays. It was built from massive logs stacked as high as the third story of the central tower, where Ivy and her family lived. The tower was constructed from black stones that were gathered from the cliffs of Onyx Cover at the eastern edge of town. Carved with immense care on the Great Hall's door the Four Gods stood guarding the entrance.

Ivy had been told to stay in her bedchamber for the night, but instead, she climbed out her window. There was a massive maple tree outside her chambers that stretched its thick arms over the roof of the hall. Ivy carefully made her way through the tree, out onto a branch.

Perching just above the star window in the roof of the Great Hall, Ivy could see her father sitting in his place atop the dais. The king's throne was made of Blackwood tree. They only grew in the Blackwood Forest just outside the gates of Godstone.

Blackwood trees grew tall, twisting from the base of the trunk up to the highest branches. The tree used for her father's throne had been cut from the bottom up to the lowest branches, giving the throne a height of three meters. The dark-wood throne stood like a shadow hovering over the Hall, with its twisted fingers reaching out over the dais. Oil lanterns hung from the twisted branches, making the shadows dance to the rhythm of the flame. Among the shadowed branches sat her father's snow-white bird, Luna. She was always close to her king.

Seated on either side of the king were the leaders of the other two houses. Lady Oharra Reiburn wore a long wool dress the color of smoke. Green emeralds hung loosely from her neck, and an iron raven clasp held her fox fur cloak. She had black hair that fell straight past her shoulders and bangs that shadowed her eyes. On her hip, she wore her sword, which she appropriately named Nightmare. To the other side sat Lord Kevan Daemont, still dressed in his black armor, covering a moss green tunic. On his chestplate, just below his blond beard, was a gold medallion in the shape of the Twisted Tower, symbolizing his house.

Ivy quietly lowered herself down onto the roof for a better view. She could hear men inside arguing about the battle that had taken place. Everyone was shouting over one another.

"If you had come earlier!" one man shouted.

"The scouts should've seen something!" another yelled.

Ivy was struggling to keep up with all the voices flying around the Hall when she heard the thunder of her father's voice. "Enough!" The king stood abruptly. "We won't sit here and cast blame on each other. Lord Kevan and his men came when they could. We were ambushed and outnumbered. Even with his men, we couldn't hope to defeat them."

The men stood silent now, waiting for their king to speak again. Magnus stood at the long, wooden table in front of his throne. He unrolled a map and started scanning, looking for answers on the piece of cloth. The map showed the land on which they lived, a red line separating the North and South.

"Here," Magnus pointed. "Temple City lays just twenty-five leagues from the town of Moore. The city is neutral in the on-going war, and they've been known to take in southern raiders and northern houses alike. That's our best chance at finding the raiders we encountered on the Thunder Trail."

"Are you mad?" Lord Kevan exclaimed. "You said yourself that we don't have enough men to fight them."

Lord Kevan was never one to take risks, not when it concerned his men or his own well-being. His castle lay to the west at the base of the Spearhead Mountain range.

The Lord of the Twisted Tower always believed that the hard terrain alone would keep him out of the war. The mountains were treacherous and prone to avalanches. To get to the Twisted Tower, one would have to brave the Spearhead Mountains or go east around them, which was all grasslands with nowhere to hide. Even though the southern raiders had been attacking towns in the North for years, they'd never gone so far as to go against the castle.

That was until a few months ago when Lord Kevan spotted smoke rising outside his walls. He'd run to one of the watch-towers and saw the whole field ahead of his castle on fire. Just beyond the flames, he'd spotted raiders flying their flag. It was red with two black swords crossed at the hilt and a black raven spread out above. The burning of the field was meant as a warning.

Their message was clear. The raiders didn't need to ambush the castle because they already had enough men to take it by force. Only then did Lord Kevan understand the severity of the problem because now it concerned his own survival.

Lady Oharra walked around the table, studying the map. "Your Grace," she finally said.

"Why not send a messenger hawk to King Cenric at Kaspin's Keep?"

Magnus could feel her eyes on him as he considered.

"Look," she said, pointing at the map, "Kaspin's Keep is the closest kingdom to Temple City. Surely the king will offer his help once he understands what happened."

Magnus sighed. "My lady, Cenric Forde isn't the most giving king. Some years ago, I asked if he would provide me with an escort on a tracking mission to the South. Kaspin's Keep has a large army and plenty of men to spare. Instead, he sent back my hawk with a message denying my request and told me to *keep my problems on my side of the North.* We'll receive no help from King Cenric in this matter." Magnus could feel Lady Oharra's eyes still watching him. Her eyes never gave away what she thought. Perhaps that was why she never wore a helm into battle, though neither did the king and many other seasoned knights. The lady could look a man right in the eyes, and he would still never see his death coming.

"Perhaps we should look farther North then," Lady Oharra

offered. Magnus often looked to her for guidance in matters involving the battle for the North. The lady was renowned in the North as a fearsome warrior. Grey Raven Castle had been sworn to House Blackbourne for generations. When Lady Oharra's father died, his only son, Lord Asher, took over.

The late Lord Asher was a kind and gentle lord, much like his father. He often sent his sister to lead his army and serve as his counselor of war. He always had more interest in books and history; yet, when the raiders came to his castle, Lord Asher was forced to act. He rounded up his army with his sister in the lead and attempted to drive off the threat. The battle lasted a day and a night, leaving both sides with hundreds dead. In the end, Grey Raven won the battle but lost their ruler. Lord Asher was found on the battlefield with an arrow through his heart, leaving Lady Oharra as the only living heir.

Men said that when the lady saw her dead brother, she screamed so loudly it sent horses scattering in every direction. Magnus remembered going to the ceremony. He'd never seen the lady so broken before. Thousands gathered at the Lake of the Dead to see the great lord float to his underwater grave.

Lady Oharra was the one to shoot the flaming arrow, lighting the boat that carried her older brother to the afterlife. The next day she was sworn into service, and her first order as ruler was to hang the two guards that were meant to keep her brother safe on the battlefield. Their bodies hung on the walls of the city until the ravens had picked every bite of flesh from their bones. Magnus said nothing of it. He knew people grieved in different ways. After Lady Oharra had properly mourned her brother, she came to visit Magnus to assure the king that she would do her brother proud and defeat their common enemy.

"Earl Rorik of Tordenfall," Lady Oharra continued, bringing Magnus back to reality. "Perhaps we should look for assistance from him. The earl has a large army, and he's a friend to your kingdom, isn't he?"

"Yes, he's an old friend," Magnus admitted. "But he's not my sworn bannerman as you are. Earl Rorik owes me nothing, and to ask so much of him would be unfair. The northern clans swear to no houses, and they take no part in this war. Why should he offer his help?"

"Because he's your friend, sworn or not. And whether he takes part in this war is inevitable. Sooner or later, the raiders will get past Godstone, and the next settlement is Tordenfall. If Earl Rorik was faced with the same situation, do you think he would send his men to die in battle, knowing he was outnumbered? Or do you think he would ask an old friend for help?" Lady Oharra had always been direct. That was one reason Magnus put her on the council.

Magnus looked to Lord Kevan, "What's your opinion?" Lord Kevan looked from the king to Lady Oharra, stroking his beard while he considered the plan. Finally, he said, "I think it's worth trying, Your Grace. If the lady believes Earl Rorik would help, then I say we send a hawk. Otherwise, we have no chance of defeating the raiders. If they are, in fact, hiding out in Temple City, that will prove to be difficult. There's no fighting within the city. So, our men would need to lure them outside city walls if we have any hope of driving them back over the border." The men in the hall started shaking their heads in approval. Magnus approved as well.

"It's settled then," the king declared. "I'll send a hawk tomorrow to Earl Rorik."

Lady Oharra then suggested that Magnus invite the earl and his men to Godstone instead. "The Feast of Winter is almost upon us," she said. "The earl would surely accept an invitation to celebrate with you here. You can speak to him about the matter in person. And, should he accept, then he's already here, and we can set off for Temple City after the celebration."

Magnus agreed and invited Lord Kevan and Lady Oharra to stay for the celebration as well. Godstone had plenty of inns to hold most of their people, and the rest could set up camp on the beaches or outside the walls. Lady Oharra and Lord Kevan would reside in the king's tower for their stay.

By the time the meeting was over, Ivy was half-frozen on the roof. She watched the Hall as it emptied, men and women going to find an empty room in one of the inns. Her father was the last to leave the Hall. Ivy slowly stood up and stretched her arms overhead, letting out a silent yawn. Her left leg was asleep, and she flexed, trying to get some feeling back into her toes. Her movement loosened some snow from the roof and sent it sliding down to disappear over the edge. She heard the *plop* as it hit the ground.

"Shit," she hissed under her breath before lifting herself back into the tree and making her way to her bed-chamber window. Ivy climbed in and shook the snow from her boots, then put them near the hearth to dry out.

Just as she climbed under her furs, Ivy heard footsteps coming down the hall. She rolled over as her chamber door opened, and soft footsteps came toward her, stopping at the edge of her bed. She turned back over to see her father.

"I didn't mean to wake you, sweetling," her father said as he laid a hand on her shoulder.

Ivy sat up and rubbed at her eyes. "I couldn't sleep anyway," she lied.

Magnus looked into her pale purple eyes and grinned. "Well," he started, "Perhaps if you'd been in bed and not spying on the roof of the Hall...." Her father narrowed his eyes but never lost his smile.

"How did you know?"

"Well, it could be the pile of snow that nearly missed me after I left the Hall, or the pool of water under your window."

Ivy tried to hide her smile, but her father saw it and chuckled at her attempt.

"Since you're all caught up with me, why not tell me of your day?"

Ivy told him of her time training with Ser Osmund. When she mentioned dropping snow on Ser Osmund's head, her father chuckled with delight at the image. But when she asked him about getting a real sword, he stopped laughing.

Magnus sighed and ran his fingers through his auburn hair. "Ivy, I have a lot on my mind right now, as you know," he said, winking. "I'll make you a deal. After the celebration, you can ask me again, and we can talk about it."

"Do you promise?" she asked hopefully.

"I promise," he said, forming his right hand into a fist and placing it on his left shoulder.

It was something Ivy's father only did with her. It meant that he was swearing to something on his honor as the king and as her father. Ivy would mirror him in response to let him know she understood. They'd always had a special connection ever since Ivy was born.

Her father leaned over and kissed the top of her head before getting up. As he opened the door to leave, Ivy called out to him. "Do I have to wear a gown for the Feast of Winter?" Her father smiled and said, "Ivy, I may be king, but I'm not the boss. You can talk to your mother tomorrow." He grinned at her and winked again before closing the door behind him. Ivy lay awake for a long time before sleep finally claimed her.

Ivy dreamt she was a knight.

She fought alongside her brother and friends against the southern raiders. The field before her was chaos, unfamiliar, and yet...

The cacophony of screams and battle cries arced through the air like arrows. Ivy blinked, trying to see the whole image before her, but it was like looking through sea water, the salt burning her eyes. Suddenly, Ivy felt a stabbing pain in her chest and a shrill cry from above. Her heart hammered madly, mixing with the steady thunder of horses' hooves and stomping boots. Someone behind her shouted Ivy's name, but she was already falling to the ground, and when she hit—

Ivy shuddered awake as she landed on the stone floor of her bedchamber. Sweat coated her brow, and her pulse was fast but steadily slowing. Pulling herself up, Ivy opened the shutters and realized it was morning.

*It was just a dream,* she told herself.

The sun was just coming up over the Shadow Sea, making the water glisten like a million black jewels.

Just a dream.

## CHAPTER THREE

# THE FEAST OF WINTER

S upply wagons had been arriving at Godstone for days now, every one of them spilling over with food and livestock. Lady Oharra had sent for wine and ale to come from Grey Raven Castle for the feast. The day before, Lord Kevan had led a hunting party out to the Blackwood Forest in search of boars. A village to the south provided the last of the year's harvest, which consisted of potatoes, squash, corn, and turnips. Everyone in the kingdom was busy preparing for the arrival of Earl Rorik and his people.

The kitchen smelled of freshly baked bread, and the smith's shop rang loud with the clang of metal being worked. Hand-maids were eagerly making up guest rooms, decorating them with fur blankets, scented candles, and garlands above the canopied beds. Ivy loved this time of year—the snow, the gifts, the food, and the company. Everyone seemed in such high spirits, and it was the one time when the whole kingdom came together to celebrate the start of winter. This was the first year that her father would be hosting three houses at the same time.

Ivy woke up early to help her mother decorate the Great Hall for the upcoming feast. She got to work hanging bundles of dried berries from the branches of her father's throne. Pine garland formed a halo above the king's seat, weaved with red and gold ribbons.

Her father's white bird, Luna, liked to make a nest in the garland every year, but she would often knock it down. Last year the bird knocked it into one of the hanging lanterns, causing a fire.

This year, Ivy decided to make the bird her own nest to keep her off the decorations. She climbed up the branches of the throne to set the bird's nest on the far side away from the lanterns. She stretched her slender arms as far as they would reach. Her attempt failed; she dropped the nest and watched it roll behind the throne. "Shit." Ivy climbed down and fetched a candle from a nearby table.

While on her hands and knees looking for the nest, something caught her eye. There were markings carved into the back of her father's throne just at the base. Lifting the candle to cast some light on them, Ivy read the words but didn't understand.

"Ivy!" Queen Elana called for her. "Where are you?" Ivy blew out the candle and scrambled to her feet, snatching up the nest as she came around the throne. Her mother stood at the bottom of the dais, eyeing her with a smirk.

Ivy had always been told that she resembled her father more than her mother. King Magnus and Ivy shared the same auburn hair that hung in lazy ringlets, and both had similar eyes, though her mother said the king's eyes used to be a more vibrant shade of purple. Her father told Ivy that only Blackbournes had purple eyes, but she thought that must not be true, as their ancestors were from the South. Her mother was from the South as well—a smaller castle called Harper Hall, which lay just over the border on the east coast.

The queen's hair was a sandy blonde that grew long and curly down her back. Her eyes resembled emerald jewels, and her face was narrow and slim. She stood tall and lean, a delicate and beautiful woman.

Queen Elana crossed her arms and looked at her daughter. "What were you doing?"

Ivy held up Luna's nest as if that was all the answer her mother needed. "I dropped this behind Father's throne," Ivy replied.

"Never mind about that now," her mother said. "Earl Rorik's party has been spotted. Come, we need to get you clean and looking presentable."

Ivy rolled her eyes; she knew there was no use in arguing with her mother about what was considered "presentable." Queen Elana had given up on dressing Ivy at age seven. She'd ruined too many gowns as a small child, wrestling with her brother or climbing trees. She and her mother finally agreed that Ivy would only be required to wear a gown for special occasions.

The dress the queen chose was a rich purple that matched Ivy's eyes. The shoulders were embellished with a black lace that ran down her upper arm. Sewn within the lace were onyx gemstones that caught the candlelight, making her shoulders twinkle. The skirt fell straight and slender to the tops of her ankles, for which Ivy was grateful. In the past, she'd been forced to wear dresses that plumed out around her like a mushroom. This skirt was more streamlined and hugged closer to her legs, but still flowed enough so that she could walk comfortably. Ivy put on some black boots and tied the golden scarf from her father around her wrist while the maid braided her hair, snaking it with a purple ribbon and a string of pearls. Ivy always had the scarf on her when she wasn't practicing with Ser Osmund.

When the torture was over, Ivy looked at her reflection in the mirror and couldn't help but smirk. The dress itself was pretty enough, but it seemed wrong on her.

Ivy's mother came up behind her. "I know you dread having to dress up, darling, but you do look lovely. Let's try not to rip this one, shall we? You're exhausting your poor maid's fingers with all the sewing she must do." They both laughed at that, only because her "poor" maid had left the room. "Come along now, my lady," she said playfully, opening the door. "We don't want to keep the earl waiting."

Ivy and the queen made their way to the front gate, where the earl would be arriving at any moment. She fell in line next to her brother Rayner, her father grinning at her dress as she passed. Rayner's head was still wrapped from the blow he'd received during the ambush, but the magister said he would likely not remember much of the incident. Magister Ivann had insisted that Rayner stay in bed today, but her brother refused, saying he wouldn't miss the arrival of Earl Rorik.

Rayner was dressed in a wool doublet darker than the beaches of Godstone. An iron-spun chain held on his cloak, which hung to the snow-covered ground. Her brother was two years older than her, but they were about the same height. Ivy had always been tall for a young girl. Rayner had the same shade of auburn hair as she and their father, and his eyes were the same purple.

Rayner shot her a look and smiled. "My, my, aren't you just—"

"I suggest you swallow those words," Ivy hissed, and Rayner snapped his mouth shut but kept his mocking smile.

The gates to Godstone were massive blocks of wood carved

from the same Blackwood trees as the king's throne. The doors stood ten meters high and were latched shut with a log that took many men to lift. They stood open to receive the earl with her father's knights lining the walls, dressed in their freshly polished armor. Ivy could hear the *clip-clop* of approaching horses. She'd never met this earl or anyone from the northern clans.

As they filed in through the gates, Ivy found it hard to discern which man was their leader. Many of the men rode white stallions, their hair intricately braided and tied behind their heads. Furs of many different animals hung over their shoulders, though the rest of their clothing was plain. Ivy suddenly felt even more ridiculous, fussing with her skirts as she looked over their guests. She spotted a woman who carried an ax across her back. The woman's hair resembled ropes that hung down her spine, and Ivy realized that most people carried axes and swords.

Suddenly, the body of horses parted to make way for what Ivy could only assume was their earl. The man rode a massive horse whose hooves were twice as large as any other. In its mane were iron bells and tiny bird skulls, softly jingling as it strode across the courtyard toward the king. Earl Rorik was a large man; his chestnut hair was shaved on either side to the scalp, revealing strange markings that crawled across his pale skin. The rest was twisted in spirals and tied with a cord. The man's beard had wooden beads woven into it that fell over his brawny chest. Ivy had never seen anyone who looked like Earl Rorik or his people. A silence fell over the yard as the earl swung down from his horse and approached the king.

King Magnus stepped forward and half-bowed to the Earl of Tordenfall. The two embraced, patting each other's backs and laughing.

"Welcome, my friend," her father said as they stepped apart. "It's been many years."

"Indeed, it has," Earl Rorik replied in a strange accent. His voice was thunderous and boomed over the courtyard. "You never come North to visit your friend."

"My place is here," Magnus said, gesturing to his family. "Besides, I've invited you to Godstone plenty of times over the years."

"I do not like to leave the North. Fewer people up there starting wars."

"Well, you're here now as my honored guest, and we're happy to celebrate this holiday with you."

The woman with rope hair came forward to stand beside the earl. "This is my wife, Ingrid."

Magnus kissed the lady's hand and welcomed her before he introduced his own family. When the introductions were done, Magnus asked Ser Osmund to show the earl and his family to their room.

All honored guests stayed in the central tower, where Ivy's own family slept. The tower was large and square, with rounded turrets on all four corners. The third floor had a covered stone corridor attached, which connected to the building that housed the maids, servants, and Magister Ivann. The first floor of the tower was a shared space for all. It had a hearth and bookshelves as high as the ceiling. The second floor was currently occupied by Lady Oharra and her daughter Correlyn, who made the journey for the celebration. The third floor was for Ivy and her brother. Four levels up, Lord Kevan and his wife Laila were put in a room next to their son Piotr. Finally, at the top was a massive bed-chamber and lounge space that the king and queen kept.

The remaining two levels held Earl Rorik, his wife, their son Grimm, and some of the earl's trusted men. While the guests were refreshing and getting settled in, the kingdom leapt back into action, preparing for the feast. The Great Hall wasn't big enough to hold every person from the three houses, so a large tent was set up outside. The feast was starting soon, and Ivy's mother promised that she didn't need to wear the gown to supper in the Hall that night.

When the greetings were finished, Ivy ran as fast as she could to her bedchamber to change. After nearly tearing the gown trying to get it off, she dressed quickly. Ivy chose a green, wool tunic, and black pants; she kept her black boots. She untangled the braid and let her hair fall loose, the pearls scattering across the stone floor. Last, she draped a hooded cloak over her shoulders, held on by an iron maple leaf pin. It had been a gift from her father some years back, and it was one of Ivy's most valued possessions. The pin got its color from small bits of orange and red-dyed glass that were carefully set inside the leaf-shaped iron frame.

There was a knock at her door.

"Come in," she called. Ser Osmund stood in the doorway, wearing a leather chest piece over a brown tunic. His sword hung from his hip, and a gray fox pelt covered his shoulders. Ser Osmund had been told to dress comfortably for the feast, but he always felt the need to wear armor, just in case. Ivy would bet her maple pin that he had chainmail underneath as well.

The knight looked over Ivy and smiled. "Now, there's my favorite sparring partner. I hardly recognized you in that purple gown."

Ivy smiled. They linked arms and took the covered archway out of the castle, heading for the Hall.

"Some of the other knights have a bet going on who will start the first fight," Ser Osmund stated. "Would you care to play along?"

Ivy smiled and nodded her head. The men always fought at feasts and celebrations. Once they had too much to drink, the insults started flying along with fists and food.

Ivy stopped on the bridge and looked to her escort. "Ser Osmund, can I ask you something?"

"Of course, my lady," he replied, still smiling.

"I was decorating father's throne this morning when I dropped something." She ran her hands together nervously. "It rolled behind the throne, so I took a candle and went to find it, and I spotted something carved on the back of the throne. I was wondering…" She hesitated before asking, swallowing the lump in her throat. "Who's Helvarr?"

Ser Osmund's smile slid from his face like ice, leaving an empty mask. "How do you know that name?" he asked, furrowing his brow.

Ivy felt her heartbeat quicken. "It was carved in the back of the throne, right beside Father's name. Who is he?"

The knight stared at her; something resembling anger and fear covered his face. "My lady," he started, "some things are better left in the past. Now, I advise you to keep this to yourself and ask no further questions about it. Your father has many duties tonight and wouldn't appreciate being interrogated. You understand?"

Ivy chewed on her lip and nodded that she understood, though she didn't.

"Good," he said, his smile returning. "Now then, let's go eat some Blackwood boar."

The feast was underway when they reached the Hall. Men were outside spit-roasting the boars over a fire, the flames licking at the fatty drippings. Braziers surrounded the open tent, and men inside lifted ale-filled horns to the sky. The air smelled of charred wood and roasted meat. Ivy's stomach growled.

Inside the Hall, her father and his guests were already seated at their places upon the dais. The servers were setting platters on the table. Since the king had more honored guests than usual this year, Ivy and her brother sat at a table with the guests' children. Ivy took a seat at the end of the bench next to Rayner and across from Piotr. Lady Oharra's daughter, Correlyn, sat across from Rayner, eyeing him and blushing when their gaze met. Earl Rorik's son Grimm sat at the end of the bench, keeping to himself and drinking ale as if their stores were about to run out. Ivy narrowed her eyes on Piotr Daemont as he flashed her a wry smile. She never liked Piotr; he was always rude and poking at Ivy until she snapped.

Correlyn was the image of her mother with the same black hair and smokey eyes, though Correlyn's hair was shorter. She wore a black dress embroidered with small gray ravens that flew up her skirts to the bodice. On her hip, she wore a sword similar to Lady Oharra's. Ivy gazed at the blade with jealous eyes. Earl Rorik's son Grimm was the largest at the table. Ivy would've mistaken him for one of the earl's men if she didn't know better. Grimm was twenty years old but stood as tall and broad as his father. He had wavy blond hair that he kept braided and tied back. His eyes were frosty blue, and his red-blond beard grew tight to his face.

"You look rather dull this evening," Piotr drawled, staring at Ivy as he ran a hand through his feathery blond hair, his blue eyes intently focused on her. "Don't you know how to dress like a lady?" he mocked.

"I don't need to impress anyone," Ivy answered simply, barely keeping the bite from her voice.

"Well then, you've done your job," Piotr taunted, looking her up and down. Ivy stayed silent, her mind focused on other things. She didn't wish to engage in the back-and-forth banter that was the usual between her and Piotr. He seemed disappointed by her silence, so prodded at her further. "You'll have a hard time finding a man if you don't dress like a lady," Piotr tsked, sipping his wine.

Ivy felt her blood starting to boil as she glared at him—his mocking smile and intense eyes. "If you don't like my outfit, then stop looking," Ivy snapped. "Or I'll smack those blue stones from your fucking head."

Rayner choked on his wine, but Piotr only sat back in his chair, swirling his cup.

"You're in a bad mood this evening, Ivy."

"I'm just not in the mood for you, as a matter of fact." Ivy tapped a finger on her chin and looked to the rafters. "I'm never in the mood for you."

Piotr flashed his teeth at her, leaning forward and bracing his elbows on the table. "I could say the same about you," Piotr sneered, but it sounded like a lie.

"Then keep your eyes off me, and perhaps I won't spoon them from your head."

Rayner and Correlyn exchanged a look, trying to drown their laughter in their cups.

Piotr glared at them, then turned back to Ivy. "Watch your tongue."

"Or what?" Ivy challenged. "You'll make another smart remark for me to slap back in your face?"

Rayner snorted, and Correlyn covered her mouth to keep from smiling too wide.

Piotr only stared her down, gulping his wine, and then got to his feet without another word. Ivy could've sworn he looked hurt, but she didn't think him capable of such feelings. Rayner nudged her in the ribs, and from down the table, Grimm lifted his cup to her.

Ivy ignored him and focused on the spread of food, which was impressive. The table was piled high with bread and an assortment of cheeses. At either end stood flagons filled with winter ale and red wine. The first course was a feast from the sea. A platter piled high with lobsters, whole smoked fish, monster crabs, and a variety of mussels was set on every table.

Next was the fire-roasted boar, the skin still crackling from the heat. It was served with boiled potatoes, roasted corn, and stewed greens. A venison stew came next with carrots and onions nestled in the thick brown gravy. Finally, dessert was served with hot, spiced wine, a platter of more cheese, and some fruit from storage. Ivy was so full she didn't dare eat any dessert, but she did try some hot wine. The taste was sour on her tongue, but the more she sipped, the better it seemed to taste.

Ivy leaned closer to Rayner to be heard over the music and talking. "You really don't remember what happened during the attack?" she asked him.

"Not much," he replied. "Magister Ivann says I might not recall any of it. All I remember is men coming out of the woods, Father yelling orders, his men scrambling…then nothing. Just blackness."

"How is it that none of Father's men saw who hit you?" Ivy asked.

"Not sure," Rayner answered, stuffing a pastry in his mouth. "Everything was chaotic at the time. I can't blame them for focusing on other things."

"Were you wearing a helm?" she continued.

"Of course, little good it did, though. Magister Ivann thinks I'll have a scar like the one Father has on his cheek." He pointed just above his brow where his helm had cut into his skin.

Ivy sat and thought for a moment, watching Correlyn give her brother heated glances across the table. Rayner's cheeks were red, and Ivy knew it wasn't from the ale. She sat wringing her hands in her lap, then finally asked, "Have you ever heard the name Helvarr?"

"Who?" Rayner asked, more focused on Correlyn than the question.

"Never mind, I'm going for a walk." Rayner barely acknowledged her as Ivy got to her feet, spotting Piotr from across the room before she slipped out the door.

CHAPTER FOUR

# THE GIFT

I vy stepped outside the hall and saw that it was snowing. She smiled, pulling up the hood of her cloak, and began walking toward the beach. Men ignored her as she passed, many already too drunk to stand. The outskirts of the small kingdom were empty as everyone migrated to the center to celebrate and feast with their king. The stone walls of Godstone ended where the black cliffs rose at the start of the beach. A small, wooden wall had been built some years before; it ran from one cliff to the other, closing off the back of Godstone. Her father said it gave comfort to those who lived closest to the beach. However, the gates were almost always open as fishermen came and went all day to bring seafood to the castle and sell their day's catch in the central market.

Ivy found them open and passed under the archway. Some of Earl Rorik's men had set up tents on the beach, but they stood empty as Ivy walked through the campsite. The sand and surrounding cliffs were black as pitch. The sea was just as dark—even during the day, the water seemed to absorb the sunlight rather than reflect it, living up to its name, the Shadow Sea. Black boulders sat under the cliffs, sunken into the sand, and Ivy took a seat upon the tallest rock, listening to the crashing waves. There were no stars in the sky tonight, and no moon. No light lay beyond the kingdom's wooden gates. Only blackness and the sound of water pounding against the cliffs. Ivy loved it here, but she also longed to travel. Her mother used to tell stories of her travels around the South when she was a young girl.

One night many years ago, Ivy fell ill during the height of a winter storm. The whole kingdom lay buried in mounds of snow and ice; even part of the sea froze over. Her father ordered everyone to stay inside and wait it out. The markets, bars, and inns lay dormant until the storm passed. Queen Elana stayed with Ivy in her bedchamber the entire time, feeding her broth and keeping the fire going. Ivy listened to her mother tell stories for days during that storm and loved every moment of it.

"When I was just a girl," Elana had started, "my father brought me to visit the city of Rahama. It lays on a beach south of my childhood home: Harper Hall. Their beaches are white, and the ocean is the lightest shade of blue you ever saw." Her mother painted a beautiful picture of the city with its dream-like beaches and its trees that grew strange fruit that the North didn't have. Monkeys wandered the streets and beaches, stealing from the fishmongers every day. People dressed in silk there rather than wool and fur. Their skin was darker, their hair lighter. Mother said the city was governed by a highborn man named Lord Cylas, who employed the help of a council to run the city.

"There are only two true kings in the South, just as there are two kings in the North," her mother said.

Ivy didn't know much about the war or why it went on as

long as it had. She did know that it was preventing her from traveling to all the places she wished to visit. If any child of a northern king were to be captured in the South, they would surely be held for ransom or killed. Of course, not all southern cities were dangerous because not all of them took part in the war. King Mashu of Kame Island had managed to keep peace on his land by separating himself from the quarrels of the North and South. Ivy dreamed of visiting the island--an area with no war, battles, or bloodshed. But going South was just a dream for now.

Ivy pushed those thoughts from her mind and stood up to stretch. She noticed a light moving around the beach, swerving between the tents.

"Ivy?" a voice called out. She called back, recognizing her father's voice immediately, and watched the lantern move toward her.

When her father drew near, Ivy's eyes went to the clasp that held on his cloak. It was an ugly thing, bent and distorted—not the shape it was meant to be. It was supposed to be his bird, Luna. However, it more resembled a bird that had been sat on by an ox. Her father loved it all the same because Ivy had made it for him last year as a gift for the Feast of Winter, though she never tried to forge anything again.

Her father stood below the boulder where Ivy was perched, his auburn hair lit up by the tiny flame of the lantern. Magnus was tall and muscular, his broad shoulders covered with a black fur cloak. His matching auburn beard twinkled with melting snow. He kept it well-trimmed to his face, but it still scratched at Ivy every time her father kissed her forehead.

He smiled up at Ivy. "Why aren't you celebrating with everyone?" he asked as he climbed to take a seat next to her.

"I was, but it's too loud in there, so I decided to go for a walk," she responded.

"Ah yes, it grew quite loud at my table as well. I listened to Piotr talking of you to his father. Apparently, you threatened him?" Magnus raised his brow and smirked.

Ivy shrugged. "Maybe he deserved it."

"Yes, I'm sure." He chuckled and wrapped his cloak around her shoulders. "You know you missed the first fight of the night?"

"Who was it this year?" she asked.

"Well, Ser Ambrin from the Twisted Tower got drunk and decided to challenge one of the earl's men to an arm wrestle. A mountain of a man named Thorne, arms as big as tree branches and taller than any man I ever saw. Ser Ambrin lost the arm wrestle, of course, and sore loser that he is, he went up to Thorne and punched him in the face. The man didn't even move. He picked up Ser Ambrin like a sack of potatoes and threw him through the doors of the hall."

Ivy laughed at the image, wondering if Ser Ambrin would remember what he did when morning came.

"The hall has settled down now," Magnus went on. "How about we go back, and you can open your gift?"

Ivy agreed. Her father helped her down off the boulder, and they began the walk back to the hall. The snow was still coming down, filling in the prints they left behind.

The big tent outside the hall was quiet now. Men slumped over tables, drinking horns still in hand, while the ones still conscious lifted their horns to the king as he passed. The braziers surrounding the tent had died down to smoldering embers, and Ivy spotted Ser Ambrin propped up against the wall snoring loudly, a black circle forming around his right eye. As they entered, Ivy saw the only people left inside were passed out from too much ale and wine.

"Where is everyone?" Ivy asked, now realizing how long she'd been gone.

"Your mother went off to bed, and Rayner had too much ale, so I asked Ser Osmund to lend a hand." Ivy suddenly remembered what Ser Osmund told her before the feast. *Some things are better left in the past.*

Magnus walked up to his throne and took a seat; Luna sat perched in her new nest above. Her father asked her to sit on the queen's throne next to him, where a wooden box sat upon the dais.

"Before you open it," her father said, "I want to tell you how proud I am of the woman you're becoming. Your mother and I know that you aren't a little girl anymore, and it's time we stop treating you like one. I know from your rooftop excursions that you're curious about the war and what goes on in my council. From now on, if you have questions, all you need to do is ask. I don't want to scare you, but I won't leave you in the dark anymore. I'll never lie to you. Do you understand?" Ivy nodded her head and smiled at her father. "Good, now you may open your gift."

Ivy took the top off the box to reveal something shiny. She lifted it from the crate and held it out in front of her. It was a silk cloak, black as night. Embroidered on the back was the maple tree that sat right outside Ivy's bedchamber window. Red and orange jewels made up the leaves, expertly stitched into the branches. Among the jewels, a small white bird was stitched on one of the branches.

"Is that Luna?" Ivy asked, excitement in her voice.

"It is," her father answered, "Luna is always with me, and so long as you wear this cloak, I'll always be with you."

Ivy jumped up to hug her father, "I love it, thank you!"

Her father chuckled and patted her back. "You're welcome, my darling, but that's not all. Look at the bottom of the box."

She drew away from him, confused. Ivy set the cloak on the queen's chair and went back to the box. The cloak had covered up the straw at the bottom of the box, and Ivy could see something underneath it. She carefully dug her way to the bottom, her heart pounding with excitement as she lifted handfuls of straw. Ivy touched something cold and wrapped her fingers around the smooth object and lifted, the straw falling away as she raised it to eye level. Her eyes began to sting with tears as she gazed at what she held.

The sword was a masterful piece of art. The blade shone like nothing Ivy had ever seen. It seemed to catch every candle in the room and harness the light. The steel created a pattern that had the look of flowing water down the length of the blade. The handle was wrapped in black leather, and the pommel of the sword was adorned with an amethyst stone the size of her thumb.

Ivy couldn't believe what she was holding—she turned to her father with tears in her eyes, but no words would come to her.

"Do you like it?" he asked curiously.

"Is this really mine?"

"It is. I thought it was time you had a real blade. I've seen you disarm Ser Osmund with a practice sword plenty of times. You're very skilled, Ivy. But this is no dull blade. If Ser Osmund wishes to continue the scarf game you two have going, it must be with dull blades. You're not to use it unless you feel that you're in danger. Do you understand, Ivy?"

"I understand."

"There's a scabbard in there as well, so you may keep the sword on a belt."

Ivy reached back into the box and found the scabbard. The wooden sleeve was wound tight with leather and adorned with metalwork at the brim and bottom.

"How does it feel?" her father asked. "Is it too heavy?" Ivy weighed the sword in both hands and gave it a swing.

"It's perfect," she exclaimed.

Magnus smiled and watched his daughter practice swinging her sword around. Ivy put the sword away and went to hug her father, beaming with happiness. "This is the greatest gift, thank you."

Magnus kissed the top of her head, "You're welcome, my sweetling."

The lanterns were dying down, and it was getting late. Ivy buckled her sword to her belt while her father grabbed her cloak, draping it over his arm.

*"All you need to do is ask."*

She stood beside her father's throne, a lump forming in her throat. Ser Osmund had warned her not to mention it, but she couldn't ignore the strange feeling she had. Ivy looked at her boots, wringing her hands.

A curious look formed on Magnus's face, "What is it?"

Ivy took a breath and looked at her father. "Can I show you something?" He nodded his head, and Ivy took a step back around the throne. Her father followed, looking more curious than angry. She pointed down at the base of the throne and said, "I found this earlier today."

Magnus set down her cloak and fetched a candle off a table.

Going to one knee, he searched in the direction Ivy was pointing. The light from the flame illuminated the carved names, and Ivy got down on her knees beside her father. His face had morphed into something she'd never seen. She put a hand on his shoulder, and he sank to the floor, slumped over on his knees.

"Father?" Ivy began. "Are you alright?" He nodded his head, bringing a hand up to stroke his beard. "Who's Helvarr?" Ivy asked.

Magnus ran his fingers over the carved names, as if they were transporting him back in time.

"I remember the day Helvarr and I felled this tree," he said, his voice drifting away to the memory. "It was after my father passed, and I took his place as king. I didn't want to sit on the same throne as my father. Somehow it felt wrong. He ruled this kingdom from that throne for over thirty years. My reign was only beginning, and I thought I needed a throne of my own, so we decided to make one.

"The day was surprisingly warm. Autumn was just beginning, and the leaves were only starting to change color. Helvarr and I saddled up and rode out to the Blackwood Forest in search of the perfect tree. It took most of the day, but we finally came upon the right one. The tree had already started to die as no leaves clung to its branches.

"We took turns with the ax, chopping away at the trunk. The tree finally came loose, and we spent the rest of the afternoon trimming off the top branches. It was his idea to keep the lowest branches attached. '*You'll look mighty sitting under its twisted arms,*' he'd said. He suggested I take the rest of the wood and have a throne made for your mother as my wedding gift. She and I were betrothed at the time and were set to marry the following summer. Helvarr and I spent weeks making the perfect throne for my future queen before even starting on mine. He was my oldest friend."

Ivy dared not speak. Her father seemed far away, sucked back into the memory. Magnus suddenly stood, his legs shaking, and looked at his daughter on the floor. "I suppose it was only a matter of time before this would come to light. I told you I wouldn't lie to you, and I meant it. So, I'll tell you about Helvarr."

They retreated to Ivy's bedchamber, got a fire going in the hearth, and settled down on her bed. The rest of the night went by in a fog of stories. Magnus told Ivy everything about Helvarr, from them growing up together inside these walls, training to become knights, and fighting alongside one another against the raiders of the South. He told Ivy of the day Helvarr was banished and about the young knight named Roe--what Helvarr had done to her. All she could do was listen and take it in. She felt sorry for her father and what he had to do for the good of his kingdom. A king must make hard sacrifices if they are to rule.

The sun was beginning to rise by the time Magnus was done, turning the world gray outside of Ivy's window. "You haven't seen him since that day?"

"Not since that day," her father repeated. Ivy was silent for a moment, and when she spoke again her voice was cold. "This is his fault," she said.

Magnus looked at her with a furrowed brow and said, "What do you mean?"

She looked up, tears and anger welling in her eyes. "Helvarr," she snarled. "This is his fault. I'll never become a knight because of what he did. You made those rules because of him-- because he killed that young girl. He forced your hand and kept a sword from mine. You should've killed him."

Magnus was shocked by her words; he knew in his heart that he could never kill his old friend. He'd known this day would come, and though she may not admit it, Magnus knew Ivy blamed him. It was his decision and his rules that were keeping Ivy from knighthood. They sat for a while, neither one speaking until the fire died away, and the sun greeted them.

Ivy had finally fallen asleep, propped up on her pillows. Magnus slowly got up and drew her curtains closed, then covered his daughter with a fur blanket. He kissed the top of her head and pushed her hair back, looking at her young beauty, a smile forming on his lips. As Magnus opened the door, Ivy called to him.

"Yes?" he said, turning back. Ivy sat propped on one elbow, her face blank. "If I ever meet him... I will kill him."

Magnus sighed and forced a smile. "I don't doubt that." He glanced over to where her sword sat propped against the wall. "What will you name it?" he asked.

Ivy curled her lips into a smile. "Promise," she said. "My sword's name is Promise."

CHAPTER FIVE

# THE KING & THE QUEEN

**M**agnus had walked this path hundreds of times, yet this morning it felt different to him. His talk with Ivy had drained him completely, yet he still couldn't sleep. Too many things still tormented his mind for sleep to come easily. He walked around the back of the tower, Luna soaring up ahead. She was never far, and Magnus recalled now the day he brought Luna home.

It had been months after the birth of Rayner, and the banishment of Helvarr. Magnus had led his men on a hunting trip to the Hercynian Forest, which lay southwest of Godstone. They purchased rooms at a local inn just outside the forest's edge in the town of Moore. This forest offered something not found in the Blackwoods.

A rare creature, the size of an ox with long coarse fur, and growing from its skull was a cross between branches and antlers. It had cloven hooves and the tail of a wolf. The locals named it the Tandrycian stag. Magnus had never seen one before the hunt, but he was sure he wouldn't miss it based on the description.

They set out early in the morning to hunt. A local man named River accompanied Magnus and his men to offer a hand in tracking the beast. The forest was much different from the Blackwoods. The Blackwoods were always dark and full of even darker trees, shadows peeking out from behind every stump, the purple leaves keeping the sun hidden. But the Hercynian Forest seemed to glow.

River found some tracks and went ahead with some men who'd brought hounds to help sniff the stag out.

"The creature can change colors," River had warned. "It'll blend with the surroundings until we are close, and then BAM!" He clapped his hands together. "Its great horns can skewer a man. I've seen it done."

"Does it eat other animals?" Magnus had asked River.

"Oh yes, its teeth are as sharp as any wolf." River chuckled and walked ahead of Magnus, but Magnus wasn't laughing.

They continued to follow the track until something caught Magnus' eye. It seemed to be a firebug glowing up in the trees. The thing was casting a great light, bright enough to be seen during the day. Magnus stopped and watched the glow moving through the branches above. His men called back to him, and the king moved along, looking over his shoulder at the glowing object.

After a while, the hounds started baying and howling. The

men turned them loose. The dogs took off running toward the sound of something crashing through the brush. Magnus now ran to keep up with his men and the dogs when they came to a clearing in the forest. Grass grew up to brush against their knees. The trees around them parted, creating a circle of light. The beast was massive, standing in the center surrounded by the hounds.

It scraped at the ground with its hooves. It was cornered and angry. The stag charged the closest hound, lowering its head as it ran. An archer loosed an arrow, and it buried itself into the neck of the beast. The creature reared its head back and let out a cry. The sound was terrifying, like a horse being slaughtered. An anxious hound charged forward and sunk his teeth into a hind leg. The beast thrashed the dog loose and tore its horns through the hound before he could escape.

"Hit him again!" River yelled.

Everyone drew their swords in fear as the archer pulled back another arrow and let it fly. Magnus watched the arrow sail just above the beast's head.

"Again!" Magnus ordered. He was becoming nervous now, with one hound already dead, and the beast only growing angrier.

The archer hit the stag this time, the arrow protruding from its chest. Its brown fur was growing darker with blood as it seeped from the wound. When it stumbled, another hound took its chance. The dog leaped into the air to clamp down on the stag's neck. As the beast flailed, it kicked another in the jaw, but it was slower, less precise. It was becoming weak. The men called their dogs back as the archer drew another arrow.

It sliced across the throat of the stag and embedded itself in a tree behind it. The beast then locked its sight on Magnus, stamped its hooves, and charged. The ground shook as the beast charged; the king lifted his sword, ready to jump out of its path and slice across its body. The archer hurriedly shot another arrow, trying to stop it. Just as it was almost upon Magnus, it stopped, ripping up grass as it skidded to a halt before him. It stood two men tall, towering over the king. Magnus lowered his sword, and the beast backed away, dropping its head before collapsing.

Magnus turned around, expecting to see a more massive creature. Instead, it was the glowing object--a bird. Its feathers seemed to glow in shades of orange and yellow, its eyes shining red. The king took a step back, cautious of the strange creature. The bird flew down and landed on a limb, eye-level with Magnus. The light that seemed to surround it disappeared revealing brilliant white feathers and its red eyes turned solid black. Magnus bent down, searching his pocket for biscuits meant for the hounds. He held out his hand and the bird flew to him, perched on his hand, and began eating the crumbs.

"What sort of bird is this?" he asked River.

"That is a Hercidrius. There is an ancient legend that says kings used to keep them in their castles. The bird could heal the king should he fall ill, taking the pain onto itself. It's also told that the bird has other powers."

Magnus narrowed his eyes. "What kind of powers?"

"I don't know, Your Grace. I've never seen one this close before. Men used to tell tales of when kings lived to be hundreds of years old, and there was always mention of a particular white bird that they kept close."

Magnus looked at the man like he was mad.

"You may not believe the legend, Your Grace. But who can say that it's not true?" It was then that Magnus had decided to keep the white bird. Luna was near the size of a horned eagle by now, her wingspan longer than Magnus was tall. She was always close; that part of the legend was real. However, he never saw her glow again as she did that day in the forest. Her feathers remained snow white.

Magnus walked through the apple trees that stood behind the central tower. Their branches were bare, and fallen apples lay frozen in the snow. He continued to the northern gate, which faced the mountains, now covered in a fresh blanket of snow. The view was better from his bedchamber at the top of the tower. He could walk from window to window and gaze out upon four different worlds, reminding him of the Four Gods.

His father taught him of the gods and said that Godstone was named for them, as it was here that each of their lands converged.

"The All-Seeing God resides on mountain tops," his father told him. "He sees the whole world from up there and all that we do. The forests belong to the God of Secrets, as he's known to be a trickster. The Whispering Wood is said to have pine trees which uproot themselves to confuse people, keeping them in the God of Secret's grasp as they become lost to the woods forever."

Stories of that god used to frighten Magnus as a young boy, especially since children were told not to enter that forest alone.

The God of Judgment held the grasslands, as far as the eye could see.

"No man can hide from his punishment in a land so open and vast," his father warned. It had been said that this god would punish people of his land by setting fire to their crops. And finally, ships that go down in a storm are thought to have angered the God of Lost Souls. He controlled the waves and the storms at sea, and people left offerings to the statue of him before setting sail.

Magnus was told the God of Lost Souls kept all that is lost at sea, including men, to add to his underwater army. If a body should wash up on shore after a shipwreck, it was taken as a sign that he wasn't good enough for the god, so he gave the body back to the living.

Black, stone-carved statues of all four gods stood at every gate of the kingdom facing their land. They had stood there for hundreds of years since the first Blackbourne rose as king of those lands. Legends said that a boy was born on the black beaches, which is where the surname originated. The boy's parents were refugees from the South, escaping a civil war. They sailed as far as they could, but the mother was with child and could be at sea no longer, so there they settled.

After she'd given birth, she told her husband that they would call themselves Blackbourne and start anew. They built the kingdom from nothing and raised their son to become the first king, swearing to defend the North from harm. These tales were not known to all, but Magnus would ensure that the written history of House Blackbourne would be passed along to Rayner when he became king. The future rulers of the kingdom would always know the history of their people.

Magnus climbed the stairs of the northern gate to where sentries stood guard. The knights snapped upright to greet their king as he passed. Magnus then walked east along the wall, noticing the heavy snow clouds looming above the mountains. He found one of the towers along the way to be empty, so he stepped inside. The towers were only used when the sentries needed to stay out of bad weather. He could hear someone approaching the tower and leaned his head out to see his wife making her way along the wall.

She had always been the most beautiful woman he'd ever seen. Her golden curls cascaded down her back, and her green eyes always twinkled when she looked at Magnus. The queen wore a white fur cloak draped over her delicate shoulders. Her skirts swirled like green and gold smoke around her ankles.

"There you are," Elana said as she approached her husband. "You didn't come to bed last night." She placed a slender hand on his cheek and kissed him softly.

"I was up all night talking with our daughter," Magnus admitted. "She asked me about Helvarr."

Queen Elana took a step back and furrowed her brow. "How did she find out?"

"She stumbled upon our names carved in the back of my throne. It was only a matter of time, I suppose."

Elana twirled a golden lock around her finger nervously. Magnus knew she did that when she was thinking, so he covered her hands with his.

"What should we do?" she asked, looking up to her husband.

"It's done, my love. I told her everything and answered all of her questions. Ivy is almost eighteen. She has the right to know of any possible danger. I'll have the same talk with Rayner soon."

"What danger? Do you know something, Magnus?"

He touched the hilt of his sword before speaking. "Weeks

ago, before I called my bannerman here, there was a raven. Lady Oharra plants scouts all around the North to keep track of the raiders, and one of her scouts claims to have spotted Helvarr in Hideaway Harbor."

Elana went back to twisting her hair. "Are they sure? Was he on the North side of the harbor?" she asked.

"I'm not sure. I can only trust what the scouts tell me. We'll set off for Temple City soon, and it's only twenty leagues from the harbor. I'll take a small group to Hideaway and search the area to ask around the fishing docks. If someone saw him, they may be able to tell us where he went. Helvarr must surely stand out with his long black hair and that crooked nose. Someone will remember him, I'm sure of it."

Magnus wrapped his arms around his wife and buried his nose in her soft hair. It smelled of scented candles and pine trees.

She turned to face him and said, "I don't like this, Magnus. What if he comes farther North? I have a bad feeling about all this." Elana had always been wary of Helvarr.

When Elana's father, Lord Harald, heard that Magnus had taken his father's place in Godstone, he visited the new king. Lord Harald and King Erwin Blackbourne never truly got along. Though Harper Hall resided in the South, Lord Harald never took part in the ongoing war. Magnus's father grew stubborn with his age and had refused a betrothal between House Blackbourne and House Harper. Lord Harald tried to reason with the king, but he still refused, saying, "The North and the South will never mix."

After the king's weak heart finally took him, Magnus claimed the throne at the age of twenty. Lord Harald jumped at the opportunity to arrange a marriage for his only daughter. When the lord and his daughter arrived in Godstone, Lord Harald again asked if Magnus would take his daughter as a wife.

"My father never informed me of your request," Magnus said.

"That doesn't surprise me, Your Grace. Your father was called Erwin the Stubborn for good reason," the lord responded.

They both chuckled, and Magnus agreed to meet with his daughter and give an answer the next day. Lord Harald explained that his daughter was a few years younger than Magnus. He'd struggled to find a suitable husband down South for Elana, as he didn't want her in harm's way with a house involved in the war.

"That's quite alright, my lord. No need to explain," Magnus had replied. "I'm sure she's lovely. Could you bring her in?"

Magnus had sat on his father's throne, waiting. When Elana walked into the Hall, Magnus felt his heart begin to flutter rapidly. His hands grew sweaty, and a knot formed in his throat. All the air escaped his lungs as he gazed upon his future wife. Her hair fell in loose curls to her shoulders, a velvet dress hugging her slim body.

Magnus quickly stood up and stumbled on the step as she approached. It was enough to make her smile, and that was all it took for Magnus to agree to the betrothal on the spot. The couple spent the rest of the evening walking, arms linked, talking about everything. Elana was to return home until the wedding the following summer as preparations needed to be made; winter was fast approaching.

Just before she was to set off for home, Helvarr returned from a hunting party. He trotted up to Magnus on his white stallion, keeping his eyes on Elana as he dismounted and brushed past his friend.

"Who's this?" he asked with a wry smile.

Magnus cleared his throat and introduced his queen-to-be to his oldest friend. Helvarr licked his lips and planted a sloppy kiss on the lady's hand. Elana forced a smile but moved closer to Magnus. Helvarr never took his copper eyes off her.

"Well," he said. "I've got me a stag to skin. Your Grace." He half bowed to Magnus laughing at his own sarcasm. "I'll see you again, my lady," Helvarr addressed Elana with a hungry stare.

After that first encounter, Elana was always uncomfortable around Helvarr and never wanted to be left alone with him. Magnus tried to defend his friend, saying he was harmless, but his queen insisted. The king obeyed.

Now, Magnus stood with his queen in the tower, looking out at the white mountains. He turned her around and kissed her forehead. "I love you, Elana, and I would never let anything happen to you or our children. You have to trust that the decisions I make are for a good reason." He paused as her emerald stare pierced him. "I've been thinking, with the raiders edging closer and a possible sighting of Helvarr...I think it may be best if we send Ivy away."

Elana withdrew from his arms, tears beginning to form in her green eyes. "Away? What do you mean? Where would you have her go?"

"Do you remember the knight who trained me? Ronin?" Magnus asked. "He resides South, on Kame Island. And I—"

"Ronin?" Elana interrupted. "You haven't seen that man in nineteen years, and you want to send our daughter to him? For what?"

Magnus could see how upset she was becoming, and he never wished to be the reason for her tears. But this was the only way to keep his daughter safe. He just had to convince Elana that it was the right choice.

"I want him to train Ivy to fight," he continued. "The North is no longer as safe as it once was, and Ivy is already skilled with a sword. Ser Osmund praises her every day, and perhaps my rules have held her back. She's talked about being a knight ever since she was a young girl, beating her brother bloody with sticks in the yard." He thought Elana might smile at that picture but she didn't.

"King Mashu," he continued. "He's detached from the war and rules his island his way and sees no border across this land. The king is a good man, and he would take Ivy in as his ward. All I need to do is send a hawk explaining the position we're in."

The queen considered what Magnus said, twirling her hair around her finger. "I need to think about this," she said and quickly brushed past Magnus.

Magnus found Ser Osmund in his chambers on the top floor of the barracks. The room was small, but cozy. The only furniture was a feather bed and a desk by the window. The knight hung his armor from hooks attached to the stone walls. Magnus looked at the fire roaring in the hearth, and Ser Osmund glanced up from a book as the king entered.

"Your Grace," the knight stood, "are you alright?"

Magnus must have looked distracted. Elana took the news exactly as he'd expected, but it still hurt him to upset his wife.

"May I sit?" Magnus asked. Ser Osmund offered up his seat and went to pour a horn of ale for both of them. Magnus drank deeply before he spoke. "How well does Ivy fight?"

"Oh, Lady Ivy fights as good as any young man her age—better even. She grows stronger and quicker every day. I struggle to keep up with her." Magnus nodded his head and smiled as he thought of his daughter fighting the older man. "You love Ivy like your own. I've seen it."

Ser Osmund had been married once, but his wife died in childbirth, along with their newborn daughter. The day Ivy was born, Ser Osmund swore to protect her at any cost. They became great friends as she grew, which was why Magnus had asked him to begin training her years back. However, the knight wasn't getting any younger, and she'd soon be too skilled for him to continue training.

"Ivy may require an escort to Kame Island. I'd feel much better if it were you at her side."

The knight looked puzzled. "Your Grace?"

"You know Helvarr was spotted not long ago. And now that Ivy knows of him, I won't have her—"

Ser Osmund choked on his ale. "So, she did ask you?" he said, wiping ale from his beard.

"You knew of Ivy's discovery?" Magnus asked.

"She asked about him last night before the feast. Said she found carvings on your throne."

Magnus drained the rest of his ale and held his cup out for the knight to refill. "Well," he began, "it doesn't matter now. She knows. If the scouts are right, then Helvarr is lurking around the border. I won't have my daughter in harm's way. I think it's time she met Ronin."

Ser Osmund nodded his head, agreeing. "I'll do whatever you ask of me, Your Grace."

"I'll need you to pick a team of your best men to guard the queen when I leave for Temple City. Rayner will come with me, and, gods willing, Elana will agree to send Ivy away. Go to the docks and start asking around. We need a captain that's heading South, as far as Port Tsue if possible."

Magnus stood to take his leave.

"Your Grace," the knight said, "how do you know Ronin is there?"

Magnus sighed. "Ronin took Helvarr's banishment harshly and decided to leave soon after. He'd trained us both since we were boys, so when he told me he was leaving, I asked if he would return home to the Isle of Fire. He said no and told me he'd head for Kame Island so that he could live in peace and never train another knight."

Ser Osmund looked at him, confused, "Your Grace, if that's true, then why would he train your daughter?"

"Because Ivy isn't training for knighthood, she's learning to defend herself. She's my daughter and a Blackbourne, and Ronin will train her."

Ser Osmund only nodded and told Magnus he would start looking for a captain.

## CHAPTER SIX

# A FATHER'S CHOICE

Magnus left the barracks to find his wife, hoping she had considered his worries. Outside, the sun was dipping in and out behind heavy gray clouds. The wind picked up, swirling the powdered snow around the king's boots as he walked the streets.

"Your Grace," a voice called out from behind. Lady Oharra ran to catch up with the king.

"My lady," Magnus greeted her. "Did you enjoy the feast?" They continued along the street as Lady Oharra answered. "I did," she said with a smile. "I heard your daughter and Piotr had a... disagreement."

Magnus chuckled. "You could say that."

"She reminds me of my Correlyn." Lady Oharra had raised her daughter to be a warrior from a young age, and Correlyn was on her way to becoming a great knight. Grey Raven lived by different rules, and Grey Raven women were free to become knights if they so wished. Magnus still disliked the idea of his little girl becoming a sworn knight and riding into battle. But the battle may soon come to them, and she wasn't a little girl anymore.

The two paused in front of the maple tree next to the central tower. "I saw that you came from the barracks," the lady stated. "Discussing the plan for the upcoming battle with Ser Osmund?"

"No." Magnus paused before continuing. "I don't think it would be wise to have both my children in one spot. Not with the possible sighting of Helvarr and the raiders pushing further North into our lands. I asked Ser Osmund to escort my daughter South."

The lady nodded her head, agreeing. "I fear you're right, Your Grace. If you need any of my men, they're yours to command. We must take every precaution we can to protect the ones we love."

"Thank you," Magnus said, "but I'll need all your men with us in Temple City. We don't know what awaits us."

"As you wish. Where will you send Ivy?"

"She'll be escorted to Kame Island. The knight who trained me resides there, and she'll be safe with Ser Osmund accompanying her."

"Oh, yes, I don't doubt that. Ser Osmund is a skilled swordsman, and I'm sure Ivy will be well protected," she reassured him, placing a hand on his shoulder. "Ronin, was it? I believe I met the man at one point," she said, turning away and strolling under the low hanging branches.

"You met Helvarr on the same day," Magnus stated.

Lady Oharra rolled her eyes, "Don't remind me."

Magnus lifted his brow and smiled. "You broke his nose, my lady," he teased.

"Yes, well, he deserved it, he never bothered me again, did he?" She smiled back. "Besides, I hear you did the same not long after."

His smile faded some as he recalled their fight. "That was different," he said, lowering his eyes.

Lady Oharra stopped smiling as well, "Yes, of course," she said timidly, "Apologies, Your Grace."

"No need. If you'll excuse me, I must talk to the queen."

She bid him a good day and continued down the street toward the beach. Storm clouds were moving down from the North, and it began to snow again.

Magnus climbed the stairs of the tower, glancing in Ivy's room as he passed. The door was cracked, and he could see Ivy pulling on her cloak with Promise strapped to her side. He poked his head into her room and warned Ivy of the storm before heading upstairs to his bedchamber. He found his wife seated by the window facing the ocean, a goblet of wine in hand. Their bed sat against the north wall, and the chamber door stood at the west. Four massive pillars lifted the vaulted ceiling, making the room more spacious. It was the largest room within the tower, and it took up the entire top floor. The southern window was framed by bookshelves standing as tall as the black stone walls.

Magnus had his desk in front of that window, always looking South for raiders. On the east side of the pillars were couches and pillows atop a bear pelt. A large hearth stood beside the window, casting a warm light throughout the room. Magnus moved to the fire to add more wood, then poured himself some wine and took a seat across from his queen.

Elana spoke before Magnus could. "I've considered what you said," she began, taking a sip of wine. "I realize that the North may not be the safest place anymore. It hasn't truly been for a long time, and I agree with you that we should take every precaution in protecting our family." She paused to look at

Magnus. Her stare could make him feel as though he were a young boy rather than a king. "Rayner is the heir to Godstone, and he needs to learn what it takes to be a king, so his place is with you. I'll be fine here behind the walls. How many men will you send to escort our daughter?"

He hesitated. "One."

"One?" the queen repeated. "You want to send our daughter into enemy lands with one escort?"

"It's Ser Osmund, my love. You know he'd never let anything happen to Ivy. Besides, a large escort draws attention. It gives the impression of someone important."

"She is someone important!" Elana snapped. "She's our daughter!"

"That's not what I meant," Magnus back-pedaled, moving over to sit next to his wife. She shed no tears this time, only coldly stared out the window. Elana stood as he came over and brushed past the king to refill her goblet. "When do you plan to send her?" she asked.

"As soon as possible. I have Ser Osmund looking for a captain now to take them into southern waters. You'll have a team of guards at all times while I'm gone."

"Very well." Elana gave in to his wishes. They both agreed that it was for the best, though Magnus could see the pain in Elan's eyes and the way she worried her bottom lip.

Magnus wrote a quick letter explaining the position he was in and sent it off on a hawk. The bird would reach King Mashu in a matter of days, giving Magnus time to make the arrangements. The king and queen sat in their bedchamber for the rest of the afternoon until the sun started to fade away. Curled up in front of the fire, Elana rested her eyes as Magnus watched from his desk. Not wanting to disturb her, he quietly walked across the bearskin pelt and bent down to kiss his wife. She stirred but didn't wake. Magnus realized he hadn't eaten all day and so walked down to the kitchens searching for food.

He found Leya, one of the cooks, stirring a pot of stew. The older woman lifted her eyes and was surprised to see her king. "What can I do for you, Your Grace?"

"The queen isn't feeling well. Could you ask a server to bring a tray of broth, bread, and cheese to our chambers? And don't disturb her. She's resting."

He grabbed a heel of bread for himself and turned to leave when he spotted white roses in a basket by the door. They were left over from the centerpieces from the feast. He lifted the bundle to his nose and smiled, thinking of his wife. "Leya, would you make sure these go to the queen as well?"

The woman smiled and said she would see to it herself.

Outside, the snow was coming down in heavy flakes, quickly covering the world around him. He didn't know where he was going, but Magnus started walking and kept going until he reached the stables. He saddled his horse and commanded the front gates open. As he rode through the falling snow, his mind was brought back to the village of Ashton. It had been destroyed years back, burnt to the ground by the raiders. At the time, Magnus didn't know who led them. When he tried to question their knights, Helvarr stepped in. However, it was now nineteen years since, and Magnus had learned that King Caato Morrell commanded the raiders.

Magnus stopped his horse west of Godstone, just outside the Blackwood Forest. Luna came soaring through the snow to land on the horse's back. Night had fallen, and the sky grew even darker with storm clouds. He gazed upon his kingdom and saw the sentries lighting fires in the turrets around the walls to keep warm. He spotted a rider carrying a lantern, and as the rider drew near, Magnus saw it was Ser Osmund. The knight didn't need to ask what Magnus was doing out there. Ser Osmund knew the king was struggling with his choice to send Ivy away. It was like juggling for Magnus, and he had to decide when to be a king and when to be a father.

"Your Grace," Ser Osmund said. "I've found a captain."

"That was quick. When will he set sail?"

"In four days, Your Grace. He's sailing to Port Tsue just inside of Catcher's Cove. He says he won't go as far as the Isle of Fire. Says the winter winds will be upon the sea in just a few weeks, and he has no desire to meet the God of Lost Souls just yet."

Magnus nodded his head, knowing he would find no ship willing to sail farther. "The queen has given her consent," he stated. "Return to the captain tomorrow and tell him he'll need to fit two horses on board as well. It seems you and Ivy will have to ride the rest of the way, staying close to the eastern coast. When you reach the city of Xanheim, take a ferry across the Serpent's Pass to Kame Island. From there, go directly to the king and don't let anyone know your identity until you're both safely on the island. The messenger hawk won't return before you set sail, so I have no choice but to send you anyway. The king will understand."

Ser Osmund agreed and turned his horse to leave.

Magnus called out to him as the knight started to ride away. "Pack light clothing, Ser Osmund. You'll be wintering in the South."

# CHAPTER SEVEN

# THE VOYAGE

Queen Elana wouldn't be coming down to the docks to see her daughter off. Instead, Ivy said goodbye to her mother within the king and queen's bedchamber that morning.

Ivy had never seen her mother so distraught. The queen's eyes were red and puffy from tears shed throughout the night. Her mother tried to smile for her daughter's sake, but Ivy saw the sadness in her eyes. She tried to reassure her mother that everything would be alright and that Ser Osmund wouldn't leave her side. Elana fussed with Ivy's auburn hair as she tried to hold back her tears.

"I'll be back by spring," Ivy reassured her.

The queen hugged her daughter, telling her to be safe. "You do everything Ser Osmund tells you. Watch each other's backs. Tell no one your identity. There are enemies and outlaws on Traders Road." She glanced at Promise hanging on Ivy's hip. "And only use that if you need it."

Ivy agreed and hugged her mother for a long time, fighting to keep her own tears back.

"You'll be eighteen when you return to me," her mother said. "A woman." She smiled and sent Ivy off. Ivy walked with her father and brother down to the docks, turning back once to see her mother standing in the tower's window watching them.

When they reached the docks, Magnus stood back while Rayner said farewell. "Stay safe, and try not to beat up on Ser Osmund too much. The man is getting old."

They turned to see Ser Osmund fighting to get his horse aboard; then both burst out into laughter. Ivy's eyes began to fill with tears. Rayner pulled her close and hugged his sister tight. The two had never been apart for more than a few days. They were close in age and grew up not only as brother and sister, but as best friends. Rayner would be twenty years old when Ivy returned as their name days were close together.

Rayner sniffed as he pulled away. "I have something for you."

Rayner unbuckled his sword belt, slid his dagger off, and handed it to Ivy. It was a beautiful blade with an onyx grip. Ivy looked confused. The knife was one of Rayner's most prized possessions. He'd won it years back when competing in the yearly tournament games. Rayner had disarmed one of Magnus's knights in a sparring contest. He was becoming a great swordsman and would be knighted within the next year. Ivy always looked up to him and strived to be like her older brother.

"I want you to keep it for me until you get back. Every warrior should have two blades on their sword belt. We can spar when you come back. If you beat me, then you can keep it."

"Thank you. I'll keep it safe."

He smiled at his sister, then hugged her again, whispering against her ear, "I love you."

"I love you too, Rayner." Ivy sniffed. She clipped the dagger to her belt and watched Rayner walk back to the tower, wiping his eyes with his sleeve.

Magnus came up behind her and rested his heavy hand upon her shoulder. "That was very nice of him," he said, and then Ivy broke down. The tears started rolling down her cheeks as she turned to face her father.

"Oh, sweetling," he said as he cradled her head on his shoulder. His own eyes threatened to betray him as the tears started forming. It was the hardest decision Magnus had ever made, and he questioned it in the days leading up to the departure. How could he let his little girl go? His only daughter to be sent to such a dangerous area by his own orders. Magnus prayed to the gods to keep the seas clear and his daughter safe. "Do you know what?" he asked, wiping his own tears away.

"What?" Ivy sniffed.

"You'll ride straight through the city of Rahama. You may finally see those white-sand beaches that your mother talks of so fondly."

Ivy smiled, but then a horn rang through the air to tell the sailors to begin boarding. Magnus saw a flicker of panic in his daughter's eyes as they listened to the horn echo through the docks.

He adjusted the clip holding her cloak together. "Do you know why I named you Ivy?" She shook her head and dried her tears. "There's an ivy plant that grows up the back of the central tower. The first time I held you was in our bedchamber. I walked over to the North window with you bundled up in my arms, and I saw that ivy growing strong, its long vines clutching the window. And then you grabbed my finger and wouldn't let go."

He brushed his daughter's hair behind her ear and continued. "An ivy plant grows taller and stronger the more that they mature. It can take over whole castles if allowed to grow untamed. But no matter where it is or what it's reaching for, it never loses its roots. I knew you would become a strong woman and do great things with your life. No matter where you go, your roots are here. This will always be your home, and you'll always be my daughter."

Ivy began tearing up again, and Magnus could no longer hold back his own tears. He let them fall freely as he pulled Ivy into his chest, not wanting to let go. He cupped the back of her head and whispered in her ear, "I love you, Ivy."

"I love you too, Father."

Magnus pressed his lips to her forehead, and closed his eyes, searing the moment into his mind. "Now," he began, drying his tears, "I don't want you to be sad. Don't worry about us back here. Focus on your training and try to have fun. You're going on a great adventure, and Ser Osmund will be at your side the whole way. Listen to Ronin, and you may just yet become a knight."

Ivy's eyes lit up with excitement at that. "A knight?" she exclaimed. "But, your rules—"

"Will be revisited upon your return."

"Promise?"

"I promise," Magnus proclaimed, placing his fist across his chest, and Ivy mirrored him. The horn sounded again, giving a final warning cry.

Ivy gathered herself, and Magnus walked her to the ship that would take her away. They embraced one last time, and Magnus watched his daughter climb the ramp to the *Red Maiden*. Ser Osmund was already aboard, waving to the king as he helped Ivy onto the ship. Magnus would stay standing on the beach until the ship disappeared over the horizon. Ivy turned back to look at her father one more time, and he placed his fist across his chest again as if to say *everything will be alright*. Because it had to be.

Ivy leaned over the gunwale of the *Red Maiden*, feeling the sea spray on her cheeks. Seagulls circled above, and Ivy's auburn hair whirled around her face as the wind came off the water. It was the first time Ivy had been on a ship of this size. Most of the local fishermen of Godstone set out in rowboats to fish the Onyx Cove. Her father had the largest ship in the kingdom, but Ivy had never seen him use it.

The *Red Maiden* was massive. Her three masts stood as tall as the ship was long. Her red sails cracked and snapped with the winds of the Shadow Sea. They'd been sailing for days now and would arrive at Port Tsue tomorrow. Ser Osmund was largely confined to his cabin, as the choppy waters didn't agree with him, and he could scarcely keep anything down.

Ivy, however, spent her days above deck, following the captain around and listening to his stories. Captain Erik Seafarer was a stout man, not much older than her father, though his hair was gray. Erik had a scar across his throat, and some of his front teeth were missing.

"Was a Siren did this," the captain said one afternoon, pointing to the scar. He told Ivy the story, in a raspy voice, of how a Siren almost dragged him down to the bottom of the sea.

The Siren Sea lay to the southwest and the captain told her it got its name from the creatures that lurked in the warm green waters. Erik told Ivy how he'd sailed South years ago, and the *Red Maiden* had been caught in a storm and run aground. Erik was the last off the boat, to make sure all the men got off. When he lowered himself down into the waist-high waters, he heard someone singing.

"A young girl lay floatin' on her back, singing to herself," he said. "I thought she must be hurt. I tried to rescue her." Erik said she was the most beautiful girl he'd ever seen. Her hair was black as night, and her pale blue eyes shone in the dark storm. He pulled her to shore, and when he dragged her onto the sand, he realized she had no legs, but the tail of a fish covered in thick black scales. "I grew up hearing stories of how the song of the Sirens can put men in a trance," the captain recalled.

"I turned to run, but she had hold of my ankle. The creature clawed at me and shrieked, and her face had morphed—her teeth were sharp things, her eyes had become hollow holes. The Siren started dragging me back into the water, and no matter how much I yelled, my men couldn't hear me over the storm.

"I tried to kick the creature off, but she sliced her talon across my neck. We struggled, and my lungs filled with salty water. I could taste blood in my mouth. I don't know how, but finally I managed to pull a knife and I just slashed at the creature. The Siren retreated to the deep waters, screaming as she dove under the sea."

Ivy didn't know whether to believe Erik, but it was a good story, and she listened anyway. He had many strange stories, and

Ivy enjoyed his company during the voyage since Ser Osmund wasn't feeling well. Ser Osmund's black stallion, Eclipse, had been brought aboard and hadn't stopped screaming since. Ivy's chestnut colt, Cassius, seemed to be faring better, though he still wasn't eating much.

Later that day, Ivy could see a storm approaching from the east. Black clouds hung low to the water, and a sheet of rain cut off her view of the sea beyond. She made her way below deck to take shelter and check on Ser Osmund. The cook had left a tray outside his door—hard bread and a bowl of broth, though most of it had sloshed out due to the rough seas. She picked it up and knocked on his door. The knight sat up in his bed, still looking a little pale. Ivy offered him the food on the tray, and the knight tried a nibble of bread.

"Erik says we'll arrive at Port Tsue tomorrow. You and Eclipse should be feeling better once you're on dry land again," Ivy teased.

"Good," the knight said. "I don't know what I'd do if we had to sail all the way to Kame Island."

"How long will it take us to ride down the coast?"

"It will take more time than our voyage did. A horse can only walk so far in a day, and we're in no rush. The weather will be better down South, so we don't need to worry about snow and freezing rains."

"Will Ser Ronin be inside the castle with the king?"

"I'm not sure, my lady. We're to go straight to King Mashu, and then he'll tell us where to find Ronin."

"Why don't you call him Ser? He's a knight, isn't he?"

"He is. Though he never wanted to be called Ser."

Ivy didn't understand. What sort of knight wouldn't want the title that comes with knighthood? "Will you tell me about him?"

Outside, the rain began to beat against the window, and the wind could be heard howling through the boat.

"Very well," Ser Osmund agreed. "Light those lanterns above the bed. The sky will be black soon." Ivy did what he asked, then settled in a chair beside his bed.

"What would you like to know, my lady?"

Ivy considered. There was so much she wanted to know. She decided to start with asking how Ronin came to Godstone and started training knights. Ser Osmund told the tale as best he could recall. Ronin came to Godstone as a young man of twenty years old when Magnus was only a boy of five. He left the Isle of Fire as a boy to pursue knighthood on the mainland. He trained in Rahama and quickly earned his knighthood, as he was renowned for his style of fighting.

"I'd never fought a man like him, before or since," Ser Osmund recalled. "The way he moved was like water flowing over a rock, and I was the rock."

Word quickly spread of Ronin's skill, and King Erwin of Godstone sought him out and asked Ronin if he'd teach his son, Magnus, to fight. Ronin was reluctant but eventually agreed and soon came to train Helvarr as well. Magnus and Helvarr were inseparable as boys. Helvarr's father had been killed in battle, and King Erwin gave him a room in the tower. He became a friend and brother to Magnus.

Ronin soon grew to care for the two boys like a father. They would train every day for hours at a time, and Ser Osmund would often accompany them to ensure the future king was safe.

"I remember the day I saw a glimpse of the Helvarr I would come to know," Ser Osmund went on, eyes hooded. "They were seven years old, and Ronin took them to the beach to spar. The day was cloudy, and rain threatened to interrupt the training session, but Ronin insisted they needed to learn to fight on ground that wasn't stone."

Ser Osmund took another nibble of bread and continued. "Ronin drew a circle in the sand for the boys—the first to be pushed out of the ring lost. They began with their practice swords, meeting each other's blows and counter striking. Your father managed to disarm his friend and push him out of the circle, but Helvarr didn't like that. They reset and came together in a crash, Helvarr never giving Magnus a chance to swing his sword. I could see the anger in his eyes as he sent his sword crashing down on Magnus's leg. He screamed out in pain and dropped his sword, but Helvarr came at Magnus, sword still swinging, and shoved him out of the circle to land face down in the sand. When I started to approach, Ronin held up his hand to stop me. Helvarr threw his sword down and jumped onto Magnus. The two boys struggled in the sand until Helvarr landed a punch across his cheek and reared back for another. That was when I stepped in and grabbed hold of his arm.

"I shoved Helvarr aside to make sure Magnus was alright. When I looked to Ronin for answers as to why he let it continue, he only shook his head in disappointment. At the time, I thought it was meant for Magnus because he wouldn't fight back, but now I know it was Helvarr who disappointed Ronin." Ser Osmund looked to Ivy, who was listening to the story intently. The room had grown dark from the storm outside, and the lanterns swung on their chains above the bed. "You must never fuel your sword with hate and anger if you're to become a good knight, Ivy. It clouds your head, consuming you."

Ivy nodded.

"Let's see," the knight continued. "Ronin remained at Godstone even after he knighted your father and Helvarr. He took on a few more young boys and started training others for knighthood. But he always kept a close relationship with Magnus and especially Helvarr."

Ivy furrowed her brow at that. "Why him? If you say he was disappointed in Helvarr, then why would he continue to look after him?"

"I'm afraid I don't have an answer for that, my lady. Perhaps Ronin felt that it was his burden somehow. Perhaps he was only making sure Helvarr wouldn't lose his temper. Who's to say what reasons Ronin had? Perhaps you could ask him when we arrive."

"Was Ronin there the day my father banished Helvarr?" Ivy asked.

"No, he was back at the kingdom training future knights. However, I was there, and I remember it like it only happened yesterday."

Ser Osmund told Ivy the whole story. The battle, how her father got the scar on his cheek, the arrow that made Ser Osmund slower to swing on his left side. He described the fight in bloody detail, even describing Lady Roe better than her father had when he recalled the event. Perhaps it was a painful memory for her father, and he didn't wish to discuss it. Ser Osmund said her father took the girl's death to heart, blaming himself for what happened to her, though Ivy knew it wasn't his fault. None of it would have happened if not for Helvarr.

By the time Ser Osmund had finished his story, the world outside was black. The knight let out a yawn, and Ivy stood to take her leave. As she walked down the corridor to her cabin, she recalled everything that Ser Osmund told her. Some things just didn't make sense to her, but she'd soon ask the same questions to Ronin himself. Ivy returned to her small cabin. The room was bare, save for the bed under the round window and her bag containing some extra clothes. Her father had told her to pack light because they wouldn't be able to bring along a carriage. He'd given Ivy a leather purse with some gold coins so that she could purchase some new clothing down South to blend in, though Ivy wasn't concerned. It wasn't as if anyone was looking for them. Why should she worry? Ivy was more focused on training and getting more answers from Ronin.

The storm raged all through the night, making it difficult to sleep. When dawn broke, the rain began to die away, and Erik sent for her to be brought up on deck. Ivy strapped on her sword belt with Promise and Rayner's dagger and ran up the steps. She found Erik at the bow of the *Red Maiden*, pointing at the approaching city.

Port Tsue was like nothing Ivy had ever seen. Godstone had the one central tower and high walls, but Port Tsue had many high structures. It was no kingdom, but it was massive to behold. The city's tallest structures were built from red stone, and all around them, beautifully colored buildings stood below. Yellow, sky blue, tan, and pink, each different from the next.

As the *Red Maiden* came closer to the docks, Ivy could see two tridents carved from stone marking the city's entrance. They stood taller than the masts of the *Red Maiden*, their three spears stabbing at the sky. The city rose high on a hill from the water to stand on stone streets as far as the eye could see, making it seem like the buildings were stacked on top of each other.

Stone steps crept their way out of the water to meet the city above. A hundred different flowers grew over the wall to dangle just above the shallows of the water. The air already felt warmer as Ivy removed her cloak. It even smelled different here. The air smelt of saltwater, fish, and flowers.

"Best go and find your sick knight, little lady," Erik said, drawing her eyes away from the city. "We'll drop you at the docks, and then the *Red Maiden* will be off again as if it was never here."

Smiling, Ivy turned and ran across the deck. She was anxious to explore the city and see the South. Ivy only wished that her father was here with her, but she couldn't think of that right now. She was anxious to get off the ship and experience new things. Her adventure was beginning, and everything was alright, just as her father promised her.

CHAPTER EIGHT

# THE LEADER

It had been over a week since Ivy left for Kame Island, and Magnus could scarcely think of anything else. Every minute while on the road to Temple City, he thought of his daughter. Was she getting enough to eat? Did she have a safe place to sleep at night? Would they encounter any trouble on the road? Every night Magnus would pray to the God of Judgement. Ivy was in his hands now, and she'd need all the protection she could get.

Traders Road ran from Rahama to Xanheim, where Ivy and Ser Osmund would cross over to Kame Island. However, the road didn't get its name because people traded goods between the two cities. Traders Road got its name from the men who abducted people, made them into slaves, and then exchanged them for gold, steel, or silk. Magnus felt a sick feeling in the pit of his stomach every time he thought of what could happen, but he felt a bit of relief knowing Ser Osmund was with his daughter.

The sun was beginning to set just as Temple City came into view. Magnus's men would set up camp a few miles outside the city in case the raiders tried another ambush in the night. Here they were in grasslands. With snow covering the fields, it was much easier to spot riders. Rayner rode beside his father, looking as gallant as a knight in his new polished armor. As they made camp for the night, Magnus went around to each of his bannermen to make sure their people had enough food and water. A river ran from Lamira up to the Hercynian Forest, and Magnus decided to make camp on the east side of the river. After a warm supper of fish stew and bread, Magnus called a meeting of the council members, which now included his son Rayner.

The king's tent was large enough to fit a trestle table and chairs for all the members of his council. Rayner was seated to his father's right, followed by Lady Oharra and her daughter, Lord Kevan, and Earl Rorik with his wife and son. Magnus always thought it wise to give the floor to someone else before making his own suggestions about an upcoming battle. He valued his council's input and wanted to show them that he was a king who could listen and not just command.

"How should we proceed?" he asked his council.

Lord Kevan was the first to speak. "We could starve them out."

"How do you propose we do that when there's a river that runs straight through the city?" Lady Oharra asked.

"We could block it off. Stop the flow of water, so the raiders have no fish to eat. Or wait for the river to freeze over."

"There are civilians within the city. Do you mean to starve them as well?" When Lord Kevan didn't answer, Lady Oharra continued. "Besides, the river will likely not freeze for months. It's only the beginning of winter, and we don't have time to wait them out."

Magnus looked around the table, waiting for someone else to suggest a plan.

Earl Rorik spoke up. "Do you mean to parley with their leader?"

"It's worth a try if we can't come up with a better option, though I doubt a parley means anything to these raiders, and it would be risky."

"If they will not meet the king's demands," Grimm said, addressing the table, "then we should take the city. We should not be negotiating. The North is our land, and the people of Temple City must have known the risks they were taking by harboring our enemy."

Rayner spoke before Magnus could. "Temple City is neutral, and they see no enemy and no borders. It isn't fair to attack their land for a war they aren't fighting."

Silence crept over the table as everyone listened to the young prince. "But if my father thinks a parley won't work, then we need to try something different. Meeting with their leader might show them that we're willing to negotiate, and my father will make it known that we're not going to attack the city." Rayner looked to his father, who gave him a proud smile and nodded for him to continue.

"Once they believe that we aren't a threat is when we go in. A few of us will find a way into the city and take their leader hostage. When my father comes back from the 'parley' with the man's name and description, he shouldn't be too hard to find. This way no one gets hurt."

Everyone seemed quiet as they considered the plan.

"How will we enter the city?" Lady Oharra addressed Rayner. He stood up and went over to a rolled-up leather cloth that contained all the king's maps. He pulled out the map for Temple City and laid it in between the lady and her daughter Correlyn. "The river runs through the city, so it must be they built their wall over the running water. All we have to do is let the river bring us under the wall."

Grimm shook his head. "Such a weakness in their defenses will be guarded."

"They have no enemies to defend against," Rayner said. "They're neutral."

Grimm leaned forward and grinned. "Then why do they have walls?"

Rayner opened his mouth, then closed it again, sighing. "Fine. If there are guards on the river, I'm sure Lady Oharra could take them down silently." Rayner looked to the lady, who gave him a confident nod. "Good. I'll lead a few of us into the city."

Magnus's eyes grew wide. "No, Rayner," he commanded. "You'll stay with me."

"And who do you propose to send?" Rayner questioned his father. "Earl Rorik and Grimm will stand out too much with their shaved heads and tattoos. You can't go. You're the king and have to stay behind in case something goes wrong. I suggest—"

Magnus cut him off and stood suddenly. "And you're my son and heir. What if something should happen? You're too valuable. I can't let you go too." As those words passed his lips, Ivy's face flashed before his mind's eye, and he felt a knot form in his throat. Magnus turned away and went to pour himself a cup of wine.

"It's my plan, Father, and I can do it. I suggest Lady Oharra and Correlyn accompany me into the city. My lady," Rayner addressed Lady Oharra. "You'll bring your bow since it's quieter. Correlyn and I will conceal our swords under a cloak, and if all goes as planned, we should be able to capture their leader and be outside the walls before anyone notices he's gone."

Everyone looked to their king for an answer as he still stood at the back of the tent. Magnus came and retook his seat, stroking his beard as he thought about his son's plan. He knew Rayner wanted to prove himself. He'd be twenty years of age soon and a man grown. Magnus couldn't keep him from danger for the rest of his life, and he wouldn't pass along his own fears to Rayner.

In truth, Magnus was proud of his son; Rayner was a strong and brave young man. He'd make a great knight one day and an even better king. Magnus looked around the table, then nodded his head in agreement. "Very well," he consented. "I'll meet with their leader in the morning."

After everyone left for the night, Magnus stayed seated at the table, stroking Luna's white feathers while thinking of what was to come. Rayner had stayed behind as well to have a cup of wine with his father. Magnus was lost in thought when Rayner spoke up.

"I know you're afraid for me, Father," he started hesitantly, "but I know what I'm doing, and this is going to work. I promise."

*Promise.*

Magnus had promised Ivy that she'd be safe; he'd promised Elana the same. And Ivy had promised that she would kill Helvarr for what he'd done. But promises don't protect people. Promises were so often only a lie wearing a friendly mask to instill comfort.

Rayner reached for his father's hand, pulling him back to reality. "I miss her too, Father. But I'm not worried."

"How can you not be worried? She's your sister." Magnus didn't understand. All he'd done since Ivy left was worry about her.

"Do you remember when Ivy and I were young, and she beat up the stable boy, Timon?"

Magnus nodded his head, waiting for Rayner to explain.

"Timon was a big boy for his age, and he and a couple of friends were picking on me one day. I believe I was eight, which would make Ivy six years old at the time. Timon and his friends outnumbered me and were pelting me with rocks, shoving me around. I tried to fight back, but Timon easily overpowered me. He picked up a hook and started swinging it at me when, all of the sudden, he was hit with a rock. I looked around and spotted Ivy across the courtyard with a wooden play sword in hand. She was just a little girl, but already I could see the fighter inside her.

"Ivy charged the two friends, swinging her sword. She cracked one of them in the head, and he went down. I stood to try and help her but quickly realized that she didn't need it. The other boy ran away before Ivy could hit him with the sword. When Timon grabbed for her, Ivy slid through the mud behind the boy and whipped her sword around to strike him in the back. He went down to one knee, and Ivy jumped on him and started pounding on his head. As amusing as it was, that's when I pulled her off. Timon and his friend retreated and never bothered me again. Ivy was born a fighter, and she can handle herself. She'll be alright, Father. I know it."

The next morning Magnus set out early for Temple City. He went alone, save for Luna, flying a white peace banner, so the raiders knew he meant to confer. The city had short walls with a portcullis as their main entrance. Magnus took notice of the river running under the north side of the walls. As he drew near, he could see men standing guard on the wall and archers nocking back arrows through a slit in the stone.

One of the guards called down to Magnus. "Who are you?"

Magnus told him who he was and what he was doing there. The two guards exchanged a look but eventually lifted the portcullis to let the king pass.

Inside the walls, Magnus could see civilians and raiders alike. The raiders didn't need to take over the city because Temple welcomed all guests, so long as they paid for their stay. They were easily spotted; most wore some armor, whether it be metal or boiled leather. Many were knights, but some of the raiders were sellswords hired by King Caato or simple farmers who took up arms against the North.

The residents of the city were busy preparing for the day. Men stood at the river's edge, casting lines into the flowing water. Women carried baskets of vegetables, and children played in the streets. Magnus was escorted to a place called the Riverside Inn, where the guards claimed their leader had a room. Part of the inn expanded over the flowing river, giving guests a balcony to fish from. Indeed, their leader, Ser Marion, was staying on the top floor with one of these balconies and welcomed King Magnus.

The knight wore lobster armor, his hair golden and his eyes the color of smoke. The knight offered Magnus some ale, which he politely declined.

"Come now," said Ser Marion. "If I meant to kill you, my men would have filled you with arrows at the front gate." That wasn't any comfort to the king, but he took the horn of ale anyway and tried a sip. "Now," Ser Marion began, "to what do I owe the pleasure of this visit?"

"I'm here to give you a chance to leave Temple City and return south."

"And why would I do that?" the knight asked curiously.

"Because you won't like what comes next if you don't comply."

The knight let out a chuckle and drained his horn of ale. "Do you mean to attack this city, King Magnus?"

"Of course not," he admitted. "These people are innocent, and I won't have their blood on my hands. Surely we can negotiate a deal."

"You have nothing to offer me." Magnus knew that wasn't true; the knight would surely ask for Godstone, which Magnus would never give up. Instead, he said, "I have your life to offer you, Ser." When the knight saw that Magnus was serious, a hint of worry crept over his face. Magnus smiled and bid the knight a good day before walking away. Ser Marion shouted insults and curses at the king's back, but nothing would stop him. He'd gotten what he came for. *Ser Marion. Hair of gold and eyes of smoke.*

That night as Rayner was going over the plan once more, Magnus lit a candle and said a quick prayer to the God of Judgment for Rayner and Ivy both. He had a quick word with Lady Oharra, asking her to watch out for his son. When the sun was set, the team was ready to head out. They'd be walking to the gate, and Lady Oharra had supplied the three of them with snow-fox cloaks to blend in with the white field. The king hugged his son and told him to be careful.

"I'll see you before sunrise, Father."

## CHAPTER NINE

# HIDEAWAY

Rayner led Correlyn and her mother to the back of the city, where the river began to flow under the wall. The back of the wall wasn't as heavily guarded since the raiders expected no enemies from the South. However, as Rayner drew closer, he realized the river ran under a portcullis, not a wall. The portcullis would surely have spikes that dug into the riverbed and slowed down the water flow.

He turned to Lady Oharra and offered to go in first to see what awaited them under the freezing water.

"I'll go," she countered. "I promised your father I'd look after you. You and Correlyn stay here while I check it out." Rayner didn't have time to argue, so he reluctantly agreed and watched as she lowered herself into the river.

The lady hissed at the water's icy bite, then silently slipped below the surface. Rayner glanced at Correlyn, who smiled and nodded that she was okay. He felt a slight jitter in his belly when she smiled at him, but it vanished as Lady Oharra resurfaced, teeth chattering from the cold.

"There's slits wide enough in the portcullis. We can slip through."

Rayner and Correlyn took off their snow-fox cloaks as Oharra dove back under the water to secure the other side. They waited a moment until they thought it was safe, and then Correlyn lowered herself into the water and disappeared below the surface. Then it was Rayner's turn. The water felt like a thousand knives stabbing at his lungs. He took in what air he could and then dove. As he was trying to squeeze through the slit, he thought he felt something tug at his leg. He gave it a yank before realizing he was caught on something. Rayner tried to pull his leg free but sliced it open. He cried out under the black waters and felt the air leave his lungs to float up to the surface. Now he was panicking, clawing at the riverbed to pull himself free before starting to feel faint. He felt a pair of arms wrap around his torso just as the world went black.

Correlyn dragged him up the bank, and ferociously started breathing air into his lungs. His eyes shot open, and he coughed up what water he'd swallowed. "What happened down there?" Correlyn asked, her teeth chattering with cold.

"I...I don't know. My foot caught on something." Correlyn smoothed his hair back and glanced down.

"You're hurt," she said, examining the wound. She quickly ripped a strip of cloth and wrapped it tight around the cut. Rayner tried not to wince as she tied it off.

Lady Oharra was standing just behind with her bow out, keeping guard, and asked, "Are you alright to continue, Rayner?"

He nodded his head, suddenly realizing how bad he was trembling. There was a brazier burning outside one of the inns, but it was too exposed. They moved into the shadows and headed toward the inn. Lady Oharra suggested finding a different way out of the city, especially with a hostage.

"Let's just make sure we have a hostage first," Rayner responded.

He'd studied the map of Temple City and, sure, there were plenty of convenient ways into the city. But they were also too exposed and would likely be guarded better than the river.

As they slipped through the city, Rayner noted the raiders atop the walls. Most were faced just north where they knew Magnus was. The entrance of the inn was guarded by two raiders, but as Lady Oharra lifted her bow, Rayner put a gentle hand on her arm and whispered, "We don't need bloodstains on the wood floor. We'll knock them out and slip in."

The lady nodded, then crept forward. Rayner followed at her back with Correlyn at the rear. Oharra moved like a shadow. The poor raider didn't even see her until it was too late. Rayner pounced on the second guard before he could shout, cracking the pommel of his sword on the back of his head. After they hid the bodies, they climbed the steps of the inn where they found Ser Marion alone in his room within the Riverside Inn.

No guards stood outside his door. They quickly slipped inside without being detected. The knight was in his bed. An empty horn of ale lay beside him as he snored loudly. Ser Marion was so drunk that Lady Oharra was able to bind his hands together before he started to rouse from sleep. His eyes grew wide as he realized what was happening, but Correlyn put her knife to his throat. "One noise, and I'll cut your pretty neck."

"We have him. Let's go," Lady Oharra instructed as she gagged the knight. She dragged him to his feet, and as they turned to leave, a young woman stood in their path. She was naked save for a fur scarf she wore draped over her shoulders. The woman looked at Ser Marion, then turned and bolted from the room, Correlyn running after her.

"Let's go," Oharra hissed with more demand in her voice.

"But the woman—" Rayner started.

"Correlyn will take care of it. We need to get him out of the city." Rayner didn't have a choice; he cleared the hallway and motioned for Oharra to follow him.

Once outside the inn, they followed the east wall looking for another way out and came upon a small, iron gate. Rayner scanned the wall above and breathed a sigh of relief that the raider on guard was at least fifty yards down. However, Rayner cursed when he noticed the gate was sealed shut with a chain. Correlyn came up behind them, wiping her blade against her pants.

"What did you do?" Rayner growled. She rolled her eyes and tried to brush past him, but he grabbed her arm.

"No one was supposed to get hurt," Rayner hissed. "My father--."

"Is not my father," Correlyn finished. "And he doesn't control me."

"Stop it, both of you," Lady Oharra ordered as she dropped the knight and snatched Correlyn's sword from her.

"What are you doing?" Rayner asked.

"I'm going to break the chain."

"That'll make too much noise."

"You have a better idea?" When Rayner didn't answer, she turned away and started hacking at the chain.

The metal clang was loud and could surely be heard up on the wall and throughout the neighborhood. Someone yelled down to them from up on the wall, and soon footsteps could be heard rushing across the stone path above them. Correlyn picked up her mother's bow and dropped the first man that came around the corner.

Rayner cursed again and drew his sword as a few more men rounded the building. Lady Oharra was still hacking at the metal when the first man advanced on Rayner. The knight swung his sword, forcing Rayner to step back. Their blades met, the ring of steel clashing only added to the clang of the gate.

Rayner came at him, jabbing his sword into the weak point in his armor. He thrust his sword up through the knight's belly and watched him sink to the ground. Correlyn was busy dropping men as they ran along the wall above, their screams echoing as they fell from the wall. Another knight came around the corner carrying a crossbow.

Rayner felt sweat running down his back when he spotted the weapon. The knight pulled the trigger, and Rayner dove just as the bolt tore past him. He heard a muffled scream from behind and turned to see the bolt sticking out from Ser Marion's leg. Rayner couldn't help but grin, and the bowman looked as though he'd just watched his own death.

Distracted, Rayner advanced on him, skewering his sword through the man's throat. He was just beginning to feel the adrenaline rush of battle when a massive man wearing no armor came around the corner carrying an ax. The shouts of other raiders could be heard through the city as they came closer. Rayner glanced at Lady Oharra over his shoulder.

"Hurry!" he yelled.

The giant raider walked toward Rayner, his feet falling heavily into the snow. He raised his ax and brought it down as Rayner dove away from its blade. The man quickly yanked it from the earth and swung it just as Rayner got to his feet. He ducked and rolled to the other side of the man, but he was fast for his size. Rayner knew he couldn't hope to stop the ax with his sword. The man was much stronger, and it would only slow the blow, not stop it. He danced around the man, dodging the ax. The chains *clanged* loudly behind him as Oharra hacked at them, the rhythm mimicking his rapid heartbeat. Rayner took a swing at the giant but couldn't get close enough to cut him.

The ax came down at Rayner's side, almost cutting off his foot.

The man shoved Rayner, who lost his sword as he fell back into the snow.

He reached for it, but the giant stepped on his arm, and Rayner heard his own bone crunch.

He cried out in pain.

The man grinned and raised his ax, keeping Rayner pinned underfoot.

Rayner closed his eyes.

The giant went down with a loud thump, his ax embedding itself in the frozen earth just missing Rayner's head. A bolt stuck out from the raider's neck, and Correlyn came to help Rayner to his feet, carrying the crossbow.

"Let's go!" Lady Oharra yelled. Rayner snatched up his sword and ran through the gate just as more raiders came around the corner. The archers ceased fire once they were outside the walls for fear of hitting their leader again. It was still dark outside when the trio came hobbling back into camp. Rayner knew the raiders would be right on their trail, and they needed to be ready.

Magnus shoved men aside to get to his son. "What happened?" he demanded as he looked over Rayner's wounds.

"I'm fine, Father."

When Magnus touched his arm to have a look, Rayner cried out and snatched his father's hand away with pleading eyes.

"It's broken," Magnus growled angrily.

"At least it's not your sword arm," Correlyn offered.

"We were caught by his whore," Lady Oharra motioned to Ser Marion. She told the king all that had occurred with the portcullis, the girl, and the raiders that attacked them. Now that the raiders knew Magnus had Ser Marion, he hoped that they'd comply. The sun would be up soon, and the raiders would be gathering their forces to come and meet the king's demands.

As the sun rose, riders could be seen coming toward the camp from Temple City. Magnus still wasn't happy with how the plan had played out the night before, and he was tired.

He was tired of a lot of things.

Ser Marion had his hands tied behind his back and was bent over with his head resting on a stump. Rayner stood behind his father, his arm in a sling with Correlyn at his side. The raiders sent one man forward on horseback to talk with Magnus. The king didn't move as the man approached. He stood next to Ser Marion with his hands tapping his sword's pommel that stuck from the ground.

"What is this?" the raider demanded.

Magnus lifted his chin. "I gave your leader a chance to leave yesterday. He refused."

"Ser Marion also said that you wouldn't attack the city and harm innocent people."

"My people were only protecting themselves against your knights," Magnus stated.

"Is that so? Then why did I find a young girl with her throat slit ear to ear?" Magnus snapped his head back to find Lady Oharra in the crowd, but it was Correlyn who hung her head nervously.

"That was a mistake, and the person will be dealt with." Magnus motioned toward the border south of them. "You and your raiders will go back south, and only then will I release Ser Marion to you."

The knight looked from Ser Marion to the king before answering.

"No. I don't think we will," he said with a smile.

Magnus scrunched his nose in anger and repeated his commands.

"And what will you do if I refuse you, King Magnus?" the knight mocked. Magnus was tired of these raiders. He was tired of fighting. Perhaps people didn't take him seriously. Perhaps no one feared King Magnus from Godstone.

"I'll kill Ser Marion," he stated plainly.

"Will you?" the knight scoffed.

Magnus drew his sword from the earth and slowly walked around Ser Marion, who was mumbling something under the gag in his mouth. "Tell me, will King Caato blame you for this negligence?"

He could see the knight's mind racing as he looked over the king's army, sizing it up. Magnus had been sure to bring enough men to defend themselves against the raiders' army. Their forces were equally matched, and the knight realized this.

"You can't do that," the knight said, addressing Magnus.

"I can't?" Magnus lifted his arms and looked around. "This is our land you stand on. Did you think I would easily hand it over?"

The knight didn't answer. He sat atop his horse, looking to Ser Marion for answers. Magnus removed the gag from the knight's mouth to let him speak.

"Don't negotiate with this false king!" he roared to the mounted knight. The knight seemed to consider for a moment, looking from Ser Marion to the king. The knight looked Magnus in the eye and lifted his chin. "I won't compromise with you. You'll release Ser Marion back to us immediately."

Magnus sighed and shoved the gag back in Ser Marion's mouth before stepping to his side. "This is your last chance, Ser. Will you retreat to the South?"

"Never," the knight answered with a grin, clearly not believing the king's threat.

Magnus nodded, then lifted his sword and brought it down on Ser Marion's neck. The man's head bounced and rolled in front of the mounted knight, spooking the horse who reared up in terror. The knight had a similar look on his face as he cursed at the king.

"I'll give you a thirty-second head start to run back to your knights and tell them to retreat south, or Lady Oharra here will put an arrow through your skull."

On command, the lady nocked an arrow and eyed the knight as he turned his horse and fled back to his men. Magnus went to his son, whose mouth hung open in disbelief. He grabbed the back of Rayner's head and pulled him close.

"Sometimes, a king must make difficult decisions. And sometimes fear is the only weapon you have left." He kissed his son's head before retreating to his tent.

The next morning Magnus and Rayner set off for Hideaway

Harbor accompanied by Lady Oharra, Correlyn, and twenty escorts. The rest of his forces remained outside of Temple City with the earl and Lord Kevan to ensure the raiders didn't come back while the king was away. On the way, Magnus rode next to Rayner ahead of everyone else to speak in private. He told his son the same story he'd told Ivy a few weeks back. Rayner listened to the story intently, trying to absorb everything his father was telling him.

When Magnus was finished, they rode in silence for a while before Rayner spoke. "That trip you went on when I was only a boy...some said you were tracking something. Was it Helvarr?"

Magnus nodded and explained that he didn't wish to hurt Helvarr, only to keep him out of the North.

"And you think he'll be in Hideaway Harbor?" Rayner asked.

"I think he was there, and someone there might know where he's gone."

"But if you won't kill him, then what will you do if you ever face him again? You said a king must make difficult choices."

Magnus had thought about that a lot, but it wasn't something he liked to dwell on. He didn't have an answer for his son because, in truth, he had no idea what he'd do in that situation.

"I know what I said," was all he could muster.

The next day they arrived in Hideaway Harbor. It was a small town--many of the buildings were constructed from driftwood and lay close to the beach. The sand was covered in a sheet of snow, and the sea sent foam blowing down the beaches. Lady Oharra's scout had claimed she'd seen Helvarr drinking in one of the local inns weeks back, and it didn't look like he was planning on leaving. She'd watched him every night since spotting him and continued to send ravens to Lady Oharra until she lost him one day. A ship from the South had come in to unload their goods and restock before setting sail. The *Green Beast* was the name on the ship, and it flew green and black striped sails.

Magnus and Rayner started at the docks. Magnus sent Lady Oharra and her daughter to check around the local inns. A fishmonger told Magnus that the *Green Beast* had set sail well over a week ago and was bound for Mandalair on the southern coast. The city was a massive trading port, and it was close to Lamira. Magnus described Helvarr to the older man and asked if he was seen boarding the ship.

"Sure, I know him. He came and bought a basket of clams and mussels from me before leaving. Though this man didn't have long black hair, it was cut shorter and slicked back."

"Did this man have a crooked nose?"

"Sure did. Said he busted it fighting, tryin' to win the love of a woman."

Magnus snickered. "Of course, he did." He thanked the man for his help, then bought some fish and crabs from him.

Magnus and Rayner went in search of Lady Oharra to tell her the news. They found the lady and her daughter sharing a flagon of spiced wine at the closest inn, and Magnus and Rayner joined them. Correlyn smiled at Rayner and poured a cup for him since his arm was in a sling.

"Helvarr left," Magnus began. "He boarded the *Green Beast* and is likely already in Mandalair."

"Really?" Lady Oharra asked, taking a sip of wine. "Well, that's good news then."

"Yes. Now we can focus on the threat of the raiders." The four of them sat drinking while the rest of their escort made camp outside the town.

The sun was beginning to go down, and Magnus requested the innkeeper to cook up the fish and crab he'd bought earlier. She quickly obliged and returned with a fish stew and boiled crabs with potatoes and more wine.

Rayner had trouble cracking the crab with his arm in a sling. Though Correlyn had laughed at his efforts, she eventually helped him. Magnus knew that Correlyn had always had an eye for Rayner; they were about the same age, and she was a beautiful young woman. Magnus has known Correlyn from a young girl and had watched her grow into the strong, brave women she was now. As she cracked a crab leg for Rayner, Magnus caught his son's eye and gave him a knowing smirk. Rayner lowered his eyes, but couldn't keep the smile from his face.

Once they were finished eating, Magnus paid for rooms to be made up for all four of them. Rayner was tipsy from the wine and had to be helped into his room by Correlyn. Magnus smiled knowingly and bid them goodnight as he walked Lady Oharra to her room down the hall.

As Rayner struggled to get his cloak off, Correlyn closed the door and moved in to help him. She unbuckled his cloak and then bent down to help him with his boots.

"Why did you kill that girl?" he asked. She looked up, her cold, gray eyes staring through him.

"Because she would've gotten us all killed, Rayner. Why are you dwelling on a dead girl when I'm right here?"

He looked at her, confused, the wine making his head swim. She stood up, placing a hand on his cheek and leaning in. Correlyn smiled softly, then gently pressed her lips to his. Shocked, Rayner quickly withdrew, stepping back and stumbling onto the bed.

"We can't."

"And why not?" she said, crossing her arms over her chest. "You don't like me?"

"It's not that... I—"

"You have an eye for someone else?"

"No!" he said a little too quickly. Correlyn smiled at him, and Rayner felt his heart starting to pound and heat flooding his cheeks. He cleared his throat and stood up, stepping toward her. "I have eyes for no one else," he whispered, keeping his eyes locked with hers.

Correlyn smiled, and Rayner lifted his free hand to her soft cheek, then leaned back in. Her lips were warm and soft, and he didn't fight it this time. He ran his fingers through her black hair as his heart pounded wildly, and his neck and cheeks caught fire.

Correlyn often flirted with him, but he never thought it could be more. He wrapped his arm around Correlyn's small waist, and she twisted around, gently pushing Rayner onto the bed. Correlyn crawled on top of him, sweeping her lips across his as Rayner tried to keep from shaking. His nerves were on edge, firing off in rapid succession.

Rayner felt her delicate hands run beneath his shirt, over his core and up his chest. He smiled against her lips and Correlyn let out a nervous giggle as she sat up, brushing hair from her face. Rayner stared at her in awe for a moment before he reached up to caress her cheek, lowering her lips back to his.

"You're beautiful," he whispered, and dove back in. Correlyn brushed her tongue against his teeth, and Rayner smiled against her lips, savoring every second of the heady sensation rushing through his veins.

The next morning Magnus went to wake Rayner with some bread and bacon to soak up the wine. When he answered the door, Magnus could see the top of Correlyn's head nestled on the pillow. Rayner looked as though he'd forgotten and quickly tried to explain what happened or, rather, what didn't happen.

The king held up a hand to stop his son's babbling. "You're a grown man, Rayner, and it's none of my business." He couldn't help but smile at his son's embarrassment. "She's very beautiful," his father pointed out. Rayner's cheeks flushed with color as he turned back to look at Correlyn.

"Yes, she is."

Magnus smirked and handed him the plate of food. "You two eat up and get dressed. We're heading home."

## CHAPTER TEN

# TRADERS

Ivy felt as though she'd been traveling for months, though in reality, it had only been a few weeks. They had just left the town of Maridiyan the day before and would arrive in Xanheim in another few days. The city of Rahama was well behind them now. Ivy hadn't even had to beg Ser Osmund to walk along the white beaches. It was just as her mother had described it—soft white sand, crystal waters, and monkeys that roamed the city. They never stayed in one spot for more than a night, so Ivy savored every moment of that beautiful city, so she could share the experience with her mother when she returned home.

Ivy and Ser Osmund had purchased new clothing while in Rahama to blend in better with the Southerners. Ivy traded her wool pants for a pair of tan-colored, cotton ones, her warm tunic for a sheer colorful top. She packed away the cloak her father had given her. She couldn't part with her boots, refusing to trade them for the toeless shoes people of the cities wore, so she kept them. As for her hair, many of the southern girls wore their hair up in intricate knots, but Ivy didn't have the patience for it.

However, she needed to fit in. She settled on braiding her dark auburn hair and letting it cascade down her spine. Ser Osmund had likewise packed away his fur cloak and warmer clothing and now wore lightly colored cotton and only boiled leather. He allowed Eclipse to carry his steel armor. Cassius and Eclipse had been so excited to get off the ship that they were able to ride for a whole day and night before they began to feel tired again and slowed down.

Ivy often couldn't sleep well while on the road. She had too much on her mind…too many unanswered questions. When she was able to sleep, she dreamt of home. Her father always came to Ivy in her dreams, accompanied by Rayner. Last week she dreamt that Rayner had drowned, and she woke in a panic, heart pounding, hands sweating until Ser Osmund reassured her that Rayner was fine. But how could he know? Rayner was over one hundred leagues away while Ivy traveled through a strange world. The landscape along Traders Road was much different from back home. Though the North had grasslands, they didn't look the same.

The dirt path here was surrounded by grass on either side, usually growing up as tall as their horses' bellies. Cass didn't like to be in the tall grass; he was a wary horse and didn't like going where he couldn't see. The grass fields were a sea of color, not just light green or brown that Ivy typically saw up north. The meadows were many shades of green, tan, yellow, and even some that appeared to be blue.

"We should stop for the night, my lady," Ser Osmund called back to her. They were approaching a small town that looked to be made up of one inn, a couple nearby houses, and stables for the horses. They dismounted and tied up their horses, Eclipse taking a nip at Ser Osmund's hand as he was being tied. Ivy lowered her head to hide her smile and tied up Cass alongside the stubborn black stallion.

The inn was so small it didn't even have a name. A woman named Hapna greeted them in the dining area, and Ser Osmund paid for two rooms. He'd been helping Ivy train along the way, usually practicing for a few hours after settling in someplace and getting something to eat. There wasn't anyone else staying at the inn, so Hapna was grateful for the company and a chance to cook for someone.

Ser Osmund sharpened his sword by the hearth, which held a small fire. As winter approached, it had begun to grow chilly at night, even for the South. Ivy went into the kitchen to lend a hand to the older woman, who was glad for the help.

"Where are you and your father headed?" she asked, making conversation as Ivy peeled a carrot. Ivy hadn't told the woman of her relation to Ser Osmund but thought it best to agree with whatever the woman presumed.

"We're headed to Xanheim," Ivy half lied.

"Ah, Xanheim. A fine city it is. What will you find there?"

Ivy lied again, telling Hapna that they were seeking a new life in a new city.

"It's as good a place as any, I suppose," Hapna smiled and, with shaky hands, gave Ivy a spoon to stir the stew.

After a rabbit stew dinner, Ivy and Ser Osmund went outside to find a private place to practice. They had no practice swords with them on the journey, so Ser Osmund had found a couple of good-sized sticks and carved them down to roughly the shape of a sword. A light breeze blew through the grass as they took their positions across from one another.

Ivy rushed him before he could swing his stick sword and easily slid around to his back, jabbing at him from behind. Ivy knew she had to be quicker than the knight since he was much stronger than her. Should he land a blow, he'd knock the stick from her hand. The clack of their swords echoed through the empty fields for well over an hour as the sun began to dip behind the horizon. After, the two found a clearing and sat in the grass to catch their breath, sharing a skin of water as they watched the sun set.

Ivy was buckling on her sword belt when they heard riders approaching. She looked up to see three mounted men trotting over to where she and Ser Osmund had been practicing. They didn't appear to be raiders as none wore armor, but they did carry swords.

"Evening," the first man called out. He had long, shaggy, brown hair and dressed as plainly as the other two he rode with. He dismounted, and Ser Osmund stepped in front of Ivy, wary of the travelers.

"Can I help you?" Ser Osmund asked in a stern voice.

"That has yet to be decided as we've only just met." The man flashed his teeth. "My name's Henry, and these are my brothers, Garold and Wes." He gestured to the two horsemen who had similar, wavy, brown hair.

"And your name?" Ser Osmund hesitated before coming up with the lie that he was Erik, traveling with his daughter Hilda.

"A beautiful name for such a beauty." Henry smiled, looking around Ser Osmund to where Ivy stood.

"If you'll excuse us," Ser Osmund started to move around the man, "we have a long ride ahead of us tomorrow."

Henry held up his hand to stop Ser Osmund. "Ah, but you

haven't helped us yet." Ser Osmund put his hand to the hilt of his sword and eyed the man cautiously, and Ivy did the same. "What a pretty sword." Henry eyed Ivy's blade. "Isn't it pretty, Wes?" he called back to his brother, a scrawny man with long legs.

"Sure is," Wes answered, licking his lips. Ivy's heart began to race in her chest as she realized the men weren't going to leave willingly.

"I think we'll have the sword," Henry proclaimed, narrowing his eyes. "And the girl." Ser Osmund drew his sword at the threat and backed away to stand in front of Ivy.

"Don't make me kill you, old man. It's only business."

Ivy had a moment of panic. She knew the men were traders— men who took innocent travelers and bargained with slave owners to exchange goods. But Ivy would die before giving up the sword her father gifted her. The two brothers dismounted and drew their swords. Hapna came outside and yelled at them to stop.

Henry pointed his sword at the old woman and yelled back, "Go inside, Hapna, before I kill you as well." The woman had no choice but to retreat back inside, giving a sorrowful look to Ivy over her shoulder. "I won't ask again, old man. Hand over the girl, and I won't kill you."

"We'll see who dies here tonight," Ser Osmund responded calmly.

Henry only smiled and called back to his brothers, "Wes, Garold. Get the girl." Ser Osmund turned his head and gave Ivy a look that could only mean one thing. *Run.*

Ivy ran as fast as she could, pulling her sword from the sheath as her feet stomped heavily through the golden grass. The sun was below the horizon now, but it still gave light enough to see. Ivy could hear the two brothers chasing her, yelling from behind that they slew her father. She felt a knot in the pit of her stomach, thinking about Ser Osmund dead, but she had to keep running.

Behind Hapna's inn, there was a scarcely wooded area, and that's where Ivy headed. She crashed through the brush, as vines pulled at her feet and twigs and branches clawed at her face. A tree stood ahead with low hanging branches, and Ivy quickly swung up into it and began to climb. Her heart was beating so loud she feared it would give away her position.

Garold and Wes could be heard moving through the brush cautiously, no longer running as the woods grew darker by the minute. Ivy didn't know what to do. She thought of her father as a tear rolled down her cheek. She didn't think she was ready to kill a man. But there was no time to be ready. Death comes to find you whether you're prepared or not. Ivy wiped the tear and tried to slow her breathing as she listened to the two men approaching.

"Let's split up," one of the brothers said. "This is taking too long."

She could see a dark figure move ahead through the trees as the other brother came below the tree branches that hid Ivy. She said a silent prayer to the God of Secrets, crouched down on the branch, slowed her breathing, and let go.

She landed behind the trader, and as he turned around to the noise, without thinking, Ivy slashed at the man's belly. He cried out in pain as his innards poured out of him, but he managed to swing his sword, forcing Ivy back. She tripped over a root and fell. The man lay dying on the ground, and Ivy could hear his brother approaching, called back by the cries of pain.

Ivy's head was spinning, her eyes as wild as a hunted stag. She quickly picked up Promise and cautiously approached the trader, sticking her blade through the man's neck, silencing him.

"Ivy!" A worried cry came through the woods. She called back to Ser Osmund just as the other trader came through the brush. He looked to the ground and saw his dead brother.

"You'll die for that, you little bitch!" He came at Ivy swinging his sword.

She caught his blade on Promise and quickly stepped around him. He turned and swung, missing Ivy's face by mere inches. She countered his blows, backing away farther into the woods until she was pinned against a tree. He slashed at her, and she ducked, shards of bark falling on her head. Ivy swung her blade at the man's feet, but he kicked her hand, and Promise went flying off into the darkness. Unarmed, she sat shaking at the base of the tree, adrenaline coursing through her body.

"Maybe I'll have my way with you first," the trader sneered as he held her at sword point and started to unbuckle his pants.

Ivy's whole body was shaking with an equal mix of adrenaline and fear as the man eyed her. But then his eyes went wide, and a gurgling sound came from his mouth. Ivy looked up through tears in her eyes to see the point of a sword sticking out the front of his neck. The trader dropped his sword, and Ivy quickly moved away to see Ser Osmund pulling his blade from the man.

Ser Osmund kicked the man to the ground, where he lay bleeding out. He dropped his sword and went to Ivy, holding her face in his hands. He turned her to either side, looking for injuries.

"Are you alright?" Ser Osmund sounded panicked.

"I'm fine," Ivy responded, though she felt anything but fine. Her legs quivered as she stood.

Ser Osmund glanced at the brother that Ivy had killed and asked if the man had hurt her. She only shook her head, keeping her eyes on the ground to avoid looking at the dead man. Ser Osmund embraced her, cradling her head as Ivy forced her tears back. She didn't want to cry. Those men deserved what they got, but Ivy couldn't help but wonder what her father would think of her. Would he be proud or disgusted? Would he have told Ivy they didn't need to die? That there was another way? It didn't matter now; they were dead, and Ivy was safe.

They found Promise lying alone in the woods and picked it up before walking back to the inn. Ivy could feel Ser Osmund's eyes on her, but she wouldn't meet his gaze. He packed up their horses, saying nothing to Hapna as he took food from the kitchen. Hapna had nothing to say either; she only looked at Ivy as if to apologize, but Ivy knew it wasn't the old woman's fault. Ser Osmund had known that they might encounter traders while on the road, but he couldn't have predicted this.

The two traveled side by side, staying off the main road and keeping to the grass and woodline. Ivy had to fight to get Cassius into the tall grasses, but the horse soon relaxed and kept a steady pace. Ser Osmund and Ivy hadn't spoken much since they left Hapna's inn. He kept a close eye on her throughout the rest of the journey but wouldn't press her into talking. Ivy kept a blank stare ahead of her horse, except for the times a bird or animal stirred in the woods and she would quickly reach for Promise.

At night, Ser Osmund and Ivy would set up camp in the tall grass, making sure they kept the fire small. She slept worse since the attack. Every whisper of the wind through the grass made her heart race wildly. Ivy was annoyed with herself that she let her nerves get the better of her.

The next day they reached the city of Xanheim, the late afternoon sun beating down on their heads. A warm breeze rolled off the sea. They dismounted and led their horses down to the docks, searching for a ferry to take them across the Serpent's Pass to Kame Island. Ser Osmund instructed her to stay with the horses while he talked with the captain.

The city was much different from Rahama. The buildings were all made of the same tan and red sandstone and stood longer than they were tall. Ivy didn't see any monkeys within the city, only small children running along the rooftops, jumping from one building to another. The streets were cobblestone paths, and not many trees grew within the city. The people looked different as well—many had dark hair and narrow eyes, and their skin was tan, where Ivy's was pale.

Some spoke a language that was alien to Ivy's ears, but she listened anyway. Ser Osmund came up behind her and laid his hand on her shoulder, making her jump. "Are you ready to go?" he asked quietly.

She nodded her head, and they walked the horses down to where the ferry sat bobbing in the water.

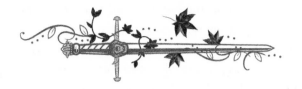

## CHAPTER ELEVEN

# KAME ISLAND

The crossing of the Serpent's Pass was much easier on the horses since the ferry was more like a floating deck than a ship. Ivy stood with Cassius, stroking his neck, and watching the city grow small behind them. Ser Osmund listened to the captain telling stories the whole ride, which lasted a few hours. The man said this part of the sea got its name from a giant sea serpent that used to drag ships under, leaving nothing behind. It was said that Captain Marlin Fairwind slew the beast on his crossing a thousand years ago and that you can see the serpent's skeleton below the water on a clear day.

Ivy didn't see anything of the sort, only a pod of dolphins that followed the ferry and a sea turtle with a red shell.

Kame Island seemed to rise from the water as they approached. The whole island looked to be one great mountain that was pushed up from the seabed. Ivy could see flat pieces of land that had been carved out along the slope to plant crops. As they drew closer, Ivy realized it wasn't a mountain but a large hill with King Mashu's castle atop it.

The main keep of the castle seemed to be grown over with plants, making it appear green from far away. There weren't many large ships in the bay, mostly small fishing boats and another ferry that was pushing off as they docked. Ser Osmund paid the captain and thanked him, leading Eclipse down the ramp and onto dry ground.

Ivy's eyes lit up as she took in her surroundings, and Ser Osmund took note. It must have been the first time she'd smiled for days. "What do you think, my lady?"

"It's beautiful here." Ivy smiled up at the knight.

"Well, come along then."

They mounted up and started for the castle. Ivy thought it must be getting late by now, but the sun seemed reluctant to set. The heat had made Ivy feel light-headed, but she was too eager to care. They trotted up the main road, Ivy's head on a swivel as she tried to look at everything they were passing.

She could see farmers on the flat hillside, pulling vegetables from the ground. Strange trees grew everywhere, some she recognized, and some she didn't. Others had flowers sprouting from their branches and leaves of different shapes and colors. Ivy plucked a fruit from a low hanging branch above and looked at Ser Osmund curiously. He only shrugged his shoulders and smiled as Ivy bit into the fuzzy fruit, letting the sticky, sweet juice drip down her chin.

As their horses trudged up the slope and more buildings came into view, Ivy could hear the familiar sound of sword fighting echoing through the trees. They came to the top of a hill and saw a practice yard off to the right. The ground was sand, and the two boys fighting wore no shoes. Large buildings surrounded the yard on three sides, and the balconies were filled with young women giggling at the fighters below.

Ivy stopped her horse to take a closer look and realized the boys appeared to be her age. The taller one had short, brown hair that swept over his forehead, broad shoulders, and a lean but muscular build. His opponent stood a foot shorter with hair as black as Lady Oharra's. The brown-haired boy turned at the sound of their horses and locked eyes with Ivy. She studied him. He had warm, brown eyes, a strong jawline, and high cheekbones. He was handsome, and Ivy felt her cheeks grow hot as his gaze lingered for a moment longer before turning away to strike his sparring partner.

"That's the king's son." Ser Osmund leaned over, gesturing at the short black-haired boy. "Prince Kal would make an excellent sparring partner for you."

Ivy nodded but found her gaze on the brown-haired boy instead until they were out of view. Trees lined the path to the main gate of the castle, which stood open and scarcely guarded. A man wearing thin black armor greeted them at the entrance. He had an odd-looking sword that he wore on his back rather than belted on his hip. His shoes appeared to be made of cloth and were tied up to his knees.

"We're here to see King Mashu," Ser Osmund told the man. "King Magnus of Godstone sent a hawk informing the king of our arrival."

The man looked from the knight to Ivy then back again. "Yes, of course," he said. "The king has been expecting you."

Two young boys came to lead their horses to the stables, where they would be watered and fed. The man called himself Akio, but claimed he was no knight when Ser Osmund referred to him as "Ser" Akio.

"Do you have many knights on the island?" Ivy asked Akio.

"Not so many. The ones we do have are from somewhere else; they've come to seek a new life. The king's guard has no knights as we don't need them."

"But if you're not a knight, then what are you?"

Akio stopped and turned to her, flashing a faint smile. "A Shadow," he answered before continuing through the castle grounds.

Akio led them to the king's court. The stone steps led up to a balcony that encircled the whole building. The door was round, and carved into the wood was a turtle, the sigil of House Tanzin. Inside, stone pillars stood supporting the ceiling, and King Mashu sat in a modest throne at the back of the court. The king stood as they approached, descending the steps to greet them. He stood eye to eye with Ivy and had long black hair that matched his beard. He wore dark pants and a colorful silk garment that came to his knees. Like Ivy's father, this king didn't wear a crown.

King Mashu welcomed his guests and introduced his wife, Queen Sarei, who sat quietly on her throne. Her hair was done up in a knot and held in place by a thin piece of metal. "How long do you plan to stay?" the king asked, not unkindly.

"Until spring, Your Grace. If it isn't a bother."

"Of course not. You're my honored guests. I've heard of the good work your father is doing in the North." He looked at Ivy. "I'm happy to help in this way. When I received a second hawk from your father, it said that you were already on your way. My people have made up rooms for both of you. Akio will show you the way."

"Your Grace," Ivy started, "when can I meet Ser... I mean, Ronin?"

"There will be time enough for that tomorrow. Right now, you both should eat and rest. The way I hear it, you'll be training very hard for the next few months." The king smiled at Ivy as they were led back out of the court.

Akio took them back the way they came and led them into one of the buildings that surrounded the practice yard.

"Someone will be by with food later," Akio said as he bowed and backed out of the doorway.

Ser Osmund's room was next door and the first one in the hall. He made sure Ivy had everything she needed and then bid her good night. Ivy explored her room; the bed was close to the ground and had only a light blanket covering it. Ivy was used to sleeping with furs, but she supposed she wouldn't need them in this heat. A small table sat in the corner of the room, and pillows were piled high near the door to the balcony. A washing room sat next to the balcony doors, only surrounded by thin curtains instead of walls.

Ivy opened the doors to the balcony and let the fresh, night air inside. She could see the road they'd come up earlier, and glowing bugs lit up in the trees all down the path. They were too far up to hear the ocean waves, but she could still smell the salt in the air. A wall of flowers and plants grew on either side of her balcony, creating a sweet-smelling privacy wall. She heard someone come onto the balcony to the left of hers and peered around the flower wall to get a look at her neighbor for the next few months.

Her cheeks grew hot when Ivy realized it was the brown-haired boy she'd seen earlier, fighting with Prince Kal. He leaned on the wall of the balcony, staring out into the yard, his eyes fixed on something she couldn't see. Ivy quickly turned away before he noticed her and sat down in the chair outside and looked up at the stars. A small woman came with a plate of food for her, and Ivy accepted it graciously. She hadn't eaten much on the road and was grateful for a hot meal. She devoured the fried fish and rice before pouring herself a cup of tea the woman had brought. The tea tasted of sweet flowers and herbs, and its foreign flavors danced across her tongue.

After a while, Ivy's eyelids grew heavy, and she realized how exhausted she was from the trip. When she got up to go inside, she knocked over the tray and sent it crashing to the ground. The boy on the next balcony poked his head out to see around the flower wall. Ivy cursed herself and stood frozen and embarrassed. The boy looked down at the tray then trailed his eyes back up to Ivy's face. A small grin spread across his lips before he stepped back and disappeared again behind the wall. "Shit," she cursed, picking up the tray and closing the door behind her.

Ivy was asleep within minutes and dreamt of Rayner. He was on horseback, barking orders to the men around him as if he were in charge. Ivy smiled, knowing her brother would make a great knight one day and an even better king. But then she saw his face. Rayner looked scared. Ivy tried to call to him, to tell him that everything was okay, but no sound came from her throat. Her brother's brow was creased with worry, one hand clenched tight around the reins and the other around the hilt of his sword. She stepped toward him, but then fire shot up from the ground, forcing Ivy back.

Her brother was inside a circle of flame, his horse desperately trying to find a way out, but the fire only grew higher. Ivy began to panic. She could do nothing but watch as a shadow, a monster, moved toward her brother.

*It's only a dream,* Ivy assured herself. She took a steady breath, closed her eyes, and jumped through the wall of fire only to land in an empty field.

Snow covered the ground and fell in large clumps, sticking to Ivy's hair as she surveyed the grounds. A large pool of blood coagulated at her feet, and a raven stood, staring at her. She felt a shudder, then heard the calls of more ravens that circled above. As Ivy tilted her head up to look, she felt something rush her. The raven was a mere inch from her face, now larger than a horse, and when it opened its beak, the only sound that came out was a terrified scream.

Ivy jolted awake and ran for the basin, splashing water on her face. The sound of practice swords clacking echoed in the yard below. She looked at herself in the mirror. At the tired eyes that stared back and the bags that hung from them. She turned away and began to strip the sweaty clothes from her back. The day was already warm, and Ivy needed to shake the dream from her head and focus on the day. Today she'd meet Ronin and begin her training. Yet as Ivy went to leave her room, she felt a chill crawl down her spine when she realized who the voice of the screaming raven belonged to.

It was hers.

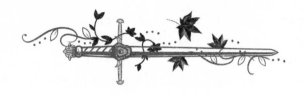

## CHAPTER TWELVE

# RONIN

The day was warm and sunny. Ivy's bare feet silently moved over the cobblestone as she approached the practice yard. Ronin was sitting in the middle of the sand circle, his bamboo staff laid on his crossed legs as he waited for his newest student. His back was to Ivy, and she knew his eyes would be closed. She quietly made her way to him, staff in hand, trying to take small breaths through her nose. Ivy lifted the staff and sent it swinging at her trainer, but he ducked his head just in time. Ronin quickly sprang up and twirled around to face Ivy. He smiled slightly and bowed to her. "Now, you are ready."

Ivy's first impression of Ronin hadn't been what she expected. The man seemed cold and distant, never speaking unless it was necessary. His dark, narrow eyes never gave away what he was thinking. She'd met Ronin the day after they arrived on Kame Island, just one week ago. He kept a small home outside the kingdom on a hillside, where no one bothered him. Ser Osmund had greeted the man warmly, and the two embraced. It had been over nineteen years since they last saw one another.

Ivy's introduction didn't receive the same reaction—he studied her as Ser Osmund told the knight of King Magnus's wishes for his daughter. She almost thought Ronin would refuse her by the look on his face, but he reluctantly agreed to train her when Ser Osmund explained that it would only be for a few months.

A week ago, Ronin had told her to meet him in the practice yard at dawn, only to send her away. She came walking through the sand to where the knight sat in the circle, but when she came closer, he held up his hand to stop her. "I heard you coming. Go away and try again later," he said without even standing to face her.

"But you told me to meet you here," Ivy said, confused.

"When you can get close enough to take a swing without me hearing you, then we will train."

"But—"

"Go away. Try again later." Ronin dismissed her with a wave of his hand, and Ivy stormed out of the yard, kicking sand as she went. It had taken over a week for Ivy to accomplish what Ronin asked, and now she could begin her training.

Ronin used his bamboo staff and had equipped Ivy with a practice sword earlier in the week, but she didn't like using it. Ivy didn't complain for fear of delaying her training even further. Ronin stood before her, burying his feet in the sand. "What have you learned this week?" he asked.

"To stay quiet—"

Ronin swung his staff so fast Ivy didn't even see it until it smacked her upper arm. She dropped her sword to grab the spot where Ronin hit her.

"What the hell was that for?" she yelled at him.

He ignored her. "You have *learned* that loud ones are always the first to die."

She stood up straight and repeated what Ronin said. He nodded and told her to pick up her sword. When Ivy reached for it, he struck her hand with the bamboo. She snapped up, clutching her hand to her chest. "You must be quicker and never take your eye off your opponent. Try again."

Ivy was growing angry but tried not to show it. She bent down slowly, watching Ronin, and quickly snatched up her practice sword and held it out in front of her.

"Now, strike me," Ronin commanded.

Ivy hesitated, and he struck her ankle with his bamboo. He put the staff behind his back and waited for her to approach. Ivy lunged, jabbing her sword at the man's head and torso. He ducked and slid out of her path, just like Ser Osmund had told her. She lifted the sword above her head and sent it crashing down into the sand as he sidestepped around Ivy.

Ronin knocked her feet out from under her, sending Ivy crashing into the sand face first. Now she was angry.

Ivy stood and narrowed her eyes on him and tried again. She swung her sword in a fury, growing angrier when the only thing she hit was sand.

"Stop!" Ronin raised his voice. "Never fuel your fight with hate and anger. Try again."

When Ivy made no move, he told her to sit down in the sand. "Close your eyes and breathe."

Ivy did what he asked, still feeling the anger coursing through her veins. "Are you still angry?" he asked.

"No," Ivy huffed.

"Liar." He smacked her shoulder with his staff. "How about now?"

She winced at the pain and stayed silent.

"Go away. Come back tomorrow."

"Tomorrow?" Ivy asked. "But we hardly did anything!"

"I think your bruises will say otherwise. Come back tomorrow when the anger has left you."

Ronin walked away down the hill, retreating to his little home.

Ivy scooped up her sword and stormed off toward her room. Ser Osmund caught up with her in the hallway to ask how her training went. She told him what happened, but he brushed it off and said it was how Ronin did things. Ivy remembered Ser Osmund's story about how hard Ronin used to be on her father when he was being trained.

When Ivy got back to her room, she took some healing balm and spread it over her sore shoulder and arm. Then she wrapped it tightly with a cloth to restrict her movement until it healed. A small woman had brought Ivy the healing cream during the week that she was learning to be silent. When she asked the woman what it was for, she only smiled and said, "You'll see."

Now she understood, and she was grateful for it. The balm felt cool on her skin as it worked its magic.

Later that day, Ivy grabbed her practice sword and went back to the yard. There were straw men in a shed off to the side of the yard used for archery practice, but Ivy dragged one out into the middle of the circle. She squared up on her straw opponent and started hacking at him with her wooden sword.

She danced around the man, trying to move her body as Ronin did. Ivy worked on holding her sword, being quicker with her swings, and dodging imaginary blows. She was beginning to feel tired when she felt a set of eyes watching her. The sun had started to dip and was now hidden behind the buildings. When she looked up, she saw the brown-haired boy standing on his balcony. He'd been watching her, but for how long she didn't know. She only stared back until he smirked down at her and retreated inside his room.

The next day when Ivy woke, her arm was tight from the previous days beating, and getting dressed took some effort. She left her boots by the door and grabbed her wooden sword. When she came around the corner, she was surprised to see that Ronin wasn't sitting in the sand waiting for her. He was sparring with the boy that had been watching Ivy yesterday. As she approached, they stopped, the boy eyeing her as she came closer.

"Lady Ivy," Ronin beckoned her over. "Come meet your new partner."

The boy snapped his head to Ronin, clearly angry. "What? You want me to fight with her?" Ronin nodded his head patiently.

"Forget it. Do you think my skills are so bad that you'd pair me with her?"

Ivy's cheeks burned with fury.

"She is the same age as you, Finn. It will be good training for both of you. I fear I won't be able to teach Ivy everything in the few short months she has here, and I thought this would be better."

Ivy stared daggers at the boy but stayed quiet.

"You two will be sparring partners, and I'll guide you," Ronin told them. "Ivy, this is Finn."

Ivy didn't know what to make of him. He seemed angry with her, though she had no part in this.

"Finn," Ronin continued, "this is Lady Ivy, and she's come a long way just as you once did."

"I don't see why I have—"

"This is how we're doing it now!" Ronin interrupted Finn. "You can accept it or find another trainer."

Finn formed his mouth in a tight line but eventually nodded his head in agreement.

The two squared up, waiting for Ronin's command to begin. Finn was a little taller than Ivy, and she knew he was strong by the muscles that peeked out from the top of his tunic. When Ronin gave the command, the two came together in a crash. Finn shoved Ivy away, causing her to stumble in the sand. She was surprised by how quick he was, but didn't let it rattle her.

Ivy crouched lower and charged, slicing her wooden sword across Finn's stomach as she passed. When he turned, she expected anger to be painted on his face, but instead, the faintest smile showed.

Finn came at her and brought his sword down as she threw hers up to block the blow. He was stronger than Ivy was and forced the sword down, where it crashed into her injured shoulder. She winced, but he didn't stop. He forced her back, Ivy parrying his attacks. Their swords crossed, and he pushed into her, leaning in close enough for Ivy to see a faint scar on his chin.

That moment of hesitation cost her, and Finn threw her back with such a force that Ivy's sword went sailing, and she landed outside the sand circle on the cobblestone road.

Her shoulder smacked the stone walkway and sent a jolt of pain coursing through her. Ronin made no move to go check on her, but Finn came and bent down in front of Ivy.

"Are you okay?" he asked, a hint of sarcasm in his voice.

"I'm fine," Ivy growled as she reached for her sword and stood. She brushed past him back into the circle, but he grabbed for her arm. "I didn't mean—"

Ivy twirled around and cracked her sword hard against his arm, forcing him to let go. Finn looked shocked and stepped away from her.

"Now, there's a fighter!" Ronin chuckled. Ivy turned her back, and Finn followed her into the yard, holding his sore arm. "Go again," Ronin ordered.

"Can you lift your arm?" Finn's voice was warmer this time.

"It's fine," she snapped at him.

The two sparred like that for another hour until Ivy could no longer swing her sword. Her right shoulder was pounding, and it felt strange to her, but she kept quiet. Ronin ended the session, telling the two to meet him back there at first light tomorrow. Ivy retreated before either one of them could say anything to her. Ser Osmund was nowhere to be found; Ivy was sure he felt safe leaving her with Ronin and had gone to explore the island. The small woman, who Ivy learned later, was named Miko, brought her a tray of food just as the sun was setting. Ivy smiled and thanked the woman but didn't touch the food. Instead, she called another serving woman and asked for a flagon of wine to be brought up. Ivy thought it might ease her pain some since the balm was no longer doing its job.

When the wine arrived, Ivy took the tray out onto the balcony and poured herself a cup. It tasted different from northern wines; this was much sweeter, and Ivy could taste all the different fruits in it. The yard was empty, and it was beginning to grow dark and chilly. Every balcony had a small brazier on it, so Ivy decided to make herself a small fire. She went to retrieve the blanket from her bed but struggled to get it over her shoulders, crying out in pain when she moved her shoulder.

"Ivy?" a voice called out from behind the wall of flowers. Ivy rolled her eyes and sighed as Finn poked his head around the wall.

"What do you want?" Ivy snapped. Before she could stop him, Finn hopped up onto the wall of the balcony and jumped the small distance over to hers. "What the hell are you doing?" she demanded.

Finn threw up his hands as if to say he meant no harm and took the seat across from Ivy. She eyed him cautiously over the brim of her cup.

"How's your shoulder?" he asked, no hint of sarcasm in his voice this time.

"What do you care?"

"Because I'm the one that hurt you. I'm sorry. I'm not used to fighting with anyone besides Ronin or Kal." He leaned his elbows on his knees, running his russet eyes to her shoulder before meeting hers again. "I know it hurts. Let me help you."

"I told you it's fine."

He sighed and said, "I'm not going to hurt you. Please, let me help."

Ivy stayed silent.

Finn sat back and sighed. "What will you tell Ronin tomorrow when you can't lift your arm?"

Ivy stared at him, noticing how the fire caught flecks of red in his brown eyes. When he smiled, she lowered her eyes. "How can you help anyway?"

"My mother was a healer in my town. She taught me a few things when I was a child."

Ivy nodded but didn't ask where he was from, though she remembered Ronin saying Finn had come to Kame Island years ago. Finn stood, and when Ivy didn't protest, he went over to her chair, leaning down.

"Let me look," he said as he gently took the blanket from her shoulders. He knelt beside her chair and pulled her short sleeve up over her shoulder. Ivy turned her head away as tears burned in her eyes.

"It's slightly dislocated," Finn said, running his fingers over her skin. Ivy felt goosebumps crawling up her arm where his rough fingers touched her. "I can fix it. The bone isn't completely out of the cavity. I need to push it back into place."

Ivy took another swallow of wine and said, "Do it."

Finn gently held her wrist with both hands and moved her arm out in front.

"This is going to hurt," he warned her, looking her in the eye to make sure she was still alright. His calloused hand cupped hers, and he gently gave her arm a push. Pain tore through Ivy's arm, kick-starting her heart.

"Stop!" she breathed, quickly gripping his hand as tears stung her eyes. "This isn't going to work."

He leaned in closer. "It'll work. I need to push harder. Ready?"

Ivy let go of him and took a deep breath before he pushed again, this time with so much force that Ivy's chair skidded back. She felt the pop, and a wave of pain crashed over her and then dispersed almost immediately. Ivy tried to lift her arm and found it moved much easier than earlier, though it was still sore. Finn stayed kneeling in front of her, his eyes never leaving hers.

"Thank you," Ivy said. Finn inclined his head then got up to leave. As he stood on the wall, ready to jump back to his balcony, Ivy stopped him. "Where are you from?"

He turned around and gave her a small smile. "The North," he answered before jumping back to his balcony and going inside.

## CHAPTER THIRTEEN

# NAME DAY

The next day, after practice was over, Ivy ran to catch up with Ronin as he headed toward his house, leaving Finn alone in the pit.

"You should go rest, Ivy," he said over his shoulder. She ignored him and came to walk beside him.

"Why did you leave Godstone?" she asked.

"It was time for me to move on," he answered.

"Didn't you like it there? Didn't you think you'd miss my father?" she prodded.

"Of course."

"Then, why?" Ronin didn't answer but only looked ahead. "Was it because of Helvarr?" He quickly glanced down, and his brow furrowed before returning his gaze to the road ahead.

"What do you know of him?" Ronin asked curiously.

"Only what Ser Osmund told me." Ronin took the bait and asked in more detail what she knew, and she told him.

When they arrived at his house, Ronin invited her in for some tea. The tea wasn't like the kind Miko brought her, and

Ivy cringed as she swallowed a sip. Ronin only confirmed all that Ser Osmund had told Ivy, but didn't add any more to the story.

"Why did you let Helvarr beat on my father that day?" she asked, referring to the story of them on the beach. Ronin stroked his beard, much like her father did when he was thinking.

"You tell me," he said, taking a sip of tea. She thought about it for a moment, remembering the painful lessons he'd given her since her training had started.

"You wanted to see if his anger would drive him to hurt someone he loved."

Ronin smiled approvingly, and Ivy blushed.

"That's enough questions for one night. Go and rest now—we have a feast to attend tomorrow."

The following evening, King Mashu was holding a small feast in honor of Ivy. Ser Osmund must've told the king that her name day was approaching and felt it worthy of a celebration. Ivy was reluctant to be the center of attention, but ultimately agreed to please Ser Osmund. He had gone through the trouble of arranging it. It was held within the king's court, which had been filled with trestle tables spanning across the room from wall to wall. Many of the locals were invited, including Ronin.

Ivy busied herself with getting ready. Miko had brought her an elegant silk gown that many of the local women wore. It was red with beautifully embroidered flowers cascading down the length of the skirts. Ivy smiled at it but put it aside and, instead, dressed in her usual clothing. She chose a green, cotton shirt and loose, black pants that flowed around her ankles.

It was getting chilly outside, so Ivy opened a chest at the end of her bed and found the cloak her father had given her. She pinned it on using the maple leaf clip and draped the cloak over one shoulder. Brushing her long hair until it shone, Ivy left it down, so it rippled over the maple tree that covered her back.

Ivy was ready faster than she anticipated and decided to go for a walk while she waited for the party to start. She strapped Promise onto her belt and left the castle grounds. The kingdom sat farther back on Kame Island, so Ivy wandered the path behind the castle that led down to the cliffs overlooking the sea. The narrow path had been worn out from years of people walking it. The hill was steep behind the castle, but it leveled out before dropping down into the sea below. The wind was strong there, and it ruffled Ivy's cloak behind her. The sun had begun to set, making the water below look as black as the sea back home.

Ivy pulled out her sword and began working on her technique along the path, stabbing at the empty air. The wind whipped her cloak around her legs as she sliced and thrashed at the wind dancing around her. The cool breeze coming over the cliff reminded Ivy of Godstone. She loved this place, but it wasn't home, and she wished to return soon. Ivy had no one on Kame Island save for Ser Osmund, and he often spent his days exploring now that she was busy training all day. Not that Ivy blamed him for that; he'd done his job and delivered her safely. The old knight deserved a break after saving her life from the traders.

Ivy felt someone watching her and turned to see Finn making his way down the narrow path. Ivy had wondered if he'd come to the feast, but didn't want to ask.

Finn wore a thin, cotton doublet the color of sand slashed with gold. His brown waves were messy from the wind, sweeping back as he approached. Ivy took note of the sword hanging from his belt. When his eyes found hers, she smiled shyly.

"Your knight sent me to find you," he called out. "The feast is about to begin."

He glanced at Promise, which Ivy still held firmly in her hand. "I see you're practicing without me," he grinned, his tone playful.

"I just wanted to practice with a real sword. The wooden swords aren't heavy enough."

Finn nodded his head. "I think Ronin only uses the wood so that he can hit us harder when we fail."

Ivy smiled at that, and Finn's eyes lowered to her lips, making her blood pump as she put Promise back into its scabbard.

"Miko won't be pleased if you refuse to wear what she brought you," Finn said with a grin as his eyes ran over her outfit.

"How did you know she brought me clothes?"

"I just had my eighteenth name day as well, not long before you and your knight arrived. Miko made me wear some colorful garments that I see King Mashu wearing often."

Ivy shrugged. "I suppose Miko will be disappointed then."

"Yes. I suppose she will," Finn said with a smile. "But I think you look fine as you are." He moved to touch her shoulder, a friendly touch, but by instinct, she stepped back. He quickly withdrew his hand, embarrassed. "I'm sorry," he said, lowering his head. "Ronin didn't tell me I'd be sparring with you. I've been here for a long time and was afraid you'd hold me back from my training. I couldn't have known how well you fight. I'm sorry for how I reacted and for hurting you, Ivy."

She studied his face. He seemed sincere in his apology, so Ivy accepted.

"Can we start over?" he asked, holding out his hand. "My name's Finnick, but everyone knows me as Finn. It's a pleasure to meet you."

Ivy smiled and shook his hand. "Nice to meet you, Finn." His hand lingered against hers for a long moment and their eyes locked. Finn smiled softly, creating a dimple in his cheek.

Ivy withdrew her hand, and Finn cleared his throat. "Well," he said, running a hand through his hair, "we should be getting to the feast."

The two walked up the path toward the king's court, where music could be heard pouring out from the open doors.

As they walked into the court, Ivy spotted Ser Osmund seated upon the dais with Ronin and King Mashu. He motioned for her to come over, but when Ivy turned back, Finn wasn't following her. "Aren't you coming?" she called back.

"My place isn't up there." He slightly bowed to her, his eyes dancing with a smile. "Enjoy your celebration, Lady Ivy."

She watched as Finn retreated to one of the tables filled with civilians near a wall. Joining Ser Osmund, Ivy took the empty seat beside him, just to the right of Prince Kal. She thanked the king and queen for the celebration, just as the food was being served.

It was a feast of seafood with many types of fish that Ivy had never seen before. Massive crab legs stretched out over the platter and sat in a spicy sauce that made Ivy's lips sticky. She was already growing full when the second course came, followed by a third before dessert was served. Prince Kal leaned closer to Ivy and talked about all the different foods that had been brought out. He told her of his training with Ronin, but that he only just began two years back.

The prince wished to become a Shadow guard, but his father had forbidden it, saying that his responsibilities were to the kingdom after King Mashu's reign ended.

Ivy noticed Miko pass by, who gave her a scornful look when she realized Ivy wasn't wearing the gown she'd provided.

Kal touched her hand. "Don't worry about Miko. She'll only try again; the woman is relentless."

Within the crowded court, Ivy could feel Finn's gaze upon her. She searched the tables and found him staring at her as she sat with the prince. Ivy's cheeks heated, and she withdrew her hand from Kal's grasp, but Finn was still watching.

King Mashu gave a short speech to thank everyone for coming and motioned to the musicians to start the music again. Ivy sat, sipping at a cup of wine, when a hand came over her shoulder. Ser Osmund asked Ivy to dance, and the two moved down to where some tables had been pulled back to make room. Many of the civilians were already swirling around the court, but Ivy still felt embarrassed. She wasn't used to having so many eyes on her. As uncomfortable as she was, Ivy forced a smile and took the knight's hand as he led her around the room. They moved slowly, spinning around the other dancers.

"How do you like it here, my lady?" Ser Osmund asked.

"I love it here, but I do miss home."

"I know you do. But we'll be back in no time. You should try to enjoy every minute you have here. Perhaps the best is yet to come."

Ivy only nodded her head.

Ser Osmund leaned closer to her. "I believe that boy has his eye on you," he said with a smile and motioned to the dais where Kal sat watching them.

Ivy looked away and said nothing, her eyes searching the crowd for another face. When the prince came down to ask Ser Osmund if he might have a turn, the knight willingly handed her over. Ivy had no choice but to dance with him. He was kind enough, but Ivy wasn't interested. She didn't need another distraction.

Kal moved his hand around Ivy's waist as the music slowed, and she felt herself blush as he touched her.

"You look beautiful, my lady." Kal leaned in close to her ear. She didn't know how to respond, feeling silly and uncomfortable. "Perhaps we could take our horses riding around the coast. I could show you my favorite spots around the island."

"I should focus on my training," Ivy replied.

"Ah, yes. You wouldn't want to miss that," Kal said sarcastically. He pulled her closer and twirled her around the dance floor. Ivy lifted her eyes to see Finn sitting up against a wall in the shadows, watching the two dance. He smiled and raised his glass to her before draining it and getting up to leave.

Ivy thanked Kal for the dance, and he unexpectedly kissed her on the cheek before returning to his seat. Ivy asked Ser Osmund if she could leave, saying she wasn't feeling well.

"Would you like me to walk you to your room, my lady?"

"No. I can manage. Enjoy yourself."

Back in her room, Ivy unpinned her cloak and tossed it on the bed before moving over to open the door to let the air inside. She heard movement below and peered over the balcony wall to see Finn fighting with a straw man. She quickly unlaced her boots and grabbed her wooden practice sword. Finn had changed as well; he wore plain clothing and rolled up the bottom of his pants.

Ivy came around the corner and stood there, watching him for a moment.

His movements weren't as quick as hers, but he was more

powerful. The straw man was quickly coming apart as his mighty blows tore through the rope that held it together.

"Would you like a real opponent?" Ivy called out.

Finn turned around and smiled when he spotted her but quickly withdrew it and pushed his brows together. "Why aren't you celebrating?"

"I don't like all the attention," Ivy admitted. "It was Ser Osmund's idea."

"Prince Kal will be disappointed he lost his dance partner." He seemed to be asking rather than stating something.

"This is the only dancing I want to do," Ivy said. Finn's smile returned slightly.

"Then I'd be glad to share this dance with you, my lady," he said in a playful tone as he bowed to her. She giggled and returned the bow before stepping into the sand circle with her sword in front of her.

The two danced around each other, parrying blows and striking back. Ivy noticed he didn't hit as hard as when Ronin was present. A full moon poked its face through the clouds to light up their dance floor. The night was growing late, but Ivy was enjoying herself much more than she had at the feast.

"We should do this every night," Finn said between breaths.

Ivy stopped. "What do you mean?"

"I mean if Ronin wants us to practice together so badly, then we should take our lessons from him during the day and use them at night. We'll only get better the more we practice."

Ivy considered what he said for a moment. It was a good idea, and Ronin would surely see improvement from both of them if they met here at night to practice, so she agreed. It was now getting late, and they both needed to be up early to meet Ronin.

They walked back inside together, keeping their voices low as they went past Ser Osmund's room. Finn stopped outside her room briefly, tucking his hands behind his back. He smiled at her, and Ivy felt her heart kick up.

"Well," he whispered. "Goodnight."

"Goodnight."

They stood there in the dark hallway for a moment, and Ivy felt this static air between them. Finn smiled at her, then turned and went to his room next door. She stood there for a moment, took a deep breath, then went into her room. Ivy washed her face and crawled into bed, suddenly realizing how sore she was.

Ivy dreamt that she was fighting on the cliffside behind the kingdom. Her straw opponent came alive to fight back, and the two sparred until Ivy felt eyes on the back of her head. She turned and saw Finn at the top of the hill, but he wasn't smiling. Instead, he looked scared. She turned back to the straw man and let out a yelp as she realized it had morphed into her father. Ivy's sword was bloody, and Magnus lay bleeding on the ground.

"No!" she cried, bending down to put pressure on the wound. "Father?" Ivy brought a hand to his forehead, but he was already cold, and then his face shifted.

She drew back her hand and watched as her father's face morphed into a girl she didn't recognize, with short hair. Then a boy about her age, lean and a mop of brown curls. A dark-skinned girl with stunning eyes, a blond man, a man with eyes like fire. Again and again, the faces shifted until Ivy was staring at herself.

Ivy screamed and shot up from her bed. "What the hell?" she panted, glancing out the window to see that it was still night. She couldn't take the nightmares anymore. Ivy didn't understand what they meant or why she had them, but she could only hope they didn't mean anything. And so that's what she told herself. Not wanting to fall back into a nightmare, Ivy caught her breath, grabbed her wooden sword, and made her way to the yard to await the rising sun.

## CHAPTER FOURTEEN

# THE SCOUT

It had been over two months since Ivy left and almost a month back, Rayner turned twenty, and the whole kingdom celebrated his name day. The day had been freezing and dark, but spirits were high as men and women prepared for the young prince's celebration. It wasn't as massive as the Feast of Winter since Lord Kevan and his family had departed, back to the Twisted Tower. He needed to get back and protect his own home—the raiders had already made threats to take his kingdom.

Just after Lord Kevan's party left, Earl Rorik did the same. His home was much closer to Godstone than the Twisted Tower was, however, and the earl offered his allegiance to Magnus and said he'd be happy to return should his friend need him. Earl Rorik never passed up a good battle, and it would only take him a few days to make the trip back.

Lady Oharra and her men decided to stay longer. Grey Raven lay farther north, and the lady wasn't so concerned about raiders traveling that far--not when Godstone was closer and could be taken first. However, she kept enough warriors back home to protect the elderly and children that resided there. Magnus was grateful for her help with many strong young men and women in her army; together, they were a great force. Rayner was pleased as well that Correlyn was staying. The two had grown closer since their visit to Hideaway Harbor.

Rayner and Correlyn were seated together upon the dais during his name day celebration. Correlyn dressed in an elegant dark green gown that covered her feet. Black lace ran down the gown's sleeves, which flared out at her wrists, and her hair was pinned up in a braid, decorated with silver beads. Rayner dressed in his best doublet, white as fresh snow, and slashed with red and gold.

He brushed his dark auburn hair back and hung his sword from a belt that was embellished with onyx. As the feast began, Magnus watched his son leaning close to Correlyn, whispering things to her and making her laugh. It made him smile to see his son so happy.

After the food had been served, Magnus asked his wife to dance. Elana's beauty was timeless, and Magnus still felt his heart flutter when she was near. He pulled her in close, feeling the warmth from her body as the two moved as one around the hall.

"How do you think our daughter is doing?" Elana spoke into his ear.

"I'm positive that she's fine, my love."

"How can you be so sure?"

"Because she has your wisdom, of course," Magnus said with a smile.

Then, Rayner and Correlyn joined the dancing as well, though they were clumsy, tripping over each other. Magnus chuckled and turned to Elana, who watched the young couple as well.

"What do you think of them?" he asked. She smiled as she watched the two giggling at their poor dancing skills. "I think they make a handsome couple."

"I don't know that they're a couple yet," Magnus said.

"But you told me what happened in Hideaway Harbor between them."

"I don't know anything for sure. I didn't ask."

"Well, I know," Elana proclaimed.

Magnus pulled back to look at her. "How can you know?"

She brushed his hair back from his forehead. "Because I see things you don't. And I see the way she looks at our son."

Magnus smiled softly, caressed her cheek, and kissed her deeply as the music played on and dancers moved around them.

When the feast began to wind down, and men were getting drunk enough to start the inevitable fighting, Rayner led Correlyn out of the Hall. The two walked closely together through the snowy path that led to the stables. Rayner still struggled a little to get on his horse after he'd broken his arm in Temple City. His arm had healed since then, though it felt weaker because he hadn't used it much.

They mounted up and set off through the gates, racing each other toward the forest. The night was clear and crisp. The snow had let up, and the moon was almost full, though a freezing wind was coming from the south.

The two stopped their horses just outside the Blackwoods

and got down to tie them off. They walked along the edge of the forest, Rayner stealing glances at Correlyn. She caught him looking, and he quickly turned his head to hide his blushing cheeks. Rayner hadn't kissed Correlyn again since Hideaway Harbor. He wasn't sure that starting a relationship with her was a good idea. They were in the middle of a war, and she lived farther north and would eventually return.

That night at the inn, he'd denied his own desires. The two only shared a bed together and nothing else. Rayner explained that he didn't want it to happen that way--not when he was drunk and injured. She seemed to understand and didn't hold it against him. However, she had restrained from touching him too often ever since. Rayner cared about Correlyn a lot and wanted more, but he was hesitant about it.

The wind was picking up, and Correlyn shivered against its cold bite. Rayner unhooked his fur cloak and moved to drape it over her shoulders, quickly retreating when she turned her face up to his. Her eyes appeared black in the gray light cast down from the moon's glow.

"Rayner," his name on her lips made his heart skip, "what are you thinking?"

He shoved his hands deep in his pockets and kept walking along the woodline. "I'm thinking about how you'll need to return home soon..." He hesitated for a moment. "And how I don't want to see you leave." He kept his eyes on the snow at his feet, but he could feel Correlyn watching him.

"I was thinking the same," she admitted.

Rayner's heart fluttered, and he spoke before his courage left him. "Don't go," he said, turning to face her. "My father can take you in as his ward."

She reached out to touch his cheek, and her hand was surprisingly warm. "I don't think my mother would allow it," she said with a faint smile, but it was sad.

Rayner furrowed his brow. "Why not?"

"My mother is very protective of me. She wouldn't like the idea of being separated from me."

"But you'd be safe. My father wouldn't let anything happen to you. *I* won't let anything happen to you." He reached for her hand that rested on his cheek. "Let me talk to my father before we go to your mother."

She nodded her head and withdrew her hand, staring at the ground between them.

Rayner lifted her chin to meet her eyes, which were filled with shiny tears. He wrapped his arms around her and pulled her close. "I'll fight for you to stay if that's what you want," he said softly against her ear.

"I do want to stay," Correlyn replied. The two came apart, but then Rayner leaned in closer to kiss her. She moved to meet his lips, only a breath away before a distant whinny of a horse turned their attention. It was too dark to see, but it looked to be only one horseman. They ran back to their horses, saddled up, and rushed to catch up with the horse that was headed for the gate.

They flanked the lone horse from the left and noticed that the rider's head was hanging down, and his back seemed stiff. Rayner pulled his horse in front to stop it and yelled to the rider, who didn't respond. He swung down off his horse and drew his sword.

"Who are you?" he called out. Still, the rider didn't answer, and Rayner approached him cautiously as Correlyn pulled her sword. He stood below the man and noticed dried blood crusting his coat. When Rayner shook the man, he fell from his horse and crashed into the snow. He was dead, and a branch had been tied to his back to keep him upright on the horse.

Correlyn came closer to see and gasped as Rayner pulled the man's hood back. "That's one of my mother's scouts. His name was Pollock."

"Do you know where your mother stationed him?"

"On the east coast, below the town of Ashton."

Rayner noticed a letter pinned to the man's coat and took it out to read it. His eyes grew wide.

"What is it?" Correlyn asked impatiently.

"We need to find my father."

## CHAPTER FIFTEEN

# HARPER HALL

They draped the man back over his horse, commanding the gates to open as they drew near. Rayner sent one of the knights to bring his father, Lady Oharra, and the queen immediately. Magnus came rushing through the central square to where his son stood next to the dead man.

"What is this?" the king asked. Rayner handed his father the letter, giving his mother a sorrowful look. Elana looked at her son, confused until Magnus read the letter and, with the same look, gave it to his wife.

"What?" Elana commanded them.

"Your father," Magnus said sadly. "The raiders have demanded that we give up Godstone, or they'll take Harper Hall and slay all who live there."

Elana's face flashed through emotions within the space of mere seconds: first fear, then worry, and then finally settling on anger. She balled her fists and ordered some knights to take the dead man down from his horse.

They scrambled at the queen's command. Lady Oharra went

to help, as it was her scout and friend who'd been slain.

"My love," Magnus touched his wife's shoulder, "what are you doing?"

"First, we need to bury this man and honor him. And then you will go retrieve my father and slaughter any man who tries to stop you." A fire burned in her eyes, and Magnus nodded his head, promising he would go get her father.

A week after the feast, Magnus and Rayner crossed the southern border with their men and Lady Oharra's. Harper Hall sat on the east coast, surrounded by grasslands and swamps. The snow wasn't piled as high there, but it still covered the land as far as the eye could see. Lord Harald's castle was small, and he'd managed to stay out of the war until now.

The walls rose high into the sky, forcing Magnus to crane his neck as they approached. A guard came trotting out to meet them, and they were led inside the walls, which opened to a massive training yard for the knights to practice. Snow-covered trees lined the road that led to Lord Harald's castle at the center of Harper Hall.

Lord Harald was surprised to see King Magnus, and then disappointed to see that Elana hadn't accompanied him. Lord Harald had short, gray hair and a matching beard that hugged his face. He was an older man but still looked sturdy and muscular as a knight. He asked about Elana before properly greeting Magnus, and only after he'd been assured that Elana was safe did the lord embrace his son-in-law.

He moved Magnus aside to hug his grandson, who now stood taller than the lord. Rayner greeted his grandfather warmly; it had been many years since Lord Harald had been to Godstone for a visit.

"Where's my granddaughter?" Lord Harald asked.

Magnus told him of how he'd sent Ivy away and why.

Lord Harald looked disappointed to hear the news and sat back down in his chair. "So then, to what do I owe the pleasure of this visit?"

Magnus pulled out the letter and let Lord Harald read for himself what the raiders were demanding. When he was done reading, he crumpled up the piece of paper and threw it down.

"They can bloody well try," Lord Harald scoffed.

Magnus closed his eyes and balled his fists. He'd been afraid the stubborn old man would refuse to leave.

"My lord," he started, "you don't have a choice. You have to come with me back to Godstone where—"

"I'm not going anywhere," Lord Harald interrupted. "If these raiders want my castle so badly, then they can come and take it."

Magnus sighed and took the seat next to him, where Elana's mother had once sat. Lady Kira had died in childbirth bearing Lord Harald's son, Elana's would-be younger brother. The boy had died soon after Lady Kira, and Elana had grown up an only child.

"My lord," Magnus repeated. "It wouldn't be wise to remain here. The raiders are surely lurking nearby."

"You think I'm afraid of that band of murderers? I'm staying here."

Magnus was losing his patience. "What should I tell your daughter when I return without her father?"

"You tell Elana whatever you want. I'm not leaving."

Magnus knew he couldn't return empty-handed. His wife would surely blame him should something happen to her father.

"Grandfather," Rayner spoke up, "don't you want to see Ivy when she returns home? She should be coming back in a few months, and I know she'd be glad to show you all that she's learned."

Lord Harald looked as if he was considering this. Magnus knew he had a soft spot for Ivy, just as he did. "You'll apologize to young Ivy on my behalf. I won't leave my home or my people."

Rayner spread his hands before him. "Your people are welcome as well, but we must—"

Lord Harald slammed his fist down on the arm of his chair. "I will not go! Do you hear me? I'll die before I let those people take my ancestral lands away from me!"

Magnus stood to tower over the old man. "Don't take your anger out on my son! You've always been a stubborn man, and now it's going to get you killed!"

Lord Harald abruptly stood to face the king. "Then so be it," he said as he brushed past Rayner and stormed out of his castle.

Magnus sank back down in the chair and ran his hands over his tired eyes.

Rayner came to sit next to his father and placed a hand on his shoulder. "What should we do, Father?"

Magnus shook his head, thinking of the right answer. "I'll drag him out of this castle if I have to," he said, earning a grin from Rayner.

"You know he won't go, Father."

"I know," he sighed. "Then, we have no choice but to stay and defend his lands."

After a quiet supper with Lord Harald, who drank more than

he ate, Magnus and Rayner went to walk the wall. The night was brisk and clear; no clouds lingered in the sky. Magnus had placed some of his men along the wall as well to help keep watch for raiders. He knew they were coming, just not when. Magnus didn't want to talk about Lord Harald anymore, so instead he asked his son about Correlyn.

Rayner blushed when he mentioned her name but told his father that nothing had happened between them.

"You care for her, don't you?"

"Of course I do," Rayner answered, almost angrily. Magnus stayed silent and didn't pry further. Rayner stopped walking to face his father. "I was going to ask you something last week, but then we found the dead scout, and I didn't have a chance."

"What is it?"

Rayner worried his bottom lip before speaking. "Would you take Correlyn in as your ward?"

Magnus looked at him, confused for a moment, but then understood. As king, he'd never taken a ward. Even if he did, they were usually young children who needed training, and Correlyn was already a strong warrior.

"You don't want her to leave," Magnus stated. Rayner averted his eyes and shook his head. "You would need to talk with Lady Oharra. I can say yes, but it's not up to me."

"I promised Correlyn I would come to you first."

"And you have. Now you must talk with her mother as well."

"So, is that a yes?"

Magnus leaned over the wall and stroked his beard. "I would be glad to take her in," he answered.

Rayner beamed as he thanked his father and left him on the wall to find Correlyn.

Magnus stayed outside, gazing out at the vast white ocean of land that lay before him. One of his knights came running up to him only moments after Rayner left. Ser Caster was tall with a lean face that he kept shaven. One of Magnus's best knights, he had been put in charge of the queen's guard by Ser Osmund when he left. It was the queen who insisted Magnus take Ser Caster along.

"Your Grace," he said. "Lady Oharra's scouts have come back. Raiders were seen coming this way, not two miles from here."

Magnus cursed and ordered Ser Caster to get the men ready; he needed to find Lord Harald.

Down below, men were scrambling to get their gear on while civilians ran toward the castle seeking safety. Magnus pushed through the crowd, searching the faces for Rayner and Lord Harald. Men on the wall began yelling down to the other warriors as the raiders approached. Magnus spotted Rayner helping Correlyn tighten her armor as Lady Oharra stood by, filling her quiver with arrows.

"Where's your grandfather?" Magnus shouted over the commotion. Rayner shook his head just as something exploded near the front gate.

Magnus turned back to see men on fire, screaming as the flames consumed them. He drew his sword and yelled, "Rayner, with me. Now!"

Rayner drew his sword and began to follow his father before turning back. He walked back up to Correlyn and grabbed the back of her head, pressing his lips to hers. She kissed him back for a long moment before letting him go, and Rayner ran to catch up with his father, who stood just ahead watching.

They ran up the steps and emerged atop the wall to see a

massive army gathering below. It wasn't so much the men that worried Magnus, it was the catapults standing to frame the army that could certainly bring down the walls of the castle with little effort. He watched the raiders load a boulder into the pouch, light it on fire, and cut the rope releasing the counterweight. The flaming rock soared over their heads and landed somewhere within the walls. They heard a tremendous boom and then people screaming everywhere. Rayner was as still as a statue.

Magnus shook him until he met his father's eyes. "Stay with me, Rayner! We need to find your grandfather."

Archers formed up on the wall, Lady Oharra and Correlyn among them as raiders began to charge the gates, which had been damaged by the catapults.

Correlyn loosed an arrow and dropped her first raider before he could reach the gate, and Lady Oharra did the same. Raiders brought forth a log, which they used to start ramming the gate.

"Get men down there. Now!" Lady Oharra screamed to her knights just as another flaming rock came sailing toward them.

Magnus ran with Rayner through the yard, yelling for Lord Harald. Raiders had now managed to create enough of an opening in the gate to start slipping through one by one. One raider threw an ax and nearly took off the king's nose. Magnus pushed Rayner behind him as a raider charged and threw an ax. He threw his sword up, slashing the man's arm, and stabbed his blade through the raider's chest.

"Go find your grandfather!" Magnus commanded his son.

"I'm not leaving you!"

"Go! Now!" he screamed as another raider approached. Rayner turned and ran, leaving his father to fight alone.

Magnus's armor was well made, and he was grateful for that

when the raider landed an otherwise killing blow to his back.

Magnus stumbled under the man's blow but recovered quickly and swung his sword back to meet the raider's throat just as another raider came plowing into him. Magnus was knocked off his feet but kept hold of his sword. He struggled with the raider on the ground and noticed the man had a familiar look about him.

"Helvarr?" he half said to himself. The man looked at him curiously before punching Magnus in the side of his head. He realized it wasn't Helvarr, but the resemblance made him falter, and the raider was on top of him, pounding on his skull.

Magnus drew a knife from his boot and thrust it up under the man's chin, spilling blood onto his face. He choked on the other man's blood as he sat up and wiped his face, looking around at the destruction. A flaming barrel came flying overhead and exploded on impact behind him, sending liquid fire raining down on civilians. His heart was pounding along with his head, but he forced himself to stand.

He cut his way to the front gate, yelling at civilians along the way to run and take shelter. The gate was nearly open now, and raiders were pouring through, a river of steel. Magnus glanced up the wall to try to spot Lady Oharra or Correlyn, but there was too much chaos. He could only hope that they were alright as he advanced on another raider. Their swords slashed at one another, then Magnus saw another barrel on fire out of the corner of his eye. It sailed too low and crashed into the building next to them, sending fire and splinters of wood everywhere. He felt a sudden pain in his lower leg but ignored it.

One of the raiders was on fire and came running toward Magnus. The raider he'd been fighting shoved Magnus into the flaming man's path. Magnus twirled around him, plunging his sword into the man's scorched back, and led him toward the first raider, who didn't hesitate to cut the man's head from his body. Magnus leapt over the raider's flaming corpse and stabbed his blade down through the raider's chest.

The adrenaline coursing through his veins was like lightning, a feeling he always got when in a battle. Above him, a man fell from the wall and landed with a sickening crunch in front of Magnus. Another man ran to escape the fire that consumed his body. Carnage surrounded him. He took a deep breath and focused on the next raider.

## CHAPTER SIXTEEN

# THE FALL

Rayner ran through the streets of what was once Harper Hall. Civilians rushed past him to escape the death that was coming. Dead bodies lay burning in the streets. His mind was on his father, whom he'd left to defend himself and Correlyn, still vulnerable up on the wall. He shook his head as if that would help him refocus just as a fire barrel came crashing down behind him. The explosion threw him off his feet, and the wind was knocked out of his lungs as he hit the ground. His ears were ringing, his pulse racing. Muffled screams surrounded him. Somewhere off in the distance, another explosion erupted, lighting up the smoke that filled the streets.

Rayner got back to his feet and ran toward the castle, where he hoped to find his grandfather. As he reached for the door, a sword came down and nearly sliced off his hand. The raider jabbed at him, but Rayner dodged his blade and slipped in the snow beneath his feet. He dug his sword into the ground and flung it up quickly, sending slush and dirt at the man's face. Rayner took advantage of his temporary blindness and charged, plunging his blade through the raider's throat.

Rayner flew through the door of the castle to see civilians huddled together on the floor. Bleeding and panting, he asked the nearest person where Lord Harald was.

Rayner found his grandfather dressed in shining armor with a sword belted on his hip, staring out the window of his bed-chamber.

His room faced the sea, and from there he couldn't witness the destruction that was taking place at the front of his castle.

"Grandfather," Rayner said, out of breath. "We have to go."

The lord made no move to leave, so Rayner ran to him and turned him around. Lord Harald's eyes were wet with tears, but the man looked angry. "Grandfather, please. We have to go. The raiders have broken through the gates."

Still, Lord Harald stayed silent.

"They have a catapult! Can't you hear what they're doing to your people outside?" Rayner yelled, his hands shaking with anger and adrenaline.

Lord Harald flared his nose. "I hear just fine, boy. It's you who isn't listening."

Rayner released him and stepped back. "What are you talking about? What kind of lord leaves his people to die?"

Lord Harald stepped up to him. "Don't presume to know what it takes to be a lord! You're only now just a man!" He fussed with his armor and calmed himself. "This fight is already lost." His voice held all the defeat to match his words. Rayner felt the anger rising inside him as he grabbed hold of his grandfather's breastplate.

"Good men and women are out there risking their lives for you, and you won't even do them the honor of fighting alongside them?" Rayner shoved him back. "You're a coward. Stay hidden in your castle. I'll let the raiders know you won't fight back." Rayner turned and stormed out of the room, leaving his grandfather to ponder his words.

Outside, the battle didn't seem to slow, and Rayner quickly made his way back to the gate to find his father. Anger fueled him as he slashed through any raider that came his way. He found his father fighting with another knight and ran to help him. Rayner thrust his sword into the man's back and yanked him off his father. He looked down and was taken aback by his father's state: his face was red with blood, and he appeared to be limping.

"Where is he?" Magnus asked.

"Hiding in his castle like a coward," Rayner snapped.

"We have to get him," Magnus said as he started toward the castle.

Rayner held a hand to his chest to stop him. "He isn't coming, Father. He regrets turning away your offer, and now it's too late. He's given up."

"We still have to try, Rayner."

"I did try!" Rayner roared. "Do you think I'd be here without him if I didn't try? Did you expect me to drag him from his castle, kicking and screaming like a child?"

Magnus stepped back and looked at his son, mouth open. Rayner's eyes widened as a raider came barreling toward them. He quickly sidestepped and hacked the man's arm off before finishing him with a blade through the heart. "We need to focus on getting our people out of here now," Rayner said. "Harper Hall has fallen, and we have to get out before we fall with it." In the middle of the chaos and destruction Rayner saw a spark of pride in his father's eyes and then he nodded.

"You're right, son. I'll start telling our men. Go and find Correlyn and her mother," Magnus told his son.

Rayner found Correlyn loosing arrows on the raiders that stormed the wall. Some had tried to put ladders up against the walls and climb over, but not many got past Lady Oharra. She was slaying a man when Rayner ran up to her and told her what happened. She called down the wall to Correlyn and her men, who gathered up their weapons and retreated. They were rallying with Magnus in the central square with as many of their men as they could find when the gates blew fully open. Raiders came pouring through to surround Magnus and his men. A boulder came flying over the wall and tore through a nearby building as Magnus yelled for his men to attack.

The two sides blended, and Rayner fought alongside his father. Rayner was out of breath and was beginning to slow down when a horse came charging through the fight to stand next to his father. Magnus looked up with a look of surprise to see Lord Harald atop the stallion.

He smiled at Rayner, but it seemed off, and then he turned toward Magnus and said, "Your son will make a fine king one day." And then the lord charged into the sea of raiders.

Magnus yelled to him, but it was too late, and the lord's horse was quickly swarmed. Rayner watched in horror and felt a stab of guilt at having left his grandfather with such harsh words.

Magnus grabbed Rayner by the collar and began to run.

"We have to go!" Magnus yelled to Lady Oharra, who pushed Correlyn along, her men following her. They ran to the stables in the back, mounted their horses, and retreated through the back gate. Harper Hall was ablaze and flaming barrels could still be seen exploding against what was left of the walls that were now crumbling.

Magnus could feel his stomach churning as the gates of Godstone opened before him. Elana stood at the front of the crowd, a look of relief and happiness on her face, but her features soon crumpled when she saw the look on Magnus's face. As Magnus slid from his horse and approached Elana, she was already shaking her head and letting tears pool in her eyes.

"No—" she croaked. Magnus reached for her, taking her small frame into his arms as he whispered, "I'm sorry, Elana. I'm so sorry."

The queen wilted in his arms, and Magnus had to hold Elana to keep her from collapsing. She screamed then, and Magnus felt his heart crack clean in two. Around them, people began to slowly disperse, heads down as they passed by their suffering queen. Magnus glanced back to see Rayner standing in front of the men and women who'd made it out of Harper Hall.

He knew Rayner felt somewhat responsible for his grandfather's death, and Magnus felt responsible as well. But in the end, Lord Harald had saved their lives and the lives of his people who managed to escape. Many of them had gone off on their own, though a few clusters had come back with them to Godstone.

After her father's death, Elana refused to eat for days. Eventually, Magnus called upon Magister Ivann to help soothe his mourning wife. Elana's hair was tangled; bags hung under her eyes, which were red and swollen from tears. Magnus's heart broke all over again at the sight of Elana suffering. He'd tried to comfort his wife, saying that he and Rayner did all they could to save her father, but to no avail.

Magister Ivann could only try to coerce her into eating and give her herbs to help her sleep. However, it wasn't working, and Magnus had given Magister Ivann permission to use more of the herbs so that his wife could rest.

A week after they arrived home, Magnus stood with Rayner on the dais in the Great Hall. Magnus recited the oath for his son to repeat and just like that, Rayner was a knight. The entire room exploded with cheers, whistles, and laughter, all except one.

Magnus and Rayner both looked to Elana, who had come to see her son be knighted. After she kissed him on the cheek and said her congratulations, Elana retreated to her bedchamber. Magnus didn't try to stop her, knowing that Elana wouldn't have it in her to celebrate when she was still mourning.

Rayner seemed to understand and smiled at his mother until she was gone, before turning to Magnus. His heart swelled with pride as he looked at his son. Rayner had showed courage, strength, and wisdom during the battle at Harper Hall, and Lord Harald had recognized something in Rayner that Magnus already knew. He would make a great king one day, and Magnus felt secure in handing over the kingdom to his son, whenever his reign should end.

## CHAPTER SEVENTEEN

# THE NEWS

S er Osmund stroked his beard nervously, folded the piece of paper, and tucked it away in his coat. The afternoon had been pleasant, with a strong breeze coming up from the coast. The knight took a swallow of ale, buckled his boots, and went off to find Ivy. He walked with heavy footfalls down the stone steps of the building where he slept. Turning the corner, he stopped for a moment to watch Ivy at practice with the young man who was Ronin's other student.

Finn was slightly taller than Ivy, though that didn't give him much of an advantage against her. Ivy had grown a lot in the past weeks. Ser Osmund was overwhelmed with pride. He'd always thought of her as a daughter--the one he never had. Everything she accomplished filled his heart with the joy of a father. Ivy looked happy, sparring with Finn and effortlessly landing blows left and right. Ser Osmund's heart sank as he approached the sand circle to deliver the news.

Ivy stopped when she spotted the knight and smiled at him. He could never refuse a smile from Ivy; her long auburn hair was falling from her braid, but her eyes were bright with cheer. She looked a mess from having sparred all day, but she was still a beauty to behold. He hesitated before approaching, not wanting to be the reason for her sadness. He'd withheld the news from Ivy, thinking he might be able to spare her, but as the days went on, Ser Osmund knew it had been the wrong choice. Ivy just seemed so happy, so free from the worries of the world. So, why burden her with bad news? But even that was just an excuse. He saw that now.

"My lady," he started, "we've received a hawk from Godstone."

"Oh?" Ivy closed the space between them, still clutching her wooden sword. Ser Osmund swallowed and grabbed the letter from his coat pocket before hesitating to hand it over. Ivy took the message and unfolded it. Ser Osmund looked to Ronin, who was observing Ivy but showed no emotion on his face. Shifting on his feet uncomfortably, Ser Osmund watched in silence as Ivy read the letter. He could see her smile as she read of Rayner and Correlyn during his name day celebration. But then her smile began to fade as she read on—the battle of Harper Hall was more of a massacre, but Magnus had spared her the details. Ivy's brow began to furrow, and she looked broken as tears started to run down her cheeks.

"No…" Ivy whispered to herself. She snapped her head up to look at Ser Osmund. "When did this come?"

"My lady, I didn't want… I didn't think—"

"When?" she asked again, her voice growing panicked. Ser Osmund lowered his head and told Ivy he received the letter three days ago, then watched as her eyes grew and her fist clenched tight around the paper.

"Three days? And you only now thought to show me? My

grandfather is dead!" she yelled, tears now flowing down her rosy cheeks.

Ser Osmund felt his heart snap. "I'm truly sorry, my lady. I never meant to upset you."

"How could you keep this from me?" she cried, her body trembling.

"I was only trying to protect—"

"Well, I don't need your protection!" Ivy exploded, her anger and sorrow seeming to forge. Ser Osmund didn't blame her.

"Ivy!" Ronin called from behind. "That's enough. Control your anger."

"Oh, screw you!" Ivy yelled over her shoulder, then shoved the letter into Ser Osmund's chest before running off.

Finn had been standing by the whole time silently, his eyes never leaving Ivy. He started to go after her, but Ser Osmund put his hand to Finn's shoulder to stop him. "No. Leave her be. She's grieving." Ser Osmund sounded defeated and exhausted from delivering the news.

"What happened?" Ronin came forward to stand before the old knight. Ser Osmund told them what happened, but Finn kept his eye on the direction where Ivy ran off.

"That's unfortunate," Ronin said calmly. "She may take a day to mourn her loss."

Ronin told Finn they were done for the day and headed off toward his little house on the hillside. Ser Osmund eyed Finn, curious about the young man who seemed to be growing close to Ivy. He decided not to say anything and retreated to his room for the night, feeling as though he was the one who created Ivy's pain.

The sun was setting, and Finn went off in search of food from the kitchen. He asked a serving woman for a platter of fish and rice with a flagon of wine and two cups. Miko walked by the kitchen as the food was being prepared. She smiled at Finn shyly before disappearing around the corner. Finn knew that Miko was only a few years older than him, and she was often present up in the balconies of the buildings that surrounded the sandpit. That was until Ivy arrived and started sparring with Finn.

He used to have a flock of women that would come to watch him practice with Prince Kal, always giggling and whispering things to each other as the two fought. Ivy's presence in the sandpit warded off Finn's admirers, but he couldn't say that he was sad about it.

His thoughts were pushed out of his head as Kal entered the kitchen. Kal wore a long, colorful doublet, similar to the one Miko had tried to get Finn to wear not long ago for his name day. He greeted Finn with a smile and patted his shoulder before asking after Ivy.

"I don't know where she is," Finn responded.

"That's too bad. I was going to take her for a long ride around the island. Do you think she'd like to share a horse? The winds can be chilly at night." Kal winked, and Finn felt a surge of anger at the image of them riding together, but quickly doused it.

"How would I know what she likes?"

"You've cast me aside to train with her. You spend all day with Ivy. Surely you must talk?"

"I didn't cast you aside," Finn argued. "It wasn't my idea to get a new partner."

"Yes, well, I'm sure Ronin had a reason." Kal snatched a piece of bread from a basket and stuffed it in his mouth. "If you see Ivy, would you tell her I'm looking for her?" He turned to leave before Finn could give him an answer, which was a hard no.

He walked up the steps of their building with the tray of food and knocked on Ivy's door. When she didn't answer, he put his ear up to the wood to listen for any movement but heard none. With a huff of disappointment, he set the tray down in the hall before going to his room. Later, Finn waited for Ivy to show up in the practice yard. They hadn't missed one session together since beginning their nightly training until now. When she didn't show, Finn got worried and went back to his room to retrieve his blade and put on some shoes and a cloak before making his way to the stables.

He mounted a horse and went off to search the island.

After a while, he found Ivy at the back of the castle on the cliffside. Ivy was sitting in the grass and staring out to sea. He swung down from the saddle and let the horse graze in the nearby field. Ivy didn't move as he approached, so he sat down beside her, leaving a few feet of space between them. He noticed that she was still barefoot and dressed in the light clothing she'd been wearing at practice that day. Finn unhooked his cloak and went to drape it over her shoulders, but she brushed him off.

"I'm fine," she said, her voice hoarse like she'd been crying.

"You didn't show up for practice," Finn said, putting the cloak beside her. "I was worried."

She stayed silent and kept her gaze on the water. Finn could see her shaking, but still, she refused to take the cloak.

"Ivy, please take this, it's cold." He picked it up again, and she smacked his hand away.

"I'm fine," she repeated.

"You're so stubborn!" Finn snapped. "I'm just trying to help."

Finn turned his eyes to the water as well. They sat in silence for a long moment before Finn could feel her watching him. Ivy turned her body slightly toward him, hanging her head.

"I'm sorry," she whispered. "I shouldn't take my anger out on you." Ivy picked up Finn's cloak and draped it over her shoulders, pulling it close to her face.

"You shouldn't take it out on your knight, either. It's not his fault."

"He told you what happened?"

Finn nodded his head. "I'm sorry for your loss. This war has taken much from many people." He ran his finger over the scar on his chin. "Were you close to your grandfather?"

"What does it matter? He's dead." Ivy wiped a tear from her cheek. "I think I should go home."

Finn's heart kicked up, and his neck grew hot, but he quickly turned away before she could see the worry on his face. "You can't go," he said quietly.

"Why not?" He couldn't come up with an answer that wasn't selfish, so he opted to stay quiet. "Ser Osmund can't keep me here if I wish to leave."

"The North isn't safe anymore. No matter who your father is or how high his walls are."

"How would you know? You live here." She spread her arms out. "This place hasn't been touched by the war."

Finn turned away, a frown forming on his mouth. "I told you I'm from the North. I've seen what this war has done."

Ivy looked at him again, angling her body closer, making Finn's heart flutter. "Where are you from, Finn?" Ivy waited the seconds it took him to answer. Finn kept his eyes on the sea as memories came flooding back.

"Tonsburg," he said quietly.

"I've never heard of it," Ivy admitted.

"Of course, you haven't. It was on the west coast, behind the Spearhead Mountains."

"Was?" Ivy scooted even closer to Finn and placed a hand on his shoulder. "What happened to it?" Finn sucked in a deep breath before beginning his story.

## CHAPTER EIGHTEEN

# THE NORTH

"I was nine years old when they came to my village," Finn began. "Tonsburg was only a small fishing community, and we didn't have many fighting men. My village was well isolated from others in the North. Moat Birger is only twenty leagues farther north, but we rarely saw them. It was the start of winter, and the coastline had not yet frozen over, so many fishermen decided to travel south one last time in hopes of a big catch.

"I was inside watching my mother…" He hesitated. "She was working to heal a local boy who'd fallen ill when we heard screaming outside. My father came rushing into the house, panicked. He told my mother to grab me and follow him to the docks to find a boat. My mother wouldn't leave the little boy, and they argued about it. I didn't know what was going on, but I could see houses on fire when I looked out the window. My mother pulled a fur coat over my head and told my father to take me and go. But they'd spent too much time arguing about what to do, and a raider came bursting through the door. He kicked it open so forcefully that it flew from the hinges.

"I watched my mother grab a knife from her kit and move to the sleeping boy. My father stepped in front of me, but the raider lunged. He threw my father to the ground, and the two wrestled as the raider tried to stab him." Finn cringed at the memory but kept going. "I was so scared, and I stood there trembling, not knowing what to do. My mother yelled at me to run, but my legs were stone; I couldn't move. The raider got free and grabbed me just as my father got to his feet.

"The raider threw his knife up, slashing my face, as he tried to stop my father." Finn touched his scar without realizing it. "My father slammed into the raider and knocked him down, throwing me aside. I watched the raider slip his knife between my father's ribs before tossing him aside like a sack of flour. My mother looked like she was screaming, but I couldn't hear it, only a muffled ringing in my ears and the sound of my heart pounding. The raider seemed to forget about me and moved to silence my mother, who slashed wildly at him with her knife. He cut her throat before stabbing the sleeping boy beside her."

Ivy sat silently in horror as Finn choked back tears. "I got to my feet and ran outside, slipping in a pool of blood. Raiders were in every house, and the village was filled with screaming people. They were burning every house, some that still had living people inside. I ran for the docks, just as a fishing boat was taking off. I didn't think to look back or search for anyone else because it was clear that they were all gone. I ran through the freezing water and pulled myself into the boat, startling the fisherman. He asked where my parents were, but I couldn't answer him.

"We sailed for weeks, staying well out to sea and away from the shoreline. The man tried to sew up my face with a fishing line, but he did a poor job." Finn paused for a moment and lifted his hand to the scar again but stopped and placed it in his lap. "We stopped in the city of Mandalair since we'd run out of fresh water and food. It turns out the man wasn't a skilled fisherman, and he could barely keep us fed on the journey. The man said the only reason he came south was to find his brother, who'd left before the raiders came to fish in southern waters. I didn't want to stay with him for fear that he would go back north, so I left and stole a horse from a stable outside the city.

"I rode for another week to Xanheim before trading the horse for passage to Kame Island from a local fisherman. He dropped me at a small dock, hidden below the cliffs on the western side of the island that wasn't used anymore. My father used to tell me stories of different kingdoms and cities before I went to sleep. I always loved how he described Kame Island and wished to travel here one day, though I never thought this would be the reason. I had no money, and nothing left to trade, so I stayed close to the docks and begged for food. I was starving and weak when Ronin found me. He came to get his tea from a trading boat, imported from the Isle of Fire, when he saw me and asked where I was from. I briefly told him what happened, so he took me back to his house. I collapsed halfway up the hill and woke up in a bed a few days later.

"Ronin fed me and cared for me until I was healthy again. He brought me before King Mashu and asked the king for his protection and a safe spot for me to live on the island. The king agreed and put me up in the building we're in now, which is usually reserved for guests. Maybe he agreed so that Prince Kal could have a friend since there weren't yet many children on the island. The more refugees the king took in, the more children came. Ronin started training me, and this became my home.

I've never thought about going back because I know there's nothing left for me now." Finn paused and cast his gaze to the ocean, his voice growing quieter as he spoke his next words. "Well, that's not completely true. Some people may have survived, but I could never bring myself to return for fear of what I might find."

Finn shook his head, as if banishing the thoughts of his past and seemed to be thinking of something else. When he turned back to Ivy, his russet eyes were intense. "I know you said you want to leave, but I don't want you to go," Finn admitted.

Ivy felt her heart skip as the words sunk in, and the way he looked at her—it was like he was losing something precious all over again.

When Ivy didn't respond, Finn continued. "Kal has been a friend to me over the years, and Ronin a good mentor, but I haven't had a real connection with anyone. Not until you came." Finn averted his eyes as tears began to well up, and Ivy lowered her head, not wanting to see his pain. She reached out and placed her hand on top of his, making Finn jump.

"I'm sorry, Finn. I didn't know what you've suffered." She moved closer to him, gripping his hand, which had grown cold in the night wind. She felt bad for Finn. If he truly had no family left and no one close to him, then how could she go?

Ivy struggled with her thoughts but finally concluded that she still needed to leave. Perhaps she could come back and visit when it was safer. "I still have to go home, Finn," she said quietly, hoping he wouldn't hear her. He turned to face Ivy then, their faces mere inches apart, and Ivy felt her heart fluttering wildly like a caged bird. Finn parted his lips slightly, and Ivy desperately wanted to lean in and feel them against hers. Instead, she quickly stood up and handed him back his cloak.

"Where are you going?" he asked, sounding somewhat disappointed.

"To find Ser Osmund. I have to apologize and tell him I want to leave."

Finn stood and grabbed her hand, but then froze. He held her there. She was trapped in his gaze for a long moment, and Ivy wondered if he'd convince her to stay somehow. Instead, he released her hand and took a step back.

"Come," he said. "I'll bring you to him." Finn mounted the horse and pulled Ivy up behind him. She scooched closer, wrapping her hands around his waist as the horse began to navigate the rocky slope. She felt Finn take in a deep breath and then release it, his shoulders relaxing as Ivy inched closer to the warmth of his body.

When they arrived at their building, Ivy pounded on Ser Osmund's door, but no one answered. Finn shrugged his shoulders, and Ivy went to her door to get some boots on. She saw the platter of food and looked back to Finn with a faint smile. His cheeks flushed but he didn't say anything as she went inside to change. Ivy came back out wearing her black boots, Promise on her hip, and the maple tree cloak her father had given her. They walked over to the court, where Ivy had her name day celebration last month.

King Mashu sat on his throne next to Queen Sarei and Prince Kal. Ser Osmund and Ronin sat below them, and a few Shadows lingered along the walls. Ivy thought Kal looked upset but didn't know why.

"Ivy!" Ser Osmund walked briskly toward her. "We've been looking for you." He shot a look at Finn. "It seems he knew right where you were." Finn lowered his eyes and stood to the side of Ivy.

She went up to embrace Ser Osmund, throwing her arms around his neck. "I'm sorry," she whispered, "I shouldn't have—"

But Ser Osmund hushed her, crushing Ivy against his chest. When they came apart, Ivy looked the knight in the eye and said, "I want to go home, Ser Osmund."

"I'm afraid that's not possible, my lady." Queen Sarei spoke softly, but her voice carried throughout the court.

Kal spoke up. "There are raiders in Xanheim." Ser Osmund beckoned Ivy to sit and Ivy watched Kal's eyes narrow as Finn sat beside her.

"My lady," Ser Osmund started, "it appears that raiders have taken hold of Xanheim. They've stopped the ferries from coming over, and no boats are going out."

"Why can't we just sail around them?" she asked.

"They're watching the island, Ivy," Ronin cut in.

"Watching? For what?" she questioned him.

Ser Osmund placed a hand on Ivy's shoulder. "For you, my lady," he said, worry spilling over his voice. Ivy only looked at him, confused, until he explained himself. "It seems that someone may have given away your position and sent the raiders to take you."

"What? Why me?"

"You're the daughter of King Magnus the Mighty," King Mashu said. "They would be glad to hold you captive to gain your father's lands. Or kill you to break him and send him on a path of rage and revenge. A path that would surely get him killed as well."

Ivy's head spun, and her stomach churned. She couldn't let herself be taken if it meant the fall of Godstone. She'd end her own life before she allowed that to happen. "Your brother isn't so easy to capture as he's always by the king's side. But they know you're here, and they will not leave until they have you," King Mashu continued.

"That's not going to happen," Ser Osmund tried to reassure her.

"We have Shadows stationed around the island," Kal proclaimed. "And my father has ordered his fleet to sink any raider ship that tries to land. Don't worry, my lady," Kal said, but he seemed to be talking to Finn. "They cannot have you. I won't let them."

Ivy glanced at Finn, who balled his fists under the table.

"What should we do?" Ivy turned back to Ser Osmund, but it was Ronin who spoke.

"You won't do anything. You'll rest tomorrow, and then we'll continue your training as normal the following day. There's nothing you can do, so don't dwell on it."

"But… when can we leave?" She looked to Ser Osmund.

"I'm afraid I don't have an answer, my lady. It's not safe to travel now. Perhaps if King Mashu's forces can drive them off, then we may leave as you like. But not sooner than that. I swore your father that I'd protect you, so if you wish to leave, we must wait. I'll bring you home. I promise."

Ivy nodded her head but kept her eyes on the table. "I'll post a Shadow outside your room at night until the threat has passed," King Mashu stated. Ivy thanked the king and queen for their help and retreated to her room, feeling numb.

Finn stood to leave when he felt Ser Osmund's hand latch on his shoulder. "I'd like to talk to you," he said. Finn and the knight moved to another table in the back of the court while everyone else left. He looked at Finn for a long moment before speaking. "Why are you always watching Ivy?" he demanded.

"What?"

"Don't play me for a fool. I have eyes as well. Answer me."

"She's my partner," Finn defended. "I'm only looking out for her."

Ser Osmund grumbled and stroked his long white beard. "She's like my daughter, and I must look out for her as well." Finn stayed silent, waiting for the man to speak again. "Prince Kal has shown an interest in Ivy, wouldn't you say?"

"I suppose," Finn said, shrugging his shoulders. "What's your point?"

"Does that bother you?"

"No," he lied. "Why would it?" Ser Osmund stared at him from across the table, a knowing smile forming on his lips. "Are we done?" Finn asked, getting to his feet.

"I suppose. For now."

Kal was waiting outside and ran to catch up to Finn as he stormed out of the court.

"Finn!"

"Fuck," he hissed and kicked a rock in front of him.

"What were you doing with Ivy tonight? You knew I was looking for her."

"I just went to find her after she missed practice." Finn felt the anger making his cheeks hot.

"I think you're lying," Kal accused. Finn stopped abruptly and turned to look down at Kal.

"I don't care what you think!" he roared. "Or what her knight thinks. If you want her so badly, why are you standing here talking with me? Go and preach your feelings to her because I don't want to hear them anymore." He stormed off before Kal could say anything to make Finn lose his temper and strike the prince.

He blew past Ivy's door and slammed his behind him before going out to his balcony. Finn leaned on the wall and took some deep breaths, staring down at the yard where he should be practicing. He had decided to take his anger out on one of the straw men when he heard his name.

Ivy peered around the flower wall, her hair swirling around her face as a breeze came up from behind her. "Are you alright?" she asked, concerned.

"I'm fine," he replied.

"Would you like some wine?" she offered.

"I shouldn't."

"Why not?" He didn't answer but kept his eyes on her. "It was you who brought me the platter, wasn't it?"

He nodded.

"Then come. You brought two cups," she said, holding them up and jingling them together. Ivy smiled at him, knowing he had no excuse, and he couldn't help but smile back. Finn climbed the wall to jump over to Ivy's balcony. She poured him a cup of wine and handed it to him, their fingertips brushing together, sending electricity through Finn's body.

"So," Ivy began, moving over to her chair. "What's bothering you? I heard you slam the door when you came in." She watched him over the brim of her cup, her beautiful eyes shining in the fire that filled the brazier.

He looked down so as not to get lost in them. "Your knight

doesn't want me…" He stopped and tried again. "He's very protective of you."

"Did he say something to you?"

"Only that he worries for your safety." He took a sip of wine to fill his mouth before more words came out. He could feel Ivy staring at him, like she knew he was holding something back.

"Well," she said, "I'm with you and Ronin all day. And I can take care of myself. He's always treated me as his daughter. I can't fault him for being concerned." Finn nodded his head, agreeing with her.

They sat together for a long time, drinking wine and talking. Ivy asked Finn if he missed the North, which he did, but he loved it here. She told him about Rayner being knighted and her dreams of becoming a knight herself. Finn told her that he never thought about being a knight since King Mashu didn't hire any, and he never imagined leaving Kame Island and assumed he would stay there forever, with Ronin. Finn admitted he was glad to have her as a partner. "You fight better than Kal. It's nice to have a challenge."

He gave her a warm smile. Ivy blushed at the compliment. "I thought you were angry to be fighting with a woman," she teased.

Finn frowned. "You being a woman had nothing to do with it, and I'm sorry if it appeared that way. I just didn't want a partner." He cleared his throat and smiled at her. "You're a great fighter, and your knight shouldn't worry so much." The fire began to die down, and Ivy shivered at the chill creeping in. Finn instantly got up and fetched her the blanket from her bed and draped it over her shoulders, but she grabbed his hand before he could move away.

"What was really upsetting you earlier? It can't be that Ser Osmund fears for my safety."

Her hand was soft and cold against his, which were callused and rough. He savored the feeling before he broke free of her grip and moved to lean over the wall. Ivy came and stood next to him, their shoulders brushing together. "It wasn't your knight who upset me," he finally admitted. "It was Kal."

"Why would he upset you?"

Finn rubbed at his scar. "He wanted to go riding with you tonight and show you around the island." Finn bounced his foot nervously, waiting for Ivy to say something. Instead, she snorted then began to chuckle as she returned to her seat. Finn furrowed his brow and turned to look at her. "Why are you laughing?" he asked, embarrassment coloring his cheeks.

"Are you jealous of the prince?" she teased.

Finn felt his neck grow hot. "That's ridiculous."

"Is it?"

Finn scowled and turned around. "You're a free woman, and you can do as you please."

"Finn—" Ivy lost some of her smile and patted his chair. "Come sit."

Finn looked back and considered but resisted. "I should go back. I have practice tomorrow."

"You mean we have practice tomorrow. I don't care what Ronin said. I'm not missing our session again."

Finn smiled, and inclined his head. "Well, I'll see you tomorrow then."

Ivy stood and walked to him. "Thank you for the wine. And the company, I think we both needed it." She reached for his hand again, which he brought up to his lips.

"Of course, my Lady Ivy," he said, gently kissing the back of her hand. Ivy's breath hitched slightly as Finn lowered her hand and gave her a shy smile. Just as he turned to leave, Ivy reached up and cupped his cheek, and to Finn's shock she leaned in. He stood so still that he wasn't even sure he was breathing anymore. Ivy pressed her lips to his cheek, just above his scar. Finn swore his cheeks would catch fire, but a cool spot stayed where Ivy's lips had touched. Feeling drunk and giddy, Finn stepped back before he could embarrass himself and jumped up on the wall.

"I'll see you tomorrow," she said softly to him.

Finn bowed his head in acknowledgement. "Goodnight, Ivy."

That night Finn dreamt of Ivy. Of her shiny auburn hair that appeared dark in the shadows but burned like fire in the light. Of her eyes that twinkled every time he smiled at her. Her soft, pale skin that he could still feel on his fingers. He dreamt they were sparring together under a full moon. They laughed and twirled around the yard, their own sort of dance floor, as Ivy once said. But then Kal showed up in the yard and stole Ivy away, and she went, laughing as Finn stood in the sand alone. The sound of yelling penetrated his dream, and Finn jerked awake. Outside, he could hear the yells more clearly and quickly dressed and ran out of his room.

## CHAPTER NINETEEN

# ANYWHERE

Finn ran toward the commotion with his sword drawn. When he got to the cobblestone road, he could see many ships in the harbor below. A few of the ships were burning, and he could see people by the docks scrambling. They were too far away to make out, but he assumed they were local fishmongers fleeing the approaching raiders. He started to head toward the shore when a strong hand took hold of his arm.

"What do you think you're doing?" Ronin asked, calm as ever.

"There are raiders in the bay." Finn pointed with his sword.

"I didn't ask you what you saw. I asked what you were doing."

"I'm going to help," he said, breaking free of Ronin's grip.

"No, you aren't."

Finn noticed that Ronin was wearing his sword down his back. He rarely ever saw his trainer with a real weapon unless it was made of bamboo. Finn sheathed his sword but made no move to leave.

"Are you going to fight?" he asked Ronin. His trainer nodded his head as he tied his hair back out of his face.

"But King Mashu has his Shadows for that. Why should you risk your life?"

"I could ask you the same thing," Ronin said with a faint smile. "Though I think I know the answer." Finn looked down at his feet to spare himself Ronin's gaze. Did everyone know of his feelings for Ivy? Everyone except for Kal, it would seem.

"Stay here," Ronin ordered. "I don't want to see you near this battle. The king has been informed that some raiders may have made it ashore already. His Shadows are hunting them down."

Finn stood and watched Ronin walk off to battle, as calm as if he was going to pick up his tea.

Back at the barracks, Finn saw a Shadow standing guard at Ivy's door. He went to move past him, but the Shadow blocked his path.

"May I enter?" Finn asked sarcastically.

"No," he said, keeping his gaze on the wall across from him.

"Why not?"

"I have orders from Ser Osmund not to let anyone in or out of this door."

Finn shook his head. "You can't keep her locked up in there! She's not a child!"

"No one in or out," the Shadow repeated.

Finn growled and went down the hall, pounding on Ser Osmund's door. The old knight answered immediately, then looked angry when he realized it was Finn who stood there. "Oh. What do you want?"

"Let Ivy out. We're supposed to practice today."

"I don't care about your practice. There are raiders on the island!"

"She isn't a child!" Finn yelled. "I'll keep her safe, and we'll only—"

Ser Osmund scoffed. "*You'll* keep her safe? I wouldn't place her life in your hands. I barely know you."

"You know me well enough, it would seem," Finn said, taking a step toward him.

"Feelings don't protect people, Finn. Now go away. I have to meet with the king." Ser Osmund closed the door on Finn.

He walked past the Shadow, shooting him a glare as he entered his room, then went outside and jumped over to Ivy's side to see her leaning against her door. Finn cleared his throat, and she twirled around. "Were you listening?" he asked. She nodded her head. Finn suddenly felt embarrassed, knowing she heard him talking with Ser Osmund.

*Feelings don't protect people.*

Finn blushed and looked away from her. "Ronin has gone to fight," he told her.

Ivy tied on her boots and strapped her sword belt around her waist, keeping her gold scarf tied around the belt.

"What are you doing?" Finn asked.

"Didn't you come to get me?"

"I was just…I just wanted to—"

"See if I was alright? I'm fine, so let's go."

"Go where?"

"Don't you want to see Ronin fighting?"

"Ivy." Finn lowered his voice. "If the Shadow knows you're gone—"

"They'll what? Lock me in my room?" She smiled up at him, and Finn couldn't resist her spirit. He grinned and relented, telling her to hurry.

They climbed down the flower wall to the first-floor balcony and ran through the practice yard, staying hidden behind the trees off the main road. Ivy hadn't been down this road since she arrived here on Kame Island over two months ago.

Ivy and Finn raced through the trees down the hill, stopping to duck as Shadows rode by on horses as black as night. They could hear the commotion and the sounds of battle as they drew near. Finn grabbed her hand and pulled her into a bamboo forest, and Ivy allowed him to lead her deeper into the woods, savoring the warmth of his hand wrapped around hers.

They found a spot to crouch down just above the harbor. The civilians had all cleared out, and King Mashu's warships could be seen in the distance, shooting flaming arrows at the raiders' ships. A few caught fire and men could be seen jumping overboard, but a clash of steel drew their attention to the dirt street where fishmongers had set up their tables. Shadows were fighting against a small boat that was unloading raiders. They spotted Ronin off by himself, fighting three raiders at once. Ivy watched with excitement in her eyes; it was true that the man moved like water.

He was too far away for Ivy to see his face, but she knew Ronin gave away nothing. The raiders wouldn't know where he was moving until he was already there. Ronin guided his thin sword to meet the first raider, easily slashing through the raider's arm, flowing around him, and then stabbed his sword through the back of his neck. The other two came at him at once. Ronin ducked as the first blade sailed over his head, almost hitting his fellow raider. He moved about them on feet lighter than feathers. Ivy would bet he made no noise when he moved like that.

The second man charged, and Ronin didn't even turn around

as he slid his sword back, skewering the man through the chest. He pulled his sword out and stood still, waiting for the raider to come to him. Ronin didn't lead his enemy, nor back away from them. He only killed when he was approached. The lone raider stood hesitating, waiting for Ronin to make a move.

Instead, Ronin held his sword behind his back and stood completely still. The raider thought he had a chance and squared up with Ronin, who still didn't move. The raider swung his sword down, and Ronin slid from its path, letting the sword hit the dirt as if Ronin was never there. The raider swung his sword up, and Ronin sidestepped. As the raider aimed for Ronin's head, he ducked and slid around the raider before he could do anything.

Ronin gripped his sword with both hands and swung at the man's torso. Ivy couldn't believe it. Had Ronin missed the man? The raider was still standing, seemingly untouched. He took a few steps toward Ronin before the top half of the man slid off, the legs buckling before going down. Finn and Ivy looked at each other, shock written on both of their faces. Neither one of them had ever seen Ronin truly fight, but they had heard the stories. Now they had witnessed for themselves how truly dangerous their trainer was.

Later that evening, Ivy walked out the door of her room and met Finn in the hallway for their nightly practice. The Shadow had been taken off her door soon after the fighting ended. The king told Ser Osmund that the immediate threat was gone for now, and Ivy would be safe.

King Mashu's Shadows informed him that the raiders had all been killed or driven back to Xanheim. It was still early in the evening, and the sun wasn't fully set, but Finn and Ivy were too excited for practice after watching Ronin fight earlier. They squared up immediately, both smiling at the other before Ivy attacked.

Ivy lunged and jabbed her sword into Finn's thigh, twirling around him as she swung her sword overhead and stopped it at his neck.

"That was a lucky shot," Finn said. "I was distracted."

"By what?" she teased, shrugging her shoulder.

Finn shook his head, a blush creeping up his cheeks before they tapped swords to let each other know they were ready this time. They came together, blocking and landing hits each as frequently as the other. He was stronger than Ivy, but she knew he'd been holding back. Ivy landed another killing blow, slashing at the artery in his leg. She stopped and stood in front of him, crossing her arms.

"What?" he asked innocently.

"Stop holding back. How will I learn if you don't use your full strength? Do you think every man I fight will be of equal strength to my own?"

"Fine," he relented. "I won't hold back."

"Promise?" She held her hand out for him to shake. He took it and repeated the word.

This time when they came together, Finn almost knocked Ivy off her feet. He swung his sword down, and she dodged it just in time, sliding in the sand to get behind him. He turned around and brought his sword down to meet Ivy's. With their swords crossing, Ivy was struggling to keep his weight off her. His russet eyes smiled at her as Ivy struggled. Finn pushed harder, and Ivy felt her knees buckle, but she swept her leg to trip him just as she was falling.

They crashed to the sand, and Finn tried to get back up, but she kicked the back of his knee, and he came crashing down in the sand again. "What the—"

Ivy leaped on his back and flung her weight backward, bringing him down with her. The two struggled in the sand, out of breath and laughing so hard their lungs were on fire.

The two rolled in the sand for what seemed like a long time before Finn tried to crawl to his sword, but Ivy held his ankle. Finn launched himself back and pinned her to the sand, holding her wrists down so she couldn't hit him. Ivy struggled against his strength, but the two were laughing so hard that Ivy could hardly fight back anymore.

"Why did you tackle me?" Finn asked between breaths, still smiling.

"Fighting isn't only meant for swords," Ivy breathed. "Besides, if I go down, you're coming with me."

"I'd follow you anywhere," Finn blurted, half to himself.

Ivy stopped giggling and stared up at him for a long moment. He felt her shift under his weight and lift her head slightly. They were close enough that he could see shards of gray that cut through the purple in her eyes. Finn felt her breath brush across his lips and quickly released her wrists, moving off her to sit in the sand.

Ivy sat up and shook the sand from her hair, which was knotted from their fight. Finn lay back in the sand, trying to catch his breath, though it wasn't the fight that stole it—it was Ivy. He battled with himself every day inside his head. Part of him wanted more with her, but he knew she would be leaving as soon as it was safe. Sometimes he felt it was a mistake getting to know her, for it could only bring pain. But Ivy was like a pool of cold water on a hot summer day, and he couldn't stay away.

Finn buried his shaky hands under the sand, feeling the cold spots that hadn't seen the sun all day. Ivy lay back as well, and they stared up at the darkening sky above them, neither one speaking.

A jolt of electricity shot through Finn when he felt Ivy's hand grab hold of his underneath the sand. He laced their fingers together, running his thumb over her soft skin as his heart beat out of control. Ivy's cheeks were rosy, and Finn felt drawn to her. He couldn't take it anymore.

He gave in to his feelings and scooched closer to her, feeling the warmth of Ivy alongside his body. When his gaze drifted to her lips, Ivy smiled sweetly, and Finn gladly moved toward them. When she didn't pull away, he thought his heart might burst and kill him before he could kiss her. They were only a few inches apart, a shared breath away. The electricity between them was palpable, all-consuming, but then Finn saw a figure out of the corner of his eye.

## CHAPTER TWENTY

# THE SHADOWS

Finn shot up, releasing Ivy's hand and grabbing for his wooden sword.

"I didn't mean to... interrupt." A Shadow stood before them. "Lady Ivy, the king wishes to see you right away. I'm here to escort you."

Ivy stood up and brushed herself off before grabbing her practice sword.

"Wait," Finn said, standing next to Ivy. "It's getting late. Why does King Mashu want to see her?"

"That's none of your business, I'm afraid."

Ivy gave Finn a confused look but insisted she'd see him later. Finn felt a chill on the back of his neck and grabbed her arm, pulling Ivy back behind him.

"No," he said, then directed his attention to the Shadow. "Why is half your face covered? No Shadow hides his face."

"A sword slashed my cheek during the fight, and I didn't want to upset the lady at the sight of it."

Finn wasn't buying it. "I know every Shadow on this island.

What's your name?"

The man put his hand to the hilt of his sword and eyed Finn.

"Move aside. You're delaying the king's business."

"Not until you give me your name."

The Shadow drew his sword, and Finn felt a sudden panic as he realized neither he nor Ivy had their real swords. And this man was no Shadow.

"Finn," Ivy whispered from behind, but the raider was already moving. Finn shoved Ivy back and threw up his wooden sword to parry the attacks. They struggled against each other, the raider hacking away a piece of Finn's sword.

"Go, Ivy!" he yelled over his shoulder, but she wouldn't leave. Instead, she attacked the man from the back, swinging her sword as hard as she could. The raider groaned as she landed a blow to his middle back, cracking the practice sword in half. The raider grabbed for Ivy, but she slipped around him to stand with Finn. He tried to push her behind him again, but the raider grabbed Finn's arm and twisted, forcing him to drop his sword.

Ivy swung, but the man caught the wood and punched her in the face. She dropped to the ground. Finn felt a wave of rage coursing through him. He kicked the man's legs out from under him, sending him crashing down in the sand. They struggled, kicking and punching at each other. The raider reached for his sword. Finn grabbed his arm, and the raider brought his elbow to Finn's face. The blow slammed Finn's head into the sand, filling his eyes with stars, but he still tried to fight the raider, who now straddled him. The raider slammed Finn's head into the sand again and punched him in the temple over and over. He was starting to black out, watching his world slip away as Ivy lay unconscious in the sand. Finn tried to fight it, but his vision turned black, and he was slipping away, Ivy's name dying on his lips. The raider stood up and snatched his sword before scooping up Ivy and throwing her over his shoulder.

The sun had set, and a faint wind whistled around the yard when Finn woke up. His head spun when he tried to sit up, and he groaned at the pain as if his brain was pounding to get out. He frantically searched the yard for Ivy and the raider but saw nothing. Finn tried to stand but stumbled as he slowly regained his vision. Voice hoarse, he called her name. No answer came. Panic and fear began working their way in, closing in on Finn from all sides until tears boiled in his eyes. Finn forced himself up, clutching his ribs where the raider had kicked him, then moved as fast as he could to his room to retrieve his real blade.

There was no time to find help. Ivy could be across the water by now. He wasn't sure how long he'd been knocked out, but more than a moment was too long, and Ivy could be dead. Finn pushed that thought from his head and stumbled to the stables to find a horse. He mounted Ivy's horse, Cassius, since he was nearest to the gate. The horse raged through the night, as if he could feel that Ivy was in danger as well. Finn rode straight to the docks in search of the boat that would carry Ivy away from him.

When he got down to the water, he saw no sign of any boat. He turned Cass and kicked at the horse to run west, to the dock he'd first arrived at the island at. When he got there, he tied Cass to a tree and made his way down the steep slope. Peering over the edge, Finn saw a man carrying something on his shoulder.

Anger took hold of him again as he watched the man throw Ivy down and begin binding her feet and wrists. Finn crept down the slope to get as close as possible without being detected. Ivy was just beginning to stir awake when Finn came around a rock and met her gaze. He held his finger to his lips as the raider finished binding her. Finn moved silently toward the man, keeping his movements slow and sure.

When he was close enough, Finn jabbed his sword through the raider's shoulder. The raider screamed out in pain, and Ivy kicked her feet at his legs, making him stumble. The raider roared in anger.

"Stupid bitch!" he screamed, and kicked Ivy in the ribs, forcing her to curl up.

Finn slashed his blade across the man's arm but only managed to cut him. His head was still pounding, and his vision unfocused as he fought for Ivy's life.

The raider swung, and Finn threw his head back, the blade just missing his throat. He quickly threw up his sword only to meet the raiders. Their swords shot sparks as they crashed together, and they were face to face. Finn put all his strength into the blade. He tried to force the man to drop his sword, but he was powerful. Finn moved one foot through the sand and kicked out the raider's leg, giving Finn enough to overpower the man. As soon as the raider hit the ground, Finn thrust his sword down into his heart and twisted his blade, killing the man instantly.

Finn moved to untie Ivy, gently cutting away at the ropes on her feet and wrists. As soon as she was free, Ivy jumped up and wrapped her arms around his neck. Finn could feel her shaking. He leaned back, bringing his hands to her face, and turning it to see the injuries.

"Are you alright?" he asked her, something catching in his throat. Ivy nodded as tears slid down her cheeks. Something inside Finn broke at the sight of her. He leaned in and kissed her forehead, then pulled her into his chest. The thought of Ivy coming so close to death was almost enough to break him.

Finn allowed Ivy to sob as he stroked her head. They sank to the ground together, and Finn cradled Ivy in his lap for what seemed like hours. When she finally pulled away, her hand came up to meet his face; he winced at the pain and pulled her hand away. "Finn…" she began.

"It's alright. I'm fine," he assured her.

"What should we do with him?" She motioned toward the dead raider.

"Bring him to the king."

Finn woke the king and queen, violently pounding on their door. When King Mashu opened the door, Finn stood there, bloodied, beaten, and breathing heavily.

"What is this?" the king demanded.

"Come with me. Now." Finn didn't wait for an answer before he strode away from the king.

Ivy had already gathered Ser Osmund to meet in the king's courtroom.

She sat slumped over on a bench when Finn came storming in with the king trailing behind him. He immediately went to Ivy and knelt in front of her, speaking softly and taking her hand in his.

"Is someone going to tell us what happened?" Ser Osmund's voice was laced with rage.

Finn stood, placing his hand on Ivy's shoulder and eyeing the king.

"Who is that?" King Mashu demanded as he gestured to the slumped body below the dais.

Finn walked up and pulled the cloth from the dead raider's face. "This is the raider who captured Ivy tonight."

The king and Ser Osmund exchanged a look.

"He's wearing the uniform of the Shadows," King Mashu mentioned.

"He's a wolf disguised as a sheep!" Finn roared. "He killed one of your Shadows and stole his uniform to trick Ivy into coming with him!"

"Calm down, Finn." Ser Osmund put his hands up.

"Don't tell me to calm down!" he roared. "Ivy could've been killed tonight! And where were you?"

He turned to the king. "Where were the Shadows if not keeping an eye out for Ivy?"

"I thought you always had your eye on Ivy," Ser Osmund stated calmly.

Finn stepped toward the old knight, but Ivy quickly grabbed his hand. "I do," Finn replied. "I care about Ivy. And I was the only one there to defend her tonight."

Ser Osmund looked to Ivy, who lowered her eyes to her boots. "Lady Ivy." Ser Osmund got to his knees before her. "I've broken my promise to your father. I failed, and for that, I'm sorry."

Ivy got down to embrace the man. Finn knew he was like a second father to her.

"You couldn't have known," she said in a soft voice as she wrapped her arms around Ser Osmund.

Finn continued to eye King Mashu, who looked overwhelmed at what had happened.

"What are you going to do?" Finn demanded of the king.

"I'll put a guard on Ivy, day and night she'll be—"

"No," Finn interrupted. "Your Shadows proved useless when it truly mattered. What will you do about the raiders that reside in Xanheim?"

"We can send a small force to drive them off," the king offered.

Finn pondered that a moment and then suggested that Ronin go along.

"Ronin?" Ser Osmund asked.

"We watched him cut a man in half today with little effort. If Ronin can't instill fear in them, then your Shadows will certainly fail as well."

Ser Osmund stood up. "When did Ivy leave her room?"

"I left soon after the guard was put on my door." Ivy stood, gripping her bruised ribs. "Right after you told Finn that feelings don't protect people. If that's true, then no one can protect me."

Finn looked at Ivy, then to Ser Osmund who looked ashamed of what he said earlier.

"Very well." King Mashu broke the silence. "I'll put together a small force, Ronin included, and send them across the water."

The king bowed to Ivy and sincerely apologized for the harm that had come to find her. She seemed to accept, and then the king left the court, retreating to his bedchamber. Ser Osmund stood between them and the door and looked from Ivy to Finn. "My lady," he began, "I believe you're in good hands and put my trust in Finn to see you back to your room safely."

Finn and Ivy walked in silence to their building. He peered around the corner into the yard, expecting to see the raider. All that remained were the wooden practice swords and the disturbed sand from the struggle.

Finn put Ivy's arm around his neck and helped her up the steps to her room. He opened the door, sat her down on the bed, and then moved to pour her a cup of water She waved it away and laid her head on the pillow. Finn covered her up and turned to leave when he felt her hand in his.

"Stay with me," she whispered. "Please."

Finn hesitated, but the look of fear in her eyes overpowered him. He nodded and went to close the door, then stuck a chair under the handle, still worried about another raider lurking in the shadows. He did the same to the doors that led out to the balcony before climbing in the bed beside Ivy. The heat from her made his cheeks flush, and he was glad for the darkness of the room. She turned to face him, and Finn froze as she nuzzled her head under his chin. He gently slid his arm under Ivy's head and cradled her against him, hoping she couldn't feel how madly his heart was pounding.

After a while, Finn felt her breathing slow as she began to fall into a deep sleep. He stayed awake, not wanting to take his eyes off her for fear of losing her again. She stirred slightly and spoke something into his chest, but he couldn't hear it. As he tilted his head down to listen to her, she asked, "Will you stay with me?"

Finn blinked at her, figuring she must be dreaming or dazed from her wounds.

"Yes, my Ivy," he whispered against her temple, pulling the blanket up over her shoulder. "I'll stay."

"Always?"

Finn smiled and kissed the top of her head, stroking her hair until her breathing became deep and relaxed again. "I'll always be here," he spoke softly to himself. "I promise."

Finn watched the shadows grow across the stone floor as the

sun came up; only then did he relax and fall into a deep sleep, with Ivy curled up in his arms.

CHAPTER TWENTY-ONE

# THE YOUNG KNIGHT

"Don't tense up so much. That's it, hold your breath and release."

The stitches in Rayner's hand itched as he gripped the bow, held his breath, and released the arrow. It had been just over a week since the battle of Harper Hall, and Rayner hadn't slept soundly since. He closed his eyes at night and saw the faces of the people burning alive; saw his grandfather ride into the sea of raiders.

His mother hadn't been the same since they brought back the news of her father's fall and had been residing in the magister's healing quarters. To Rayner, she looked like she might follow her father to the afterlife. Queen Elana hadn't eaten much in the past week, and the meat was beginning to fall from her bones. Rayner couldn't bear to look at her; it pained him to see his mother that way. She'd always held herself with a sense of authority and wisdom. Now she only resembled defeat. He took some comfort in Magister Ivann's assurances that she was only grieving.

A warm trickle of blood ran down his hand as one of the

stitches came loose. The raider who left this mark now lay in his grave, but that gave Rayner no comfort. He knew there were many more of them, their armies still lurking around the southern border. They were growing bolder. It was only a matter of time before they came for Godstone.

Correlyn walked up to Rayner to steady his elbow as he drew back another arrow. She'd been teaching him to use a bow, so he didn't have to rely only on his sword. He let the arrow fly and watched it stick into the foot of the straw man.

"Shit," he cursed under his breath. He threw down the bow, walking over to the shed to buckle on his sword.

"It's alright," Correlyn assured him. "You're only just starting. You'll get it with more practice."

Correlyn reminded Rayner of his mother in some ways. She could be calm and caring, but he knew a bright fire burned in her chest when it came to battle. His mother was no warrior, but she was wise in many ways that he didn't understand.

Correlyn came and rested her hand upon his shoulder. Rayner turned and pulled her in, squeezing her tight around the waist, not wanting to let go.

"When does your mother plan to leave?" he asked quietly as if that would bring a different answer.

"At sunrise tomorrow," Correlyn admitted, her voice choked with sadness.

"Then we have to speak with her tonight." Rayner pulled away and brushed the hair from her face before leaning in, kissing her deeply.

Magnus strolled across the covered bridge that led from the central tower to the building where his wife had been staying. He paused and watched as Rayner and Correlyn stood below the roof of the shed, wrapped in each other's arms. Magnus knew Rayner hadn't talked with Lady Oharra yet but decided not to push him to do so. If he truly cared for Correlyn, Magnus knew his son would put up a fight to keep her by his side. He smiled as he watched the two together, but it soon turned into a frown as he remembered the news he had yet to tell Rayner.

Magnus buried his hands in the pockets of his fur cloak and started down the walkway again. The only noise to drown the chaos in his head were his footsteps, echoing on the stone floor. He knocked softly on the door, and Magister Ivann answered, looking almost as sickly as the queen. The magister had been working tirelessly to keep Elana comfortable and fed but with little success.

"How is she?" Magnus asked, peering around the old man in search of his wife. Ivann was reluctant to answer but told the king that Elana had improved slightly. "May I see her?"

"Of course. She's your wife." Ivann stood aside to let Magnus in and closed the door behind him, keeping the cold, gripping fingers of winter out.

Magnus walked over to the bed, where his wife had been sleeping the past week, though it felt like a year to Magnus. He didn't sleep well when he wasn't beside his wife. The warmth of her under the furs and the smell of pine needles lingering in her hair was something he ached for. Magnus kissed the top of her head and sat down on the stool beside her. Elana stirred awake and let a faint smile escape as her red-rimmed eyes spotted her husband.

"How do you feel, my love?" Magnus asked, stroking her long, golden hair. Elana shrugged but didn't answer. "Ivy has surely gotten my letter by now. Perhaps she'll return sooner than planned. Would that make you happy?"

"Ivy?" Elana spoke softly, her voice hoarse from crying. "Ivy can't come back. Not now. It isn't safe here." Worry crept over her face.

"This is her home, darling. She'll be safe by my side and Rayner's."

"No."

Magnus sighed and took his hand away. "Don't you want to see your daughter?"

"Of course, but…" The words caught. Magnus knew she wasn't only mourning the death of her father. She was fearful for her children and what this war might bring to their home. Her father's death had only made it clear that no one was safe. The raiders would stop at nothing and have no mercy for anyone. Not even the king's daughter.

"I promise you she's fine." Magnus cradled her hand in his.

"How can you know that?" Magnus didn't know how to describe it to her, and he searched his head for the right words before continuing. "I can feel her." Tears began to form in the queen's eyes, and she sat up, wrapping her arms around Magnus's neck. "Please," he whispered to her. "Come home."

She nodded her head in agreement, and Magnus hugged her a little tighter.

"Will you attend the feast?" he asked.

That night the kingdom was holding a feast for Lady Oharra and her warriors to repay them for their help in the battle. It was also a send-off, as Lady Oharra wished to return home to Grey

Raven. Magnus couldn't argue with her duty to her people. The winter would be long, and she needed to ensure they were prepared to weather it.

"I don't think I feel up to it," Elana responded. "Please wish Lady Oharra safe travels for me," she said, before squeezing Magnus's hand and retreating to their bedchamber.

Rayner and Correlyn walked to the Hall holding hands. The snow was falling, making everything around the kingdom appear soft and at peace. Inside, torches lined the walls. Benches were filled with men and women who cheered at something Lady Oharra had said.

Magnus sat on his throne; Luna perched up in the branches that crept out over the dais. Lady Oharra was seated at the king's table, taking the seat beside him that was usually reserved for the queen. Rayner walked Correlyn to the table and took the seat on the other side of his father, eyeing Lady Oharra cautiously.

After the food had been served and cleared away, a poet stood to tell of the Battle of Harper Hall. He painted a heroic picture of Magnus and Rayner fighting off raiders as the city burned around them. Rayner was glad for his mother's absence as the story surely would've upset her. When the poet finished, Rayner got up to sit next to Lady Oharra, catching his father's eye as he approached. Correlyn carefully watched from down the table, nervously sipping wine from a goblet.

"My lady," Rayner greeted her as he took the seat beside her.

"May I speak with you?"

"Of course, Ser Rayner." She smiled at him as he sat down. "What an honor to sit beside such a heroic knight. This poet tells the tale true. I witnessed for myself your skills in the battle."

Her praise made his cheeks flush with color. He still wasn't used to the new title that came with the honor of being knighted.

"I hear you're leaving tomorrow morning," he stated, moving straight to the point.

"Yes. I've been away too long and must check on my people."

Rayner sat, wringing his hands nervously under the table. "I was hoping that Correlyn might stay here. With me."

Lady Oharra looked confused for a moment, then smiled and reached out to put her hand on Rayner's cheek before saying no.

He furrowed his brow. "Why not? My father has already given his consent, and she'll be safe. There's no reason—"

"No, Rayner. Nowhere is safe, but I'd feel better if she were back home."

Rayner saw Correlyn coming over and tried to wave her off, but she came anyway.

"Mother," she said, standing beside Rayner. "I want to stay."

Lady Oharra looked from Rayner to Correlyn, her gray eyes clouding over. "I don't care what you want. You're my daughter, and I won't lose you."

"Mother, please. Don't treat me like a child. I'm old enough to make my own decisions, and I have been for a long time. But you need to let me make them."

Lady Oharra was growing angry, and the darkness showed on her face. "No, Correlyn. We can return in the spring if you like, but we must go home."

"Why?" Correlyn questioned her mother. When Lady Oharra

didn't answer, Correlyn told her she was staying, and there was nothing that she could do about it. "I care for Rayner," she said, placing a hand on his shoulder. "And I want to be with him. Will you deny your daughter happiness?"

Lady Oharra didn't have an answer, and after a moment, she stood up and walked out of the Hall, her black hair swirling behind her like a shadow.

The next morning Correlyn stood in the crowd that formed to see off Lady Oharra and her warriors. She watched as her mother made the rounds, embracing King Magnus with a smile, kissing Queen Elana on the cheek, and shaking hands with some of Magnus's knights that she'd grown to know.

When she stopped in front of Rayner and Correlyn, the smile faded from her face. She spoke only to Correlyn, telling her to keep herself safe, no matter what. Lady Oharra began to tear up as she pulled her daughter in, stroking her hair.

"Please," Lady Oharra said into her ear. "This is your last chance."

"I'll see you in the spring when you return, Mother," Correlyn answered.

Forcing herself to let go, Lady Oharra wiped the tears from her cheeks and glared at Rayner for a long moment before turning away and mounting her horse. Lady Oharra never looked back, and Correlyn stayed to watch them ride off until they were out of sight.

"She's angry with you," Correlyn said, her eyes still on the snow path now torn up by horses.

"I took her daughter away. I can't blame her for being upset."

It wasn't until the following day that Magnus told Rayner the news that would take him away from Correlyn. After Rayner was knighted, Magnus had given him control of a small force of knights. All were older than Rayner, but he was the king's son. The knights treated him as such. That morning, the king and his son ate breakfast together in the Hall to talk, and Magnus told Rayner that he needed him to take his men to the town of Ashton for a scouting mission.

Lady Oharra had called back many of her scouts from around the border, which left Godstone vulnerable to an attack. Ashton sat north of Harper Hall, and Magnus was sure that the raiders hadn't ventured very far from Harper Hall since they didn't get what they came for last time.

"I'm sending scouts to the Town of Moore and Temple City as well," Magnus explained to Rayner. "But I need you in Ashton. Your mother is still mourning, and I need to stay by her side," Magnus explained.

"It's alright, Father. I understand. When do we leave?"

"Tomorrow," he said gently.

Rayner looked down, realizing he'd have to leave Correlyn. His father had promised Lady Oharra that Correlyn wouldn't go anywhere that might be dangerous, so she would have to stay in Godstone while he ventured South. Rayner understood this, but still he hated to leave Correlyn so soon after he fought to keep her here with him.

CHAPTER TWENTY- TWO

# THE TOWN OF ASHTON

Rayner went to see his mother the following morning as his men were mounting up to leave. Elana looked a little better, but sadness still haunted her eyes. Rayner was taller than his mother now, and she had to reach up to kiss his cheek.

"You take care of yourself, Rayner," she said. "My sweet son, my young knight."

He hugged his mother for a long moment, assuring her that he'd be back before she knew it. Then, he turned to leave and join his men. He knew his mother would stand in her window of the tower and watch him ride away, just as she had when the boat took away her daughter.

At the gates, Rayner embraced his father.

"I'm so proud of you, son," Magnus whispered in his ear, then stepped back as Correlyn approached. Tears slipped down her cheeks as Rayner hugged her and said that he'd be back in only a few weeks. He tried to assure her that it was just a scouting mission and that his men would likely grow bored.

Rayner leaned back and caressed her cheek, smiling despite the growing pain in his heart. "Correlyn, I—"

She cut off his words, pressing her lips to his. Rayner drew her in closer, running a gloved hand through her midnight hair. His stomach danced as Correlyn parted her lips, inviting Rayner in for another kiss. He wished so badly to stay in this moment forever, but Rayner knew that forever was just around the corner. Forcing himself to step back, Rayner pressed his lips to her brow. "I'll see you soon."

Correlyn smiled, her gray eyes sparkling, "Come back to me."

"Always."

Rayner mounted his horse and rode through the gates with his men, looking back every few minutes until Correlyn was just a dot on the horizon. Godstone was gone.

It took only two days for Rayner and his men to reach the town of Ashton. They set up camp. A few men went down to the river to break up the ice so that they could fish. Ser Caster was Rayner's second in command. He was about the same age as Rayner's father but with more gray running through his dark hair. Rayner had a tent to himself that had been set up on a hill overlooking the town. He'd never been to this town before, but it seemed familiar to him. He remembered his father telling the story of Helvarr's banishment and the battle that had taken place there over nineteen years ago.

The town was small, but it was alive with people at work doing their daily chores. Rayner walked through the town alone, looking at the new houses and workshops that lined the dirt street. The village had fallen to a fire set by the raiders back then. His father had been too late to save them all. Many of the villagers had perished in the fire or been slaughtered by the raiders that stormed the village.

Looking at it now, one could never tell that it was once the victim of war. No scorched wood touched the houses, no charred bodies lay in the street. The only noises belonged to the wind, children laughing, and the occasional whinny of a horse. Rayner couldn't imagine how hard it must've been for his father to banish his closest friend. Magnus had only been a few years older than Rayner was now, but with the entirety of a kingdom resting on his shoulders. Rayner was in no rush to claim his father's throne and would be glad to see his father's reign last until Rayner had a son of his own.

They spent their days sparring in the open field, fishing the river, and hunting the nearby wooded areas surrounding the village. A local innkeeper had been happy to offer Rayner a room for his stay, saying that they were forever indebted to House Blackbourne. Rayner was grateful but declined the offer, preferring to stay with his men at the camp. He thought of Correlyn every minute and wondered how she was doing back home. Their relationship was very new, but already Rayner knew that he had fallen deeply for her.

He often wondered if their trip to Temple City had brought them together. Rayner even considered the fact that it was the raiders who had brought them together. If it hadn't been for them, Lady Oharra wouldn't have come to Godstone so often over the past few years. He pushed that thought out of his head, not wanting something so bad to be the reason for something good. Surely the gods had brought Correlyn to him for a reason— one he couldn't figure out yet.

He also thought about Ivy down in Kame Island, wondering how she'd taken the news of their grandfather's death. He hoped their father told of his sacrifice. A pit had been forming in Rayner's stomach since that day, and guilt consumed him. He couldn't help but think that his harsh words had caused Lord Harald to sacrifice his life. He had been unable to look at his mother in the days that followed, fearing that she'd sense his guilt and blame him for killing her father. Somewhere inside, he knew that wasn't true, but those were the dark thoughts that crept around him at night when he was alone, trapped inside his own mind.

Rayner tucked his hands into his chest plate as he walked down the streets of Ashton. They'd been there for over a week now and would begin to break down camp in a few days to head back home. He heard the clang of metal being pounded and followed the noise down the street, sticking his head into a small shed at the end of the road. A man not much older than Rayner was working at a sword. He dropped it into a pail of water, the sword hissing at the liquid that cooled it. The smith stopped his work when Rayner entered the shed and greeted the young knight.

Many of the villagers knew him by now in the small amount of time that he'd spent there. There was a feeling of respect that emanated from them that Rayner felt he hadn't earned. If his father weren't King Magnus, these villagers might not treat him so well. Rayner was careful not to take advantage of their kindness.

The smith smiled at him. "Can I help you with something, Ser?" Rayner pulled out a small piece of cloth that held an obsidian stone and told the smith what he wanted. The man smiled at him and said that he would be honored to make it, telling Rayner to come back in two days.

Rayner walked back to his tent, feeling nervous about what he was going to say to Correlyn when he returned home. He'd found the smooth stone lying on the beach of Godstone just before he was knighted. He'd been feeling anxious about the ceremony and had decided to take a walk on the beach to clear his head. Rayner sat down on one of the many boulders that lined the shore when the stone caught his eye. The beach used to be filled with them, or so his father claimed. But people had been digging them for years to sell or trade for other goods.

When Rayner spotted the obsidian stone sitting on top of the sand, he decided that it had to be a sign from the gods. Anyone else could have easily spotted its smooth black surface that still shone in the light. He picked it up and decided then that he would save it and make it into a ring.

Rayner had come to know Correlyn over the past few years but had only grown to love her in the last few months. Though he hadn't spoken the words to her yet, he was sure she felt the same. Rayner spent many nights in his tent going over what he'd say to her, how he would propose and what her reaction might be. He feared that she would say no, out of fear of what Lady Oharra might say. He wondered what his father would think, and how his mother would react. He was so afraid that the queen would spiral into the darkness that sucked her in after the fall of Harper Hall. Rayner never wanted to see his mother like that again.

His mind drifted to Ivy, and he smiled, thinking about how she would react to the news. His sister was his best friend, and Rayner knew that she'd be happy for him and Correlyn. Rayner wondered how much she'd changed over the last few months, if at all. Rayner could still picture her standing before him at the docks, tears welling her eyes as Rayner gifted her the dagger he'd won years ago. It broke his heart to let his sister go, but he wanted her to be safe. He had no choice but to trust his father and pray to the gods to keep his sister safe on her journey.

The night before they left Ashton, Rayner sparred with Ser Caster in an open field. The night was cold, but the crisp wind felt good on his face and filled him with life. Fires from the camp cast an orange glow on the thin sheet of snow that covered the field, and shadows of his men danced around them as they cheered on the two knights. Rayner made the first move, slicing toward Ser Caster's chest. His armor screeched under the blade, and he slid away, throwing up his sword as Rayner's came crashing down. The men cheered Rayner on, and his eyes grew with excitement as the adrenaline began to run through him. He swung his sword over the knight's head, dropping him to one knee.

Ser Caster thrust his blade forward, landing it in Rayner's chest. The swords were dull, but Ser Caster's strength managed to put a dent into Rayner's new armor. He grunted and brought his sword down, catching the knight on his hand as he tried to block the blow. Ser Caster dropped his sword, and Rayner held his blade to the knight's throat before giving him a playful tap on the cheek. The men cheered to Rayner's victory, and he threw his hands in the air to accept their praise as Ser Caster plowed into him.

His sword was thrown from his grasp as he landed in the snow. The men cheered even louder, their laughter filling the air as Ser Caster crawled on top of Rayner, laughing at his negligence.

"Keep your eye on the enemy, young knight," Ser Caster said as he struggled to pin Rayner. He couldn't help but smile, and his men's cheers only filled him with more fight. They rolled through the snow, flattening it beneath their weight until Rayner came within reach of his sword. Ser Caster snatched his arm back, and Rayner shifted a leg loose and threw his knee into the knight's side.

They both grunted with pain, and Rayner made a break for it. He slipped in the snow, his cheeks hot from laughter and exertion. Ser Caster grabbed at his foot from behind, and Rayner quickly scooped up a pile of snow and turned, throwing it in the knight's face. His gloves and boots were soaked through, but he didn't care. As soon as Rayner touched the hilt of his sword, something sharp cut down his back, and the men burst into laughter. Ser Caster shoved a pile of snow down his armor, and the cold was like a hundred piercing daggers.

Ser Caster was forming another piece of snow when Rayner grabbed the sword and swung it around, holding it to the knight's face. Ser Caster smirked and dropped the snow, throwing his hands up in submission. They both burst out into tears, clutching their stomachs as they laughed.

The next day was their last in Ashton, and Rayner went back to the smith's shop to fetch the ring. The day was bright and unusually warm for winter, the first sign that spring was on the way. The field where he fought Ser Caster the night before was slick with mud and melted snow. He breathed in the fresh air and knocked on the door to the shed. When the smith answered, Rayner greeted the man and followed him into the workspace. He unfolded the piece of cloth that Rayner had given him a few days ago.

A small silver ring sat inside it with the obsidian stone set in the middle. When Rayner held it up, the sun coming in from the door caught the silver, and it shone like a star. His heart fluttered at the thought that his plan was coming into play, and this was real. He was going to ask the woman he loved for her hand in marriage. He paid the smith handsomely for the ring and thanked him before leaving. He couldn't keep his eyes off the small silver band as he walked back up to the camp that was already being torn down. Rayner put the ring into the piece of cloth and tucked it into the pocket of his jacket, safe below his armor.

The next day, with Ashton well behind them, Rayner ordered his men to stop and camp for the night. They would reach home tomorrow, and the thought of that filled his head with excitement. The land was scarcely wooded, mostly consisting of open fields and a few swamps that still lay frozen. After his men set up a tent for Rayner, a few of them went off to hunt the wooded areas and came back hours later, dragging a boar behind them.

That night they feasted on the massive boar, and Ser Caster made a toast in honor of Rayner and his future happiness with Correlyn. Rayner blushed as the men cheered and hooted from around the camp but lifted his horn to the sky anyway, accepting their good fortune. Rayner slept soundly that night, dreaming of Correlyn's beautifully dark hair and sharp gray eyes that haunted him in the most wonderful way. Instead of being greeted by the sun that morning, Rayner was jerked awake to the sound of a horn. The call ran through him down to his bones. It only meant one thing. *Raiders.*

# CHAPTER TWENTY-THREE

# SLIPPING

Miko lifted Ivy's light cotton shirt to examine her ribs. They were severely bruised by the raider who'd taken her a week ago, and a yellow and green ring surrounded Ivy's left eye and crept down to her cheekbone. She winced at the pain as Miko wrapped a cloth around her ribs, restricting Ivy's movement. Miko was a healer and had told Ivy that no bones were broken but that she'd still have pain for a while.

"You look like you've been kicked by a horse," Miko mentioned as she tied off the cloth.

"It feels like it," Ivy said through clenched teeth.

Finn had stayed in bed for a few days following the attack. His wounds were worse than Ivy's, and she felt a stab of guilt every time she saw him. His face was badly bruised and cut. Miko said he had a slight concussion but that he should heal just fine. Ivy had been in the doorway of Finn's room when Miko was caring for his injured ribs. Ivy's eyes ran down his bare chest, over the corded muscles of his arms and broad shoulders that hunched when Miko touched at his ribs.

Miko's fingers roamed over his abdomen, and Ivy felt her cheeks grow hot, but Finn didn't seem to notice Miko at all as soon as Ivy walked through the door. Miko turned and gave Ivy an icy look as she packed up her supplies, brushing past Ivy out the door. Finn pulled his shirt back on, wincing at the pain.

"Hey," he said, his cheeks turning pink.

She hadn't slept well in the past week, usually waking to nightmares, and turning to see her bed empty. Finn had stayed with her the night of the attack but had since retreated to his room. Ivy didn't want to ask him to stay. That was selfish, and she knew he needed to heal. He hadn't tried to kiss her again since that night either, and every day that passed, Ivy could feel Finn slipping away.

They spent their days seated up on her balcony, talking about little things, and watching some other men use the sparring pit. Prince Kal took advantage of their absence and fought there nearly every day, smiling up at Ivy every time he took a break. She could see that it bothered Finn, but he remained silent. They didn't speak of that night in the sandpit or what might have happened, but she still felt Finn's eyes on her every time she looked away.

Now, she approached Finn as he stood up. "Hey. Are you feeling well enough for a walk? Ronin is leaving today with King Mashu's Shadows, and we should go see him off."

"Sure." He grabbed his sword belt and strapped it on, Ivy watching his fingers work the buckle. Heat crawled up her neck, and she turned to lead the way when she felt Finn's hand wrap around hers.

"Are you feeling well?" he asked in return.

"I'm fine," Ivy replied.

"You always say that." Finn let go of her hand, and brought

his up to caress her cheek, looking at the healing bruise around her eye. She could see the pain in his features as his thumb brushed over the bruise. "I'm sorry for this," he said quietly.

"You saved my life, Finn, so stop saying that you're sorry. I could never repay you for what you did."

He took a deep breath and withdrew his hand before following her out the door.

The sun was high in the sky, and pink flower petals drifted through the air, covering the cobblestone road. Ivy could smell the flowers and the ocean in the breeze and let herself smile as she took it in. Finn plucked a flower from a low hanging branch and tucked it behind her ear, his fingers lingering and sending heat up Ivy's neck.

"Beautiful," he whispered. His russet eyes drifted down to her lips, and Ivy's pulse spiked. The way Finn looked at her was like nothing else around them even existed. She could feel herself being pulled to him, gravitating closer, but Ivy turned away, and they continued to stroll down the road toward the docks.

"When do you think he'll return?" Ivy kept her eyes on the boats that sat bobbing in the water below.

"I don't know. It could only take a few days or a few weeks."

"Ronin told us not to wait for his return to continue with our training."

"I don't think either of us is in any shape to train," Finn argued. Ivy felt disappointed at the thought of delaying their nightly practice any longer. It had been a week now, and she couldn't take sitting on her balcony one more night, looking down at the empty circle.

"We could start slow," Ivy persisted. "We've already missed a week."

"Fine," Finn said with a smile. "But only straw men, I won't fight you. Not yet."

Ivy agreed, and her heart beat a little faster as she thought about tonight.

Ronin was helping the Shadows load weapons and supplies onto the ferry when Ivy and Finn approached, but stopped when he saw them. Ronin had come to visit them a few days ago as they lay abed, nursing their wounds. He praised Ivy on her fighting skills and courage during the attack as he heard the story from Ser Osmund. Finn didn't take the praise as well. Ivy had been listening through the wall when Ronin went to his room. Finn felt insulted by Ronin's words and yelled at him to get out, telling him no one seemed as concerned for Ivy's life as he was. When she heard Finn say that, she wondered if it were true.

Ser Osmund had made a promise to her father, though he admitted that he failed. Then she remembered the traders that almost killed her and how Ser Osmund had fought for her life. She knew the Ser Osmund would do anything to keep her safe, but he also seemed to trust Finn more and so relaxed about keeping an eye on her all the time.

"Are you feeling better?" Ronin addressed them both. Finn stayed silent, and Ivy assured her trainer that she'd be ready when he returned. "And you, Finn?"

"Just as Ivy said. We'll be ready," Finn replied coldly.

Ronin nodded his head and put a hand on Ivy's shoulder. "Your father will be proud of you. I doubted your commitment when you arrived, but you've shown me the warrior inside of you. Your father should reconsider his rules about female knights."

Ivy's heart fluttered at that. Her father had promised to re-consider upon her return, and if Ronin thought Ivy good enough to be a knight, perhaps that would be enough to persuade her father.

"Thank you, Ronin." Ivy slightly bowed to him.

Ronin turned to Finn and told him to keep Ivy close, to which Finn replied, "Always."

The ferry pulled away from the docks just as Ser Osmund was walking up, out of breath.

"Did you run here?" Ivy asked. The knight nodded his head, trying to regain some air to his lungs. "Why didn't you ride Eclipse?"

"That horse grows more stubborn by the day," Ser Osmund complained as he held up a bloody hand where Eclipse had bitten him. Ivy giggled at him. Ser Osmund and Eclipse had been feuding for years, and he'd surely drive the knight mad by the time they reached home.

"Maybe you should retire Eclipse when we get back to Godstone," Ivy offered, still smiling at him, but when she turned to Finn, he wasn't smiling. Every time Ivy mentioned going home, he grew quiet.

"Yes, well, let's hope that stubborn horse doesn't kill me on the road home," Ser Osmund joked.

The three of them walked back up the hill together. Ser Osmund retreating when he caught the scent of fried fish leaking out from the kitchen. The walk had made Ivy lightheaded, and she remembered that she hadn't had anything to eat or drink today.

"So, what now?" Finn asked.

Ivy shrugged her shoulders and stumbled on the steps of the barracks. Finn caught her by the elbow and helped her up. "Are you alright?" he asked.

"I'm—"

"Fine. Yes, I know," Finn teased her. "When was the last time you had something to eat?"

"Yesterday, I think. I just got lightheaded."

"I know the feeling. Why do you think I stayed in bed for so many days?"

Finn walked Ivy to her room then left, saying he'd be back with some food. She poured a small cup of wine to ease her head and went to sit on the balcony. The familiar clack of wooden swords crawled up the terraces to where Ivy sat. She peered over the edge to see Prince Kal sparring with a Shadow that Ivy frequently saw lingering around the prince. She figured Kal had asked his guard to train with him since Ronin seemed to have little time for the prince these days. Ivy watched the two sparring and had to admit to herself that Kal was a skilled fighter. He wasn't nearly as strong as Finn, but he was quick.

Ivy heard someone scoff behind her and turned around to see Finn holding a tray of food, his eyes on the prince below. She gestured for him to join her on the balcony, but he put the tray down inside and asked if she needed anything else, his tone cold. "Only your company," she said with a timid smile.

"You should rest before practice," Finn replied. Ivy stood to block his view of the men below, and only then did he meet her eyes, helpless to return her smile. Ivy thanked him for the food, went inside, and closed the door behind her, shutting out the prince and his Shadow.

Ivy looked at the array of food Finn had brought her. "Would you like some?"

Finn shook his head and started for the door. "Eat and get some rest. I'll see you tonight." When he was gone, Ivy devoured most of the food and some water. Her head already felt better, but she decided to lie down anyway.

She fell asleep almost immediately and dreamed of her attacker again. This time Finn wasn't there to save her, and the raider slit her throat and dumped Ivy into the sea. The black water surrounded her as she watched her life escape from her in the form of tiny bubbles. When she tried to swim up, she felt something wrap around her ankle and pull her down deeper. A distant voice crept toward her through the water, yet it sounded as though the person was right next to her. Then a woman came into view, and Ivy smiled, feeling a warmth wrap around her, and she began to swim off with the woman, but then another voice called to her. It was Finn.

"Ivy!" he screamed, over and over. Ivy tried to swim to him, but the woman flashed her fanglike teeth, and Ivy screamed, her mouth filling with water. Ivy watched the inky water rising above her as she was dragged down. Above the surface, the stars began to flick out, one by one.

Ivy woke up to Miko shaking her ankle. She offered Ivy a cold cloth for her head, and Ivy noticed she had sweated through her clothes.

"Nightmare again?" Miko asked in a small voice.

"Why are you here?" Ivy took the cloth and held it to her brow.

"Finn asked me to wake you at sunset. So you don't miss

practice." She thanked Miko as she gathered Ivy's bedclothes to be washed. Ivy changed her clothes, slipping on a blue cotton shirt and some dark pants, then strapped on Promise and ran her finger over the handle of the knife Rayner had given her. The sun was already gone, pushed away by the moon when Ivy arrived at the sandpit, but Finn wasn't there.

## CHAPTER TWENTY-FOUR

# EVERYTHING

Finn was nowhere in sight, but Ivy figured he must be on his way. She kicked off her boots before entering the pit and went to the shed to drag out two straw men for her and Finn. The weight of them pulled at her ribs, and she took a minute to regain her breath before taking off her sword belt and picking up her wooden blade. Finn still hadn't shown up, so Ivy took the time to stretch, but when she bent over her ribs screamed for her to stop. She pushed until she couldn't take anymore and stood upright to see Kal entering the pit.

Ivy cursed in her head and shot a worried glance at Finn's balcony to see if he was there. Kal was dressed in his usual colorful clothing, his black hair freshly washed and slicked back.

"What are you doing here by yourself?" he inquired as he closed the space between them.

"I'm waiting for Finn. We're supposed to practice," Ivy said, gripping her wooden sword. Kal looked around as if to state the obvious, that Finn wasn't here. "I came early," Ivy told him before he could say anything.

"Aren't you still injured?" he said, looking at her healing eye, but Ivy didn't answer. "It's a beautiful night," Kal opened his arms and looked at the moon. "Come riding with me instead."

Ivy tried to hide her grimace. "That's kind of you to offer, but I need to practice." She narrowed her gaze on Kal as he took a step closer.

He reached for her face, but she moved away. "My lady, why do you punish yourself? You've already been beaten. Why would you continue to fight?"

Anger rose in her chest as she looked down at Kal.

"What's that supposed to mean?" Her voice was hostile.

"You're so beautiful," he said ignoring her question. "Come, ride with me, and I'll show you why I'm a better choice than he is."

Ivy opened her mouth, about to curse him to hell when Kal grabbed the back of her head and pulled her in. He pressed his lips to hers while his other hand snaked around Ivy's waist, drawing her closer.

Ivy shoved her hands into his chest, forcing the prince to stagger back. "What the fuck is wrong with you?" she yelled, wiping her mouth, but her heart stopped dead when she spotted Finn, standing outside the circle, watching them. Her heart sank into her feet, and her anger turned to worry.

Kal turned and smiled at Finn, waving as he greeted his friend. "Ah, Finn! I'm afraid Ivy will miss practice," Kal said as Finn stormed through the sandpit, fire in his eyes. "I've asked her to go riding—"

His words were cut off as Finn's fist crashed into the prince's jaw, blood flying from his mouth. Ivy tried to catch him as he fell, but he slipped through her hands. She looked at Finn, who was vibrating with rage, but he said nothing and brushed by her, disappearing into the night.

Ivy turned her anger back on the prince who lay in the sand, feeling at his broken lip.

"Why did you do that?" Ivy demanded.

Kal stood up and scowled at her. "I should've kissed you sooner, and I don't regret it."

Ivy balled up her fists, wanting to punch him herself, but instead took a step away. She put on her boots and gathered up her sword before heading to the road.

"Go and run to your northern orphan then! I'll be waiting when he rejects you!"

Ivy felt tears burning her eyes as she searched the cobblestone road but blinked them away. The moon made shadows among the trees that danced and grabbed at her feet as she ran up the road. She went around the castle to the cliffs on the south side, where Finn had found her months before, but he wasn't there. The waves crashed down below the cliffs as Ivy searched the coastline.

When she decided he wasn't near, she climbed the slope back to the castle and made her way to the docks. Her mind was racing. Ivy didn't know what to say or how to explain that *Kal* had kissed *her*. The past week she had feared him slipping away, and now Kal may have pushed Finn from her grasp for good. Her cheeks grew hot with anger again as she thought about Kal's lips pressing into hers.

The docks were empty save for the few fishermen that lived along the shoreline. A few boats sat lightly bobbing in the waves, and Ivy searched them for Finn. As she searched the island, and her legs were beginning to tire from climbing the many steep hills. After a while, Ivy sat down under a flowering tree and brought her knees up to her chest. She sat there for a long time, listening as the wind rustled the leaves above her. A flower came loose and drifted down to her lap. She picked it up and smiled, thinking of Finn and his fingers brushing her skin as he tucked the flower behind her ear. Tucking it in her braid, Ivy got back to her feet.

She was almost back at the sand circle when she realized that there was one spot she hadn't checked. Turning on her heels, Ivy sprinted back down the road before cutting through the trees, heading west. The moon lit up her path, leading her forward through the trees and to the western dock. She came crashing through the brush and ran to the cliffside that looked down to the small beach. Her heart was beating rapidly from running, but it seemed to stop when she spotted a figure sitting on the beach. She climbed down the slope and took off her boots before stepping into the sand, a habit that would be hard to break, thanks to Ronin. The sand was cold beneath her feet as she approached Finn.

He sat facing the ocean, and buried a hand in the sand, lifted a pile of it before letting the sand fall between his fingers.

"Finn," she called to him. He didn't turn to look at her but got to his feet and started to walk away. Ivy blocked his path, placing a hand on his chest, where she could feel his heartbeat quicken. He went back to his spot and hugged his knees into his chest, focusing his stare on the ocean. Ivy approached nervously and sat beside him, leaving a few inches of space. His brows were furrowed, and she could tell that he was still angry.

"I've been looking for you all night," she told him. Finn stayed silent and didn't move. Ivy desperately explained what happened, that she was waiting for him when Kal showed up and had denied his request to go riding. "*He* kissed *me*."

Finn flinched like she'd hit him but finally turned to look at her. "I know," was all he said. Ivy didn't understand.

"You know?" Finn lowered his eyes to the sand covering his feet.

"I watched the whole thing," he admitted. "I came around the corner and saw you standing with Kal. I was about to call to you but decided not to."

"Why?" Ivy asked.

"I...I needed to know if you had any feelings for Kal."

Ivy shook her head, trying to understand. "If you saw everything, then why the hell did you punch him and run away from me?"

Finn picked up some more sand and handed it to Ivy, letting it fall through her fingers.

"This is the place where I almost lost you," he said quietly, eyes filled with sorrow. "I just couldn't handle it if I lost you again. I shouldn't have hit him," Finn admitted, running a hand through his wavy hair. "But when I saw him kiss you..." He stopped, shaking his head and turning back to the ocean.

"Finn," Ivy said quietly. "You aren't going to lose me."

Finn turned to face her again. "How can you say that when you and I both know that you're leaving?" Now Ivy turned away, her eyes on the lapping waves. She didn't want to be reminded of home.

Not now.

"I don't know what to say, Finn," she whispered.

"I know that you're leaving soon, but I can't let you go without telling you how much I care about you." Ivy turned to look at him, mouth open, but he continued before she could speak.

"Ivy... I can't stop thinking about you, and I don't even pretend to try." Finn angled toward her, taking Ivy's hand. Her breath hitched. "Not since I first saw you and your knight riding up that road. It caught me completely by surprise, and I'd catch myself looking for you when we weren't together or wondering what you were thinking, whether you were thinking about me. You're the first thing I think about when I wake up and the only reason I get out of bed. I'm always excited to see you; that smile you get when you beat me in training is... breathtaking."

Finn smiled, lifting his hand to brush away a lock of hair that drifted across her cheek. Ivy couldn't speak. She was barely breathing as his skin shot jolts of electricity through her.

"And every time I look at you, *every single time*, I think, 'My gods, she's the most beautiful girl I've ever seen.' I'm sorry it took me so long to tell you, but I'll be here for you, always," Finn continued. "I've protected you with my life, and I'll continue to do so, no matter what you choose or where you go, that will never change. Just... don't tell me that it's one-sided. That you don't feel anything for me. That you don't want to be with me."

They stared at one another for a long time, and when Ivy said nothing, Finn's cheeks turned rosy. He let go of her hand and stood, but Ivy quickly shot to her feet.

"Wait." She smiled shyly, stepping closer. Ivy didn't know what to say; so many thoughts raced through her mind, but she tried to focus on what she needed to tell him. "Finn... I—"

Before Ivy could finish, Finn grabbed her cheeks, pulled her in, and kissed her.

Their lips crashed together, Ivy's eyes still open in shock. Finn ran his fingers through her hair, pulling her closer, and Ivy smiled, throwing her arms around his neck. She parted her lips against his, deepening the kiss as he held her, as if he was the only stable thing to keep her from soaring away into the receding moon. Finn tilted her head back, and Ivy welcomed the second kiss, then a third. Ivy savored the moment: every brush of her lips to his, the way his tongue brushed against her teeth. It was everything; *Finn* was everything. Ivy grabbed a handful of his shirt, pulling his body flush against hers. Finn spoke between their joined lips, his voice a husky whisper. "I've wanted to kiss you for months."

Ivy leaned back, and Finn opened his eyes. "Why didn't you?"

Finn ran his thumb over her bottom lip, sending fire to Ivy's core. "You know why. This—" he gestured between them. "I mean… you're leaving—"

"Stop," Ivy begged, resting her forehead against his. "I can't think about that right now, just…I just want to live here. In this moment, with you."

Finn smiled sweetly and nodded. "Me too." Ivy brought a hand up to his cheek, and leaned back in, stealing another long kiss. The moon was nearly gone, and the world around them turned gray and blue in the first light of morning.

They walked hand in hand back up the cobblestone road. Finn couldn't take his eyes off Ivy. Now that he'd kissed the woman he'd desired for months, Finn didn't want to let her out of his sight for one second.

"Will you come to my balcony to watch the sunrise?" she asked him.

"Of course," he said and wrapped an arm around her shoulder, kissing her temple as they continued walking.

Just then, Prince Kal stepped out into the road, blocking their path. His lip was cut, and part of his face bruised. Finn could tell he was fuming with anger. Kal stepped toward them, and Finn instinctively put a hand to Ivy's side, pushing her back.

"You." Kal pointed a finger in Finn's face. "You've dishonored me, and I challenge you to a fight."

Ivy stepped forward. "Don't do this, Kal." But he didn't even look at Ivy. All he saw was Finn standing in front of him.

"Kal, I'm sorry for hitting you," Finn said, trying to calm down the angry prince.

"Sorry isn't good enough. You will fight me."

"I won't," Finn's voice lowered to a growl. Kal scrunched his nose up and drew his sword from the scabbard down his back.

"Kal, stop!" Ivy yelled at him, but still, he wouldn't look at her. Finn had no choice. If Kal meant to hurt him, then Finn had to defend himself. He put his hand to the hilt of his sword and warned Kal one last time to stop and walk away. When Kal made no move to back down, Finn took a breath and drew his sword.

"Kal," Ivy pleaded. "Don't do this!"

Kal started to move toward Finn, anger covering his face like a mask. Ivy stepped between them and shoved her hands to Kal's chest, trying to force him back. Rage taking over, Kal threw up his hand and cracked Ivy across the cheek, knocking her to the ground. An explosion of rage erupted inside Finn, and he charged. The two came together, swords crashing in the silent morning.

Finn was angry, but still, he didn't counterstrike, only blocked the blows that came from Kal's sword. Kal swung, and almost sliced Finn across the chest. This wasn't a practice session, and Kal looked like he meant to hurt Finn. Their blades slid over one another, and Finn grabbed hold of Kal's arm and wrenched it behind his back. He kicked the prince in the back and dropped him to his knees.

Before Kal could swing his sword around, Finn was on him, pulling him to the ground and smashing his hand against the road until it opened, releasing the sword. Each struggled to pin the other down, both grunting with anger. Kal got a hand free and sent it into Finn's bruised ribs. He cried out in pain and rolled off Kal. The prince scrambled for his sword, but Ivy ran to it before he could reach it. She picked it up and held it to his throat, commanding him to stand. Shock painted his features as the prince did what she asked, keeping an eye on Finn, who was still keeled over from the pain.

Ivy had a wild look in her eyes as she held the sword to Kal's skin. Finn stood up, clutching his ribs, and eased closer to them.

"Ivy," he said gently. She ignored Finn and pressed the point of Kal's sword to his throat until a small trickle of blood ran down his neck and into his shirt. "If you ever touch me again," Ivy's voice was calm and cold, "I will fucking kill you. Do you understand me?"

Kal shot a panicked look to Finn, but he wouldn't find any help from him. "Do you understand me?" Ivy pressed the sword in a little harder. Kal nodded his head, and when Ivy dropped the sword, Kal fell to his knees, touching the spot where she'd cut him.

Ivy went to Finn, throwing his arm around her neck to help support him. They walked back to their building just as the sun was starting to peak over the horizon, kissing the treetops. Ivy helped Finn onto his bed and told him to take off his shirt. He blushed before obliging, and Ivy helped him slip it over his head. The wrap that Miko had put on the morning before was coming apart. Ivy carefully unwound it, watching Finn's face to make sure she wasn't hurting him. She ran her eyes over his chiseled chest, and Finn caught her looking, flashing her a knowing smile.

Ivy's brow creased as she focused on his side and gently pushed on his ribs, feeling for any that were broken. Finn winced as Ivy moved her hands over his side but remained silent.

"I'm sorry, Finn." He looked up at her and placed a steady hand on her cheek where Kal had struck her.

"Don't be sorry. It's my fault." Ivy wrapped a new cloth around his ribs and helped him put on a new shirt.

They moved out to his balcony and sat down together in a deep-set chair, Ivy sitting between Finn's legs. She leaned back into him, feeling the steady rhythm of his heart beating. He kissed the top of her head and wrapped her in his arms as the sun came up to greet them. They sat together, not saying a word, only existing in each other's presence. Finn forgot about the pain. How could he think of anything else when everything was bundled up in his arms?

He knew Kal wouldn't forget their altercation, but that didn't matter right now. All that mattered was Ivy, this girl that he'd fallen so hard for--the girl who'd come riding into his world and flipped it upside down. But Finn wouldn't trade a second of the time he'd spent with Ivy, not for anything because all he ever wanted was her.

## CHAPTER TWENTY-FIVE

# THE LONE KNIGHT

Ronin was calm as ever as the ferry pulled into the dock of Xanheim. It was the first time he'd been back on the mainland in what seemed like a lifetime. The Shadows strapped on their weapons and prepared themselves as they anchored the ferry. Ronin wasn't a Shadow, and he didn't work for them. He was under direct orders from King Mashu to find the leader of the raiders and kill him. While the Shadows formed up in ranks, receiving orders from their leader, Akio, Ronin stood off to the side, his hands folded behind his back.

Xanheim was a maze of tan-colored buildings, and Ronin knew the raiders could be anywhere, though they didn't need to hide--not in this city. Xanheim was primarily controlled by King Caato, who resided only forty leagues west in Lamira. When Akio finished giving his commands, the Shadows quickly dispersed into the city, climbing the rooftops, and leaping across alleys from above. Ronin set off as well, in a different direction.

He remembered the first time he came to Xanheim. He'd been only ten years of age, and the city was peaceful back then.

It was a rare time, and King Caato's father moved his raiders around the land, thinking of his next move before making it, like a game of Taffl. King Malin Morrell wasn't as ruthless as his son, who now held the crown. Ronin remembered many years of peace during King Malin's reign, but when his son took over, it seemed like the land became coated with the blood of the innocent. Raiders were present in every city across the South, demanding loyalty to King Caato. Ronin had never paid much attention to the war before. That was until it came to his home.

Ronin had come to Xanheim as a child with his father to trade swords for rare fruit, silk, and other goods that weren't found on the Isle of Fire. His father had been a smith, and Ronin took an interest in swords from a very young age. Though his father was no warrior, he'd taught Ronin what little he did know. But it wasn't enough. When raiders came to their home looking for warriors to join their army, Ronin's father had been quick to ask them to leave. The people of the island were peaceful and had no desire to participate in a war that they didn't understand. The raiders wouldn't accept this and soon rounded up all the men they could and forced them off the island, Ronin's father included.

Ronin never understood why his father didn't fight back, nor why he had seemed to submit so quickly to something he didn't believe in. A few years after his father was taken, his mother pulled him into the house and gave him the news of his father's death. A local had come back to the island to provide the news in person. Ronin's father had been well respected among the people, and they all mourned his death.

All except Ronin.

He felt ashamed that his father had died fighting someone

else's battle. And angry that his father abandoned them. He felt sorry for his mother, who'd lost a husband to something so pointless. It was then that Ronin decided to leave. His mother hadn't fought him, saying that there was nothing left for him and that he should try to have a life away from this island.

He moved to the city of Rahama in search of a trainer to teach him the way of sword, fighting where his father had failed. He quickly found a worthy trainer in the massive city and was soon gaining the attention of other trainers. Ronin progressed quickly, developing his own style of fighting, different from any knight he'd seen, and at the young age of thirteen, Ronin was knighted. His trainer spread the word of this young knight's skill across the land, and soon many men were coming to swear their sword to him. But Ronin refused them. He preferred to be alone. That was until he met Yacira.

She was from the city of Maridiyan, but had moved to Rahama when her mother fell ill and died of a fever. He recalled spotting her in a crowd and being immediately entranced by her beauty. She'd stolen his heart as quickly as the raiders had taken his father from him as a boy. Yacira was two years older than Ronin; she had his same black hair, and her skin was as pale as milk with eyes the color of copper. Soon after meeting, they wed and began a life together in Rahama. It was the happiest Ronin had ever been. He'd found the life his mother wished for him— until it was all taken away, and his world came crumbling down around him.

Ronin now walked through the streets of Xanheim, looking down every alley, around every corner, and in every open door. He didn't know who led this band of raiders, so he needed to find one to question. The streets were full of people going about their daily tasks. The sun was high in the sky, beating down on Ronin's head as he searched for a man he didn't know. Ronin was glad to be alone. He liked to escape into his mind, thinking of things that he couldn't say aloud. He'd never told anyone about his life in Rahama with Yacira, only that he went there to train and left as a knight.

He turned a corner that opened to a square where vendors had set up booths to sell their goods. He strolled past the tables filled with fish, brightly colored silks, newly forged knives, and leather armor. Ronin stopped in front of a man selling jewelry.

He picked up a copper bracelet and turned it in his hand, running his finger over the smooth surface.

"For your wife?" the jewelry man asked.

Ronin put it back and said nothing. He was walking away when something caught his eye. Ronin spotted the man across the square, and he carefully moved around the booths, trying to keep him in his line of sight. Ronin felt for the smaller sword tucked in his belt and slowly drew it. He made his way toward the man, pushing past people and tightening his grip on the hilt.

The man didn't seem to notice Ronin, but started to leave the square and head up a cobblestone street. Ronin didn't believe what he was seeing. Were his eyes playing a trick on him, or was it truly him?

He moved more quickly to keep the man in his sight when an older woman ran into him, dropping a stack of metal bowls. They crashed on the stone ground, and Ronin watched the man turn toward the commotion as the old woman stood there yelling at Ronin. The man locked eyes with Ronin, and Ronin felt his heart stop in his chest. The man recognized Ronin too and quickly spun around and darted off through the streets.

Ronin pushed past the woman and took off running through the square, just as he spotted the man turning the corner of a building. Ronin's heart was pounding as he chased the man through the streets, clutching the small sword in his palm. He didn't know what he'd do if he caught him, only that he needed to try. Ronin turned the corner and scanned the streets before taking off again. He shoved people aside to get through, glancing down alleys that he flew past. A voice in his head told him to stop. That he was ridiculous and was only imagining things. He pushed Yacira's voice from his head and ran faster through the winding streets.

Ronin came to a fork in the road and stopped, frantically searching his surroundings. He put his sword back and brought his hands up to his face, rubbing at his eyes. Sitting down in the middle of the empty street, Ronin cradled his head as it swam with too many thoughts. A cry rang out from above, and Ronin raised his head to the sky, lifting one hand to block out the sun. A horned eagle circled overhead, its massive wings casting a long shadow on Ronin. He snapped his eyes shut, trying to block the memories pounding their way back in. It'd been many years since he'd seen a horned eagle. They were rare and only resided in the South, where fishing was good all year round. Their horns grew down the back of their heads and their wingspan was twelve feet or longer. He shook the memory from his head and searched the sky again, but it was empty.

After a long time had passed, Ronin got to his feet and made his way back through the streets of Xanheim. The square had cleared out as the sun was beginning to dip, and vendors were packing up their goods for the evening. He'd heard the fighting of Shadows and raiders deeper in the city as he sat in the road, waiting for the man to come back. When he finally realized he wasn't going to return, Ronin picked himself up and started back. He didn't need to wait for the king's Shadows to return to Kame Island. Ronin was on his own mission, but he'd failed, and now he must explain his defeat to King Mashu.

He walked through the square, his head swimming with old memories being dragged from the darkest parts of his mind. Ronin almost ran into the raider that stood before him and quickly stepped back.

"You're Ronin?" the raider asked him. He wore leather armor and carried an ax on one hip and a sword on the other. Ronin searched the man's face, waiting for him to make a move. The raider pulled his ax free of the leather loop and held it tight to his side. "Our leader sends his regards," the man said with a smile before lunging toward Ronin.

CHAPTER TWENTY-SIX

# THE COPPER BRACELET

Ronin quickly sidestepped the raider as the ax came down just in front of his face. The raider swung it back as Ronin ducked, reaching for the sword on his back. He held off and let Ronin grab his sword before pulling his own. Ronin jerked his chin toward the raider, letting him know he was ready. If he knew who Ronin was, then he knew of his fighting skills and evidently wished to witness them up close.

The raider brought his ax down to meet Ronin's blade, grabbing a sword from his hip with the other hand. Armed with two weapons, the raider grinned at Ronin, believing he had an advantage. He was wrong. Ronin backed up, put his blade behind his back, and waited for the man to attack. A few more raiders came trickling in from the streets. None of them made a move to help. Instead, they stood aside, watching the fight to see which man would come away with his life.

The raider pushed forward, swinging his ax up beside Ronin's head. He seamlessly turned away from the ax's sharp blade and brought his sword around his back to slice off the head of the ax, sending it flying through the square. The raider grunted and threw the handle down. He came at Ronin, who blocked every blow and easily slid around him, like a snake moving through the grass. This was how Ronin always fought, letting his attacker tire themselves out and only striking when necessary. *Never lead, never pursue. Be still and let them come to you,* his trainer's voice came bubbling to the surface of his mind. The raider swung and stabbed at Ronin from every angle, turning wildly to keep up with him.

The raider soon grew tired as sweat beaded at his temples, and his breath came out in sharp gasps. He desperately looked out to the faces of his fellow raiders for assistance. A few of them stepped forward and unsheathed their swords before coming at Ronin from behind. They brought their swords down one after the other, Ronin leaning left and right to dodge them. He turned and ducked as a sword sailed over his head and jabbed his own blade forward, finding the softness of a raider's stomach. The man screamed and fell to the ground, clutching at the gaping hole that stained his shirt black with blood. The hot, copper scent of the blood stung Ronin's nose as it pooled before his feet.

The other raiders seemed to grow panicked as they watched their friend die. But still, they came to try and take down the lone knight.

He cut through them with little effort until all that stood was him and the first man who attacked him. The raider's shoulder was bleeding where Ronin had struck him, but he still held his sword out, ready to die fighting.

"Who's your leader?" Ronin stood before the man and waited patiently for his answer.

The raider laughed and lifted his sword. "You know who," he said with a smile as he brought it down. Ronin cut his hand from the sword and quickly stuck his blade through the man's neck and out the back. The raider dropped to his knees, coughing up blood and trying to scream at the pain. Ronin watched him drown in his own blood before wiping his sword on the man's shirt and putting it back in his scabbard.

The sun was dropping below the sea when Ronin got back to the docks. He left the square with his clothes blood-soaked and with his mind mulling the answer to his question that he already knew. He thought about what he would tell King Mahsu when he returned without having killed the leader. He hoped the Shadows had been successful in their mission to ease the disappointment from his failure. He decided to wait for them to return rather than going back to Kame Island alone.

As night crept over the city, the Shadows emerged from the streets, dropping down from the roofs without making a sound. Akio walked up to Ronin and told him that his Shadows were able to kill or chase many of the raiders from city limits, though he wasn't confident that they would stay away for very long. He looked over Ronin and noticed the blood on the front of his shirt.

"How many did you kill?" Ronin shrugged his shoulders. He never kept count but guessed that it was around twelve. They kept coming, almost as if they wished to fall upon his sword. As if being slain by him would somehow earn them credit in the afterlife.

The ferry made its way back to Kame Island in the night, Shadows pulling it along with oars as the night was absent of wind. Ronin sat by himself at the back, watching Xanheim disappear behind them. He wondered if he would ever touch the mainland again or if he would die alone on Kame Island. It wasn't the life he imagined when he was young and still had Yacira.

He remembered building their home in Rahama up on a hill that overlooked the city and the sparkling sea. She'd wanted a quiet life as well, and so Ronin built their house away from the chaos and noise of the city below them. When Yacira told him that he would be a father, he thought his heart might explode with joy. He promised that he'd be a better father to his child than his own had been to him. And he swore never to abandon his family and even considered laying down his sword and renouncing his knighthood to become a farmer.

Yacira was the only thing in the world that mattered to him, and he would do whatever it took to make her happy.

His wife was close to giving birth when Ronin went to the city, searching for the perfect gift for her and their new child. He strolled the streets, whistling a song to himself when something caught the sunlight in his gaze. He walked over to a small table where an older woman was selling jewelry and glass goblets. He found the piece that caught his eye and smiled as he picked up the copper bracelet to inspect it. He smiled at the piece, thinking of Yacira's eyes, and purchased it before setting out again to find a gift for his child. Not knowing whether it was a boy or girl yet, Ronin settled on an embroidered blanket to swaddle his baby. He spent hours walking through the streets and picking out his wife's favorite food and a flagon of wine imported from Kame Island. As he walked the path that led him away from the city, he heard his wife screaming.

Ronin dropped the baskets of food and ran to their little

house tucked away behind the trees. He burst through the door to find his wife keeled over on the floor, bleeding.

The baby was coming.

He picked her up and set her gently down on the bed then ran outside to fetch a bucket of water. She screamed in pain, and Ronin panicked, wiping her brow, and trying to hum a song to soothe her.

"Ronin…" she pleaded, but he didn't know what to do. He was a young man still and had never been around a woman giving birth.

"Should I run for help?" he'd asked, worry pouring out with his words. But Yacira only gripped him tighter and told him not to leave her.

He stayed, and for hours his wife labored in agony as the baby tried to make its way down, and Yacira grew paler and weaker every minute. Ronin reached into his pocket and pulled the copper bracelet out and put it around her delicate wrist. She smiled and touched his cheek, a fat tear rolling down her face. He felt her head and quickly pulled away—she was burning from the inside, fever coursing through her body. Ronin felt his heart sink as tears began to fill his eyes.

During the early hours of the morning, Yacira gave one final push as Ronin pulled the baby from her. It was a boy, crying madly in Ronin's arms as he cut the cord that had filled his child with life for nine months.

"It's a boy," he proudly proclaimed. But when he looked back to his wife, she was still. "Yacira?" he said over the crying baby. She didn't move; her eyes were fixed on the ceiling above. The last bit of life had been pulled from her with their son.

Ronin put the baby down and shook his wife, screaming her

name over and over again. Hot tears poured from his eyes and blurred his vision. He looked at his wife, lying in their bed that they once happily shared. Now it was a death bed, consuming Yacira and eating at Ronin's soul the longer he looked. He didn't remember screaming, but sometime later, he came out of the fog that lingered in his head, his throat sore, and his eyes burning.

His son lay crying on the ground, still naked and covered in Yacira's blood. A sudden rage filled Ronin as he looked at the thing that killed his wife--that snuffed out the only light he had. The one good thing he ever had was ripped from his grasp. It wasn't supposed to be like this, Ronin remembered thinking. The baby's cries grew louder and more urgent until Ronin couldn't take it anymore.

He stood up and grabbed his sword, and put it to the baby's throat, screaming at him to stop. But when he looked back at Yacira, he lowered his blade. He couldn't kill their son only feet from where his wife lay dead, so he gathered up the baby and carried him into the woods.

His cries echoed through the hillside, making Ronin's blood boil with anger, until his heart shattered with sorrow. He wiped a tear from his cheek and sniffed back the rest as he came to a clearing in the woods.

Ronin put his son down on the grass and turned away to leave, but a cry came from behind him—only it wasn't his son. He looked up and saw a pair of horned eagles circling the clearing. Ronin looked at his son one last time before turning his back, leaving him to the animals or the gods, whichever found him first.

He returned to his home to bury his wife, gently removing the bracelet that he'd placed on her wrist only hours before. He tucked it in his chest pocket and dug her grave behind the home he'd built for her. Ronin then said a silent prayer to the Four Gods before going to the city to buy a horse.

Five years passed, with Ronin spending his days roaming the land, never staying in one place for very long. He'd traveled to the western shore to the city of Volantar when someone came looking for him. He was a knight from Godstone who claimed to have been tracking Ronin for over a year. He brought word that King Erwin wished to hire Ronin as a private trainer for his son and heir, Magnus. Ronin refused at first, but the knight wouldn't leave until he agreed. Ronin had nothing left and so reluctantly agreed to follow the knight back to his kingdom where his first real student awaited him.

As the ferry came to a halt at the docks of Kame Island, Ronin slid back to reality and jumped off, not waiting for the Shadows to unpack. He went straight to his little house on the hillside and made himself some tea. The steam drifted up to his face, cleansing him of bad memories. He reached in the pocket that covered his heart and pulled out the copper bracelet. He'd carried it with him since the day he lost Yacira and had given up their son. Ronin ran his thumb over the smooth metal, feeling a tear escape his eye. It was the only thing he had left of his wife and of the life he'd lived before. Ronin waited patiently for the sun to come up before making his way to King Mashu's castle to deliver the news of his failure.

## CHAPTER TWENTY-SEVEN

# THE HUNTED

Outside the tent, a storm had blown in, and the world around Rayner swirled with snow, clawing at his face. Ser Caster was running toward the tent already dressed in his armor and his sword drawn. "Ser Rayner!" he called. "There're raiders just behind the tree line. They must have used the storm to conceal themselves."

Rayner felt suddenly lost. This wasn't supposed to happen. "Tell the men to leave everything," Rayner commanded. "Mount up and be ready to fight."

Ser Caster turned and ran back to the men. Rayner quickly threw on his armor, drew his sword, and checked his pocket for the ring before running out into the storm.

The camp was frenzied as the raiders were moving in. Rayner found his horse and cut it loose, swinging himself up before looking for Ser Caster. Rayner wished that he had a helm with him; it would help to keep the snow from stabbing at his eyes. He squinted against the wind and called out to his men. Many of them were mounted and ready, so Rayner led them away from the camp and out into a field. They formed up in ranks with archers at the back. Rayner took his place next to Ser Caster.

The knight looked worried, and that made Rayner feel worse. They could both feel it swirling in the air with the snow. Something was wrong. The raiders screamed through the wall of snow until they were in view.

"Archers!" Rayner's voice thundered over the howling of the wind. "Nock, draw, loose!" The arrows cut through the snow and disappeared into the storm. Rayner could just barely see the army coming through the snow ahead.

There were many of them--too many to count. He ordered the archers to fire again, but the raiders were prepared. They lifted their shields in unison to the death falling at them from above. Rayner drew his sword and said a prayer that only he could hear before looking to Ser Caster. Their screams filled the air as he led his men down the hill toward the raiders. His heart was thumping to the beat of his horse's hooves, but his head was clear. One word kept him going, kept him focused on what he had to do. *Correlyn.*

The two sides wove into one another, Rayner bloodying his sword on the first raider he passed. He could see his men fighting off the raiders and forcing them back. Rayner saw the raiders up ahead begin to split their ranks. He stopped his horse, the hooves sliding over the slick ground covered with fresh snow as the raiders parted. Rayner laid eyes on a black knight sitting atop a midnight stallion. He looked around for Ser Caster, but he was lost in the sea of men.

A sudden realization struck him the way a viper strikes a mouse. His eyes scanned the crowd, and his heart dropped to his boots—the raiders weren't fighting his men. They were only blocking their attacks, but their swords shone clean, not having tasted blood. He yelled over the storm, calling for Ser Caster, but his men were being pushed back into the storm, away from him.

Rayner sat atop his horse alone, and the black knight made no move. His helm had horns that grew down the length of his skull, and his face was completely concealed. Rayner was alone with him and had no choice but to attack. He swallowed the lump in his throat and charged. The horned knight moved just in time and kept Rayner chasing him. He slashed at the knight from behind, but his stallion was swift, and Rayner's sword only met with the falling snow.

Suddenly, a raider broke into view, holding a small barrel. Thick black liquid poured from the back of it as the raider ran his horse around Rayner and the horned knight. Rayner's eyes widened, and he kicked his horse, sending it in the direction of the raider.

But it was too late.

A flaming arrow came down, igniting the black liquid. Hungry flames shot up, licking at the hooves of Rayner's horse as it reared back. Rayner was almost thrown off the back of his panicked horse. The fire rose higher than his steed, and Rayner scanned his eyes in every direction, finally landing on the horned knight trapped in the circle with him.

"Rayner!" The cry drowned out the roar of the flames, and he turned his head to see Ser Caster outside the wall, desperately fighting off raiders who were keeping him at bay.

Rayner closed his eyes, trying to calm himself. He felt sick to his stomach as he realized how well planned this attack was. The fire crackled behind him, the wind cut through his armor, and the snow pierced his cheeks. *Not like this,* he thought. The horned knight ran out of patience and charged Rayner. He kicked his horse to meet the man, throwing up his sword as the knight's blade came down. They flew past one another, and Rayner quickly turned his horse and charged back. The horned knight was sinister looking, his long horns making him appear to be an evil spirit from a story Rayner had heard as a child. But this was no spirit, this was a real man, and he meant to kill Rayner today.

They came together, swords clashing as the snow encircled them. The knight thrust his sword forward, Rayner slashing it away just in time. He brought up his blade and sent it crashing down into the knight's armor, which took the blow. The knight swung, forcing Rayner to lay flat across his horse's back. But before Rayner could sit up, he felt a stabbing pain at his side. Rayner screamed to the sky, and his horse bucked, kicking Rayner from his back before running around the circle of fire, blood leaking from its side. As he slammed to the ground, Rayner gasped for air, and when he looked down, he could see where the knight's sword had stabbed through his armor and into his horse.

He tried to stand and stumbled as the world shifted under his feet. The knight caught Rayner's horse by the reins and didn't hesitate as he slit the beast's throat, forcing a terrified scream to come gurgling up from its mouth. Rayner pinched his eyes shut and put his sword into the ground, leaning his weight into the hilt to stand. Blood was pouring from his side, hissing as it melted the snow around him. The horned knight wiped his sword clean and came charging at Rayner. He jerked his blade from the ground and held it with both hands, the weight pulling at his arms. Rayner slashed at the man as he flew past but only just brushed his armor with the tip of his sword.

The knight turned again, and Rayner felt his heart slow. The image of the man riding toward him was blurred as the life drained out of him. His pulse thumped in his ears, and sweat poured down his temples despite the frigid conditions. As he blinked the knight into view, his head snapped back as the knight's steel covered boot swung at him, catching Rayner near his eye. He collapsed in the snow, rapidly losing blood as the knight came trotting over on his stallion.

He couldn't move, he'd lost so much blood already, and his hands violently shook as he reached for his sword. The horned knight looked down at Rayner for a long moment, as if enjoying the sight of him. Then, growing bored of Rayner's attempt to cling to life, the horned knight walked his horse forward, trampling over Rayner's bleeding body. He felt a crunch in his chest, and the air forced from his lungs as his armor crushed him under the horse's weight, squeezing out the last bit of strength that Rayner had left.

The firewall was dying down, and as quickly as they appeared, the raiders were gone. The horned knight was nowhere in sight; the raiders had disappeared into the white shield of snow. His men ran to him, seemingly unhurt as Rayner slipped in and out of consciousness. He heard his name being called, but it sounded muffled by the ringing in his head. Rayner didn't feel anything, not the broken bones in his body, the bone-deep gash to his side, or the swelling of his face.

He focused his eyes on the sky above; dark gray clouds hid the blue sky and soaring above him, an unkindness of ravens. Their calls fell upon him with the snow as he watched them, circling his body as if he were already dead. He felt himself floating above the ground, his body lifting toward the ravens as if their hunger couldn't be satisfied fast enough.

Rayner gave into their will and closed his eyes, feeling what little life remained, slipping out of every bleeding hole in his body. He gave into the God of Judgement who didn't protect him, the one who didn't hear his prayers and sent his wrath upon the young knight. Rayner didn't understand what he'd done or failed to do to anger the god, but it didn't matter anymore. The gods didn't always explain, only taking what they wanted at a whim's notice, like a hungry eagle snatching a fish from the ocean. His last thought was of Correlyn, her obsidian hair, and confident smile. The way her fingertips felt like lightning against his skin. She reached out to him, and Rayner grabbed her hand, letting a smile form in the corner of his mouth before the darkness consumed him.

Ser Caster took his hand as Rayner reached out, desperately searching for someone who wasn't there. They ran Rayner's body to the wagon used for carrying supplies and threw the door open. They quickly tossed aside tent canvases and barrels of ale to lay Rayner on the bench inside. When Ser Caster looked back at Rayner, his eyes were closed, and he wasn't moving.

"No!" he screamed as he shook the young knight, but Rayner wouldn't open his eyes. Ser Caster commanded his men to mount up and ride hard for Godstone. They had no healers among them and needed to get back and find Magister Ivann.

Ser Caster rode beside the cart as their horses pounded

through the snow, their breath visible in the cold, dead air. Ser Caster hadn't bothered to check himself or any other men, but he already knew he would find nothing. No wounds would mark their skin, no blood of their own stained their armor. The raiders were there for Rayner, hunting him like a boar in the forest. They meant to kill the heir to Godstone to win it.

King Magnus had beheaded one of their leaders as a message. Godstone wasn't for the taking, and nothing would change his mind.

But their plan had worked. Rayner lay dying or already dead in that cart, and when Magnus understood what happened today, it would send him on a path of rage and vengeance. Ser Caster knew this would kill Magnus, and a tear escaped his eye as he imagined the chaos that would follow.

He kept looking at the cart that bounced over the rough ground beside him like somehow his frequent gaze would keep the boy alive. They rode hard all day, exhausting their horses until the vision of Godstone came rising over the hill, like a palace of the gods. He kicked furiously at his horse, forcing it to run faster, and passed the cart and the men who led it. He screamed with all the air he had left. "Open the gate!" The God of Judgement stood guard at the southern gate, his eyes staring forward as if he couldn't bear to look upon his own wrath.

Magnus had been walking the walls, talking with his sentries when he spotted Rayner's party coming from the south. He smiled and called down to Correlyn, who raced up the steps to see

Rayner's arrival. The party was small, but Magnus was sure it was him. They were still a ways off, just coming over the snow-covered hill from the south. Magnus looked at Correlyn and saw the happiness shining bright in her eyes. Magnus was happy for his son and knew he'd be glad for some time spent with Correlyn.

As the men came closer, a confused look came over Magnus's face as he saw the horses were in full gallop.

"Why are they running?" Correlyn looked to the king, concerned. He didn't answer but instead moved to the towers that stood directly above the gates on either side. Correlyn followed him, keeping her eye on the riders.

"Open the gate!" The terror in that voice made Magnus's heart sink and his stomach lurch. He took off in a sprint, leaving Correlyn behind.

Magnus shoved men aside to help open the southern gate and ran out into the field as the riders approached. They didn't stop for Magnus, and the horses came raging in through the gate, pounding the earth beneath them. Magnus ran after them, his eyes madly searching the crowd. Correlyn had come down from the wall and was doing the same, calling for Rayner. Magnus couldn't breathe, he felt his heart beating in his throat, and he tried to call his son, but no words would come. Ser Caster ran to his king, panic written on his face. Magnus grabbed him by the collar of his armor.

"What happened? Where is he? Where's my son?" He shoved Ser Caster aside before the man could answer. Men ran off toward the building next to the tower, while others surrounded a wagon that they used to carry their camp supplies. No one wanted to look the king in the eye. They cleared a path to the carriage as he approached.

Magnus drew back the curtain and felt bile rising in his throat. He stepped back, not believing what his eyes were showing him. Rayner's body lay on a wooden bench, drenched in his own blood. His face was swollen beyond recognition, and one eye was the color of charcoal. His armor had been stripped from him and lay on the floor of the wagon.

Magnus picked up the bloodied armor that had been brand new when Rayner left, though now it was so dented and beaten that Magnus was terrified to ask how it got that way. He thought he could see the outline of a horse's hoof on his chest plate. Magister Ivann ran up behind Magnus and covered his mouth at the sight. Rayner's side was ripped open, and a broken rib could be seen coming out of the skin.

Shaking his head, Magnus backed away as tears poured from his eyes, and a loud ringing sounded in his ears. He heard the muffled shouting as Ivann employed men to help move Rayner's body out of the wagon; then Correlyn's scream shot through Magnus like an arrow. He spotted her running toward the wagon, but Ser Caster snatched her up around the waist, as much as she tried desperately to kick him away.

Magnus dropped to the ground; his knees stuck to the frozen earth. His eyes went down to his hands, which were covered in his son's blood. He tried to wipe them off on his pants, but the blood clung to him like a second skin. Shaking, he shoved his hands into the snow and viciously rubbed at his skin to get it off, but he knew it wouldn't come clean even if he washed and scrubbed all day. Rayner's blood would forever be on his hands.

The king broke, something inside him snapping as he snarled, pounding his fists into the frozen earth until his knuckles bled.

Ser Caster ran over and wrapped his arms around Magnus, who crumped in the knight's grip, as he wept for his son. "I... I'm so sorry, Your Grace," Ser Caster choked, sniffing back his own tears.

Magnus said nothing.

He sat there for a long while as the courtyard cleared, and the sun began to slip away.

## CHAPTER TWENTY-EIGHT

# LAST DANCE

"Attack!" Ronin's voice cut through the thin morning air. He'd returned weeks ago from Xanheim with the king's Shadows, and since then, Ivy sensed something different in him. She assumed it must be that he failed in his mission from King Mashu. But Ivy knew that Ronin would never fail at a task and wondered what truly happened in the city.

King Mashu seemed disappointed in Ronin but was otherwise content with the outcome of the mission. His Shadows were able to push out the raiders they encountered or kill them where they stood. Ronin was quiet when Ivy and Finn asked about the mission, and he insisted they get back to training as he was sure Ivy would be leaving soon.

In the past few weeks, Ronin had sped up his training and even interrupted Ivy and Finn's nightly practice with his presence. He made them fight more often, strike harder, and even wrestle with no weapons. But today was different.

Finn stood in front of Ivy, hesitant to obey Ronin's command. Their trainer put a real blade in Finn's hand and took the wooden one from Ivy's. He ordered Finn to attack Ivy, who held no weapon, and she was to dodge his blows.

"Attack!" he commanded Finn again, but still, he didn't move. Ivy thought Ronin had lost his mind when he walked up to Finn, knocked him to the ground, and took his sword before coming after Ivy. Her eyes widened as she realized he wasn't stopping.

Ronin swung the sword, and Ivy heard the whistle of the blade cutting through the air as it almost sliced her ear off.

"Ronin!" Finn called from behind, getting to his feet. Ivy shot a look to Finn that said she was alright. Ronin stepped forward again, and Ivy narrowed her gaze on her attacker. She quickly slipped around him as he jabbed the blade forward. Finn's hand gripped her waist, pulling her back to where he stood. Ronin said nothing to him, keeping his eyes on Ivy. Finn stood in his path, and Ronin quickly twisted the blade and threw it up, smacking Finn in the cheek with the broad side of the sword.

Anger rose in Ivy's chest, and she charged her trainer, ducking under the sword as it cut the air above her head. She slid in the sand and kicked her leg out, striking Ronin in the ankle. He stumbled but didn't fall. She threw her legs up and pushed her hands into the sand behind her head, flinging herself up to a crouching position. Ronin's sword came down where her hand had been only a moment ago. She thrust herself forward, grabbing his wrists. She twirled under his arms, twisting them over each other and jerked her elbow at the back of his. He barely winced, but let go of the hilt with one hand as Ivy reached for the one still holding the sword. She grabbed it and drew her other hand back before sending it flying into his wrist, and he dropped the sword. Ivy dove for it as it fell, catching it by the hilt and stood before her trainer, blade to his throat.

Ivy's chest rose and fell with her rapid breath, but Ronin gave no approving look.

"Again," was all he said, forcing Ivy and Finn to square up and fight, this time with Finn unarmed. They went at it all day, fighting one another, squaring up with Ronin and wrestling in the hot sand. Ronin didn't say much, only giving them direction and commands when needed. When the sun fell behind the buildings, Ronin decided they had enough and retreated to his little house on the hillside.

Sometime later, Ser Osmund came looking for Ivy and found her holding hands with Finn under a tree just outside the sand-pit. He watched Ivy and Finn talking in hushed tones; her smile was as bright as he'd ever seen it. It broke his heart to see Ivy so happy with the young man, whom Ser Osmund had disapproved of not long ago.

He knew it was time to leave, but he was hesitant to tell Ivy. Ser Osmund took in a quick breath and approached the couple.

"My lady," he called to her. Ivy released Finn from her gaze and looked up to meet Ser Osmund's. He struggled to get the words out, not wanting Ivy to lose her beautiful smile, but finally he said, "It's time to go home."

She said nothing, only nodding her head that she understood and let the smile slip from her face. He looked at the ground beneath his feet, feeling Ivy's stare bore into him.

Ser Osmund broke the silence. "The king wants to throw a feast for our departure. Tomorrow night will be our last on Kame Island. We'll leave the next morning and catch the first ferry out." He turned to leave but stopped just out of sight.

Ser Osmund watched Ivy turn back to Finn, whispering his name but no more words came out. Ivy looked as though she wanted to say more, her eyes searching. Finn smiled, though Ser Osmund thought it looked sad. He wrapped Ivy in his arms and cradled her to his chest, rubbing small circles on her back. The knight looked away then and left the couple alone where they sat in each other's arms under the tree.

The feast was filled with music, food, and wine. Everyone around Finn wore a smile and danced happily around the room, but all he felt was a hole in his heart. He'd kissed Ivy the night before and then retreated to his room, even after she told him he could stay. Finn fought every impulse in his body as he declined her offer and went to sleep alone. He'd been avoiding her all day, not wanting to speak about what would happen after tonight.

Finn already knew he would lose her; the only woman he'd ever cared for was being pulled from his grasp. He didn't sleep at all the night before, frequently getting up to look over the balcony, hoping to see Ivy out there waiting for him. Finn thought he could hear her sobbing through the wall sometime during the night, but still, he stayed away.

Finn now watched Ivy sitting up on the dais with Ser Osmund

and the king's family. Prince Kal kept his eyes down at his food while his Shadow lingered in the background. He'd kept his Shadow close after the fight on the road a few weeks back, and Finn noticed that Kal hadn't talked to him or Ivy since that night. He remembered the feeling he got when he realized Ivy had feelings for him. Finn thought that he'd never lose her, but perhaps he was naïve to think such a thing. Finn would lose everything tomorrow when the ferry departed.

Finn barely touched the food that sat before him, instead, filling his stomach with ale to drown out his thoughts. The feast went on late into the night; King Mashu gave a speech on what an honor it had been to have Ivy and Ser Osmund and how the island would be empty without their presence. Finn drained his cup at that, slammed it down on the table, and got up to leave.

He went to the sandpit and pulled out a straw man and began striking it with his fists. He let his anger fuel his punches and beat the straw man as if it were at fault for Ivy leaving. Tears begin to burn his eyes, and Finn let his arms slump to his sides, defeated. He let the empty hole eat him alive as the tears ran down his cheeks and wet the sand around him. Finn didn't know what he would do without Ivy in his life. He'd been alone for so many years after the death of his family. He'd never loved anyone since, that was until—

"Finn?" His heart slammed to a stop. He quickly wiped his cheeks before turning around to face Ivy. She wore her hair down, and it seemed to glow in the pale moonlight. She looked radiant, and he desperately wanted to reach out and pull her in and never let go.

Instead, he said, "You should be celebrating," his tone emotionless. "The king has worked hard to prepare this feast for you."

"I don't care," she answered as she closed the distance between them. Ivy tilted her head up to look into his eyes, which were shiny with tears. She put her arms around his neck and began to rock back and forth. "What are you doing?" Finn asked.

"This is our dance floor, remember?"

Finn recalled the first night she came to him in the sand-pit. He'd been watching her dance with Kal with jealous eyes all night. He had wondered what it would feel like to hold her like that; to be close enough to see the gray in her purple eyes or feel the softness of her hair. She was here with him now, and that should be enough. But it wasn't. Finn pushed his negative thoughts away and snaked his arms around Ivy's waist. They danced to the music of the wind and crickets chirping in the grass.

They moved through the sand soundlessly; the only noise was the beating of their hearts. Finn looked down into her eyes and placed a hand to her cheek. He leaned in, and kissed her softly, and she returned it, placing her hands on his chest. The ale swam in his head, and his heart pounded against his ribs as her hands trailed down his side. His breath came quicker as Ivy slid her lips over his, her hands resting low on his hips. He wanted her; he wanted to be with her and never to wake up alone with only the memory of Ivy to warm him at night. But he couldn't do it. He gently took her hands away from him and brought them to his lips instead, kissing her knuckles.

Finn walked Ivy back to her room, and she paused outside her door, twirling a lock of hair. "You… you can stay, Finn. If you want."

He knew he couldn't do it. If Finn stayed, he would only give in to his desires, which would make her departure even more painful. Ivy begged him with her eyes, and he felt his stomach turn at the thought of hurting her.

"I'll see you tomorrow," he said, trying to force a smile that wouldn't come.

"Do you promise?" Ivy asked.

"I promise. I'll come and see you off, my Ivy." He pulled her into his arms and kissed the top of her head before going to his bed, alone.

That night Finn didn't dream. Not of Ivy or her soft hair, not of her electric touch that made his blood pump. Not of the way her eyes paralyzed him with their sharp violet hue. Nothing, only blackness. When he woke up, he stayed sitting in his bed for a long time, watching the sun climb into the sky.

Ivy led Cass down the road toward the docks, constantly checking over her shoulder for Finn. She'd already said goodbye to the king and his family. Kal seemed cold toward her but forced a smile and waved to her as she started down the road. Ivy stopped at Ronin's little house on the way to say goodbye. He came to the door at the sound of her approach and handed Ivy a small basket with food for the ride. She thanked him for everything he taught her and assured him that she'd be back to visit.

"Stay safe and give my good wishes to your father," Ronin said in a low voice.

"I will," Ivy told him. He seemed strange toward her, but she brushed it off as other things were on her mind. They shook hands and said goodbye before Ivy started down the road again.

Ser Osmund was waiting for her. He's already put their bags

on the ferry and somehow tricked Eclipse onto the boat. Ivy tied up Cass next to Eclipse and got back off the ferry to search the road ahead of her. She'd struggled not to blurt out the question to Finn last night when he refused to stay the night in her room. Ivy knew this was the only home he'd had since his own was destroyed, and she couldn't bring herself to ask him to leave it behind and come with her.

The sun reached up higher in the sky, and the man who owned the ferry was growing impatient. Ser Osmund came up behind her and rested his hand on her shoulder. "Ivy." Her name sounded strange on his mouth. She was so used to him calling her "Lady Ivy" or "My lady."

"We have to go," he continued gently. Ivy felt a tear roll down her face and quickly wiped it away as she realized Finn wasn't coming. She couldn't blame him. Ivy knew her leaving was painful for both of them and didn't want to see him in pain. She got to her feet, wiping off the sand that she'd been sitting in for the past hour. Ser Osmund put a strong arm around her shoulders and led her away to the waiting boat.

## CHAPTER TWENTY-NINE

# THE JOURNEY HOME

The wind picked up and twirled Ivy's hair around her face, hiding her eyes that began to fill back up with tears. Ser Osmund gave her shoulder a reassuring squeeze. "I'm sorry," he whispered and sounded sincere.

Ivy brushed him away and stomped up the ramp and onto the ferry. Cass was eager to leave, and Eclipse was starting to get restless, pulling at the reins that held him in place.

Before the ferry owner could push away, Ivy heard her name being called from behind. She whipped her head around to see Finn riding down the path on a white and brown speckled horse, carrying a bag over his shoulder.

Ivy sprinted past Ser Osmund and jumped down the ramp. Finn swung down from the horse and stumbled back as Ivy came plowing into his arms. She let the tears willingly roll down her cheeks as Finn stroked her hair and looked at Ser Osmund. The knight smiled at Finn and turned around to give them some privacy.

Ivy felt his lips brush her ear as he whispered, "I'm coming with you."

Ivy leaned back to look at him, not believing the words he just spoke. "I didn't want to ask you to leave," she admitted. "This has been your home for so long…" Ivy's words broke in her throat.

Finn caressed her face and shook his head. "This is just a place; it's not my home, Ivy. I promised that I would always be there for you wherever you went. I could've left many times, but I had nowhere to go until now. I want to be with you."

Ivy had no words. The relief she felt was like a wave crashing over her head. She pressed her lips to his, both of them smiling through the kiss as Ivy's tears turned to joy.

The three left Kame Island together, heading for home. Ser Osmund seemed content that Finn's decision made Ivy happy. The knight told them that they would ride all the way to Port Tsue, where Ser Caster would be waiting with a ship to bring them the rest of the way.

Many people in Xanheim weren't leaving their ports for fear of being taken by raiders at sea. Finding a captain willing to go north had proven too difficult, so they made their way back on Traders Road. They stayed off the main roads this time.

They'd ridden past Hapna's inn a few days ago, not wanting to stop there again. When they neared Rahama, they decided to not to enter the city. Instead, they camped outside Rahama. They could still see the glow from the city at night, and Ivy told Finn of all the beautiful things she had seen the last time she was in Rahama. She told him of watching the monkeys stealing fish from people, the crystal waters, and the strange trees. The whole time, Finn's eyes never left Ivy.

Ser Osmund got a small fire going to cook up the last of their fish from Ronin. Ivy and Finn sat close together, Ser Osmund watching them through the flames. He smiled every time Ivy looked his way, and she knew that Ser Osmund had accepted Finn.

After Ser Osmund went to sleep, Finn and Ivy stayed up talking late into the night. She told him about Godstone and her family. Ivy assured him that her father would accept him as a ward and find a place for Finn to stay, maybe even giving him a room in the central tower. She told him of Rayner and Correlyn, of the maple tree outside her window, and of the Blackwoods where they could spar together. Finn listening to every word until the fire died down to nothing but smoldering coals. Deciding they should get some sleep, Ivy unrolled the furs she'd brought from home and pulled Finn down beside her.

The early spring wind rustled the grass, sending a chill up to greet them. Finn pulled the furs around them and cradled Ivy against his chest while they listened to the sounds of the night. Ivy couldn't stop imagining what it would be like to have Finn in Godstone with her. She felt his fingers twirling a strand of her hair as she nestled down, feeling her eyes growing heavy with sleep. She wanted this every night—Finn's body curled around hers, his warm breath tickling her neck, his—

"I think I'm in love with you, Ivy."

Finn's hushed words filled her ear and sent a burning sensation down her neck. Ivy's eyes shot open, and she turned around to Finn's nervous, yet confident smile beaming down at her. This boy had saved her life. He'd protected Ivy, and been there for her when she needed. And now, with his words out there, hanging between them in the dark, Ivy knew in her heart that she was meant to be with Finn.

She smiled, and ran her fingers through his soft brown hair, pulled him close, and whispered, "I love you, too."

Finn grinned from ear to ear before his lips crashed into hers. Finn kissed her deeply, making Ivy feel flushed all over, yet gooseflesh covered her skin as if she was frozen. Ivy broke the kiss before she could get lost in him. Finn smiled and pressed a gentle kiss to Ivy's cheek before she laid back down, nuzzling her cheek against Finn's chest and drifting off to sleep.

The next day, Ser Osmund couldn't take his eyes off the couple. He'd heard everything the night before and couldn't help but smile as he watched the two riding alongside one another. Finn's eyes sparkled like nothing else when he looked at Ivy, and Ser Osmund knew that look. He suspected that he'd fallen in love with Ivy long ago.

They rode around Rahama that morning, and he listened to Ivy and Finn chatting, smiled as her sweet giggles filled the air. Ser Osmund felt a small relief when they left Traders Road and continued along the small dirt path that would bring them to Port Tsue. Ser Osmund had sent a hawk to Magnus not long after Ronin came back from Xanheim. They had arranged for Ser Caster to meet them in Port Tsue as the king didn't want Ivy to see the ruins of Harper Hall.

They rode three abreast down the dirt path, laughing and telling stories all afternoon. The sun was starting its descent in the sky as they came upon a small village. Ser Osmund told them to stay back while he checked it for safety.

"Do you think your brother will accept me as your knight has?" Finn asked.

"Why wouldn't he?" Ivy knew that Rayner would be happy if she were.

"The way you talk about him. I can tell you two are close. He might not be fond of me... spending time with you." Finn blushed slightly and Ivy smirked.

"Rayner is my best friend, but he'll accept you. I promise. If I'm happy, then so is he. Besides, from the letter I got, it seems like he's spending a lot of time with Correlyn anyway."

Ser Osmund came trotting back, waving at them to follow. They brought their horses around to a stable next to an inn. A man and his son ran the inn, and they were happy to have guests, saying they didn't get many travelers through there. Ser Osmund paid for two rooms and said that they should get a good night's rest and a hot meal before arriving at Port Tsue.

They ate roasted duck and vegetables together by the hearth that night.

"I've watched you fighting these past few months," Ser Osmund said to Finn. "You're very skilled. Perhaps you would care for a different sparring partner this evening?"

Finn smiled. "I'd like that."

They all finished their supper quickly before heading outside.

It was still light, and they walked around the inn to find a clearing near the road. Ivy sat on a stump with a good view of the field where Finn and Ser Osmund would fight. Finn suggested the knight lose his armor since he was undoubtedly quicker and wanted the fight to be fair. Ser Osmund chuckled as if Finn had no chance but agreed anyway.

Ser Osmund went back to the inn to put away his armor, and

Finn went up to Ivy and kissed her softly. "I'm going to feed the horses and find our practice swords. I'll be back."

Ivy nodded, then pulled out the dagger Rayner had given her and began to sharpen it on a stone. She was filled with excitement at the thought of returning home and telling her brother everything that happened. Ivy knew Rayner would be proud of what she'd accomplished and couldn't wait to spar with him and show off her new skills.

CHAPTER THIRTY

# THE STRANGER

As Ivy sat on the stump waiting for Ser Osmund and Finn, she heard a shrill cry from above. She turned her head to the sky and spotted a horned eagle circling her. Ivy watched it for a moment, never having seen one before. When she lowered her eyes again, Ivy was startled by a stranger standing in the road. She stood up abruptly as he smiled and came over to her.

"Hello there," he said, and his voice was deep but not unkind. Ivy said nothing but held her dagger at her side as he walked closer.

He was a tall man with dark hair, and she could see a sword hanging from his belt. "Are you staying here?" The man motioned to the inn. Ivy nodded and waited for him to speak again, watching his hands for any movement to his sword. He buried his hands in his pockets and walked closer. He stood taller than she, and Ivy watched as his eyes ran up the length of her, sizing her up. The man looked around, searching the empty fields that surrounded them. "This is a lovely place, don't you think?"

Ivy gripped the dagger tighter. "I suppose."

"I love this time of year," he said, taking in a deep breath. "It's a good time to start something new. Are you heading north?"

"No," Ivy lied. "We're going to Rahama."

The man smiled and Ivy noticed he had a tooth missing. Something about him gave Ivy a strange feeling, but she dared not reach for her sword, fearing that he would do the same. "Well, I'm heading north myself," he said after a moment.

"I have some business there." Ivy wished him safe travels and began to move away from the man when she heard Ser Osmund say her name.

The way he said it made Ivy's skin crawl and sent shivers down her back. She turned to see Ser Osmund standing there with panic pulsing in his eyes as his gaze locked on the man.

"Come away, Ivy." His voice shook slightly.

"It's good to see you again," the man said to Ser Osmund.

The name hung from Ser Osmund's mouth, and he let it fall like a whisper only meant for him. "Helvarr."

Ivy's head spun around to look at the man that she'd heard so much about. Her brow furrowed, her eyes widened, her heart violently pounding inside her chest. Why hadn't she known who he was?

Helvarr had the same black hair from the stories, his nose was crooked, and his eyes were haunting. Somehow his face had morphed into something sinister when Ser Osmund spoke his name--as if he released Helvarr. Ivy tried to back away, but she couldn't move. She didn't understand what was happening.

"Ivy!" Ser Osmund let the panic fill his voice. Helvarr took his hands from his pockets and put them behind his back, making no move to grab her. He smiled at her as she slowly backed away to where Ser Osmund stood.

The knight drew his sword and waited for Helvarr to do the same. "I've been looking for you for a long time," Helvarr addressed Ivy.

"Don't do this, Helvarr," Ser Osmund growled. "There has to be another way."

"Another way?" He shook his head. "Do you think Magnus considered that when he banished me? Do you think I'd be here if there were another way to get what I want? This is the only way. Magnus will hand over Godstone to us if I have his daughter… Ivy, was it?" He smiled at her, and she stood frozen in fear.

"Magnus loved you." Ser Osmund took a step toward Helvarr. "Your banishment hurt him as much as it did you. You were his only brother."

"Ah yes, poor King Magnus, sitting in his kingdom, wasting away at the thought of me out there on my own." Helvarr narrowed his eyes. "No, that doesn't sound right. Magnus the Mighty they call him now," Helvarr said with a chuckle. "The only thing mighty about that man is the kingdom he holds."

Ivy stepped forward in a wave of anger at the insult to her father.

"Oh, you'll get your turn young, Ivy." Helvarr's crooked smile only enraged her more. He pulled his sword and winked at her before charging Ser Osmund.

The two knights came together as the sun was dipping lower in the sky. Ivy drew her sword and watched the duel unfolding, looking for an opening. Helvarr sent his sword flying at Ser Osmund's head, holding nothing back. Ivy suddenly noticed that Ser Osmund had taken his armor off and panicked as she saw that Helvarr wore light black armor.

The two struggled against each other's blows, Helvarr almost losing his hand to Ser Osmund. They stepped around the clearing, slashing at one another and grunting with anger. Helvarr jabbed his sword toward Ser Osmund's belly, but he quickly smacked the blade away and plowed his fist into Helvarr's face. He stumbled back, spitting out blood and grinning before coming back for more.

Helvarr ducked just as Ser Osmund swung, slicing a lock of black hair from Helvarr's head. Ivy thought she saw a moment of hesitation in Helvarr's eyes, but it was quickly eaten up by anger again. Helvarr slashed and cut through the shirt Ser Osmund wore, but the knight didn't slow down. Rather, he thrust all his weight into his sword and drove it through Helvarr's shoulder. He screamed in pain but quickly slashed at Ser Osmund's leg.

Ser Osmund stumbled back and looked down—blood pooled around him. Helvarr brought his fingers up to the hole in his shoulder and growled when they came away bloodied. He pursued Ser Osmund, pushing him back and staying on his right side. Ivy realized what he was doing and felt a wave of nausea wash over her. Ser Osmund had received an arrow through his right shoulder many years back. Helvarr knew that was his weak side because he was there when it happened.

Ser Osmund slipped and went down to one knee. As Helvarr raised his sword, Ser Osmund swung his forward and caught his leg. Blood now poured from each man's legs, and Ser Osmund got back on his feet and called over his shoulder to Ivy, telling her to get Finn and run. But Ivy didn't move, she couldn't leave him.

Ivy took a step toward the men, willing to die to fight for Ser Osmund. Perhaps if they both attacked, they could defeat Helvarr. But as she stepped forward, her world slowed down, and her eyes grew wider than saucers.

Helvarr bared his teeth and thrust his blade into Ser Osmund's chest. The knight fell to his knees, still clutching his sword, and Ivy felt her own knees give out. Her pulse rushed in her ears, and her vision blurred with tears. Ser Osmund turned back to look at Ivy one last time, a sad smiled forming on his lips before Helvarr swung his blade across his throat, nearly taking his head off.

"NO!" Ivy screamed as Ser Osmund fell to the ground, blood pouring from his neck. Hot tears streamed down her face. Her whole body was shaking, and she felt sick, a knot twisting her stomach. She lifted her gaze to Helvarr, who stood over the dead knight, smiling down at Ivy.

Rage filled her belly as she grabbed the hilt of her sword that lay beside her. "I promised that I'd kill you if our paths ever crossed."

Helvarr smiled, amused. "Is that so?"

Ivy launched herself from the ground with Promise in her hand. Something changed in Helvarr's eyes, but Ivy didn't care; she was going to kill him for what he did and fulfill her promise. Before she reached him, Ivy felt a hand snatch her arm and whip her around, throwing her to the ground. She saw Finn come running toward her, worry painting his face, and when she turned to see who'd prevented her from killing Helvarr, the anger on her face was replaced with confusion. Ronin stood there facing Helvarr.

Ivy felt Finn's arms pulling her to her feet as she watched the two intently staring at each other. Helvarr seemed shocked, his eyes wide, but then he let his crooked smile start to creep back across his mouth. Ronin wore no expression, but Ivy saw something change in his eyes. She tried to break free from Finn, but he wrapped his arms tighter.

"Let me go!" she roared, twisting in Finn's arms. She locked eyes with Helvarr, who watched her curiously. "I'll kill you," she screamed. "I'll fucking kill you!"

Ronin broke his eyes away from Helvarr and turned to help Finn get her to the stables. Helvarr made no move; instead, he stood over Ser Osmund's body like a statue, watching them go and wearing that strange smile of his.

Finn had to force Ivy onto Cass, then they broke into a gallop, sending up a cloud of dirt behind them. Ivy swayed in her saddle and let the tears return. She gripped the reins until they dug into her soft skin, needing to feel the pain to confirm that this was real--that it wasn't one of her nightmares. Finn kept calling her name, but it was just a faint echo compared to the steady pounding of Cass's hooves against the dirt, and all she could see was that last look Ser Osmund gave her.

She let a loud sob escape and jerked back on the reins to stop her horse.

Ivy fell from her saddle and buried her shaking hands into the dirt, rocking back and forth. "No, no, no, no, no," she muttered to herself.

Finn fell in front of her and frantically searched her face, but there was only pain there. Ronin stepped out from around Cassius, and Ivy staggered to her feet and ran to him, throwing a punch that he caught with his fist.

"I could've killed him!" she screamed as she melted into his arms. "Do you know what you just did!" Ivy pounded at his chest, and Ronin let her. "I don't care if he was your student! Helvarr killed Ser Osmund!" She choked on his name. "He killed him!"

They sat there for a while, listening to Ivy sob as the world grew dark around them. After Ivy calmed down a little and her sobs became quiet, Ronin got to his feet.

"I am sorry." He seemed to choke on the words, and Ivy looked up and thought she saw tears making his eyes shine. "You're sorry?" The anger returned to her voice. Ivy stood up to face him. "I don't give a shit if you're sorry. It won't change what you did."

Finn stepped forward, "Ivy—"

"Why did you stop me?" she demanded, her hateful gaze boring a hole in Ronin.

"Because he was your student?" She laughed. "He's a monster, and I could've—"

"He's more than my student!" Ronin interrupted, letting his anger temporarily take over. He lowered his eyes to the dirt, and Ivy waited, shaking with rage. Ronin took a deep breath and dragged his eyes back up to face her, lowering his voice. "He's my son."

## CHAPTER THIRTY-ONE

# FORGED

Ivy stood before Helvarr, his cold copper eyes telling her to do it--to kill him. She pushed off from the ground and ran as fast as she could, Promise swinging at her side, thirsty for a taste of the stranger's blood. She swung her sword and sliced Helvarr across the throat; he never moved to get out of her way. As he lay bleeding in the grass, Ivy heard a slow clapping behind her. She turned to see Helvarr sitting on the tree stump, applauding her effort. Ivy turned back to the man that Promise had slain and saw that it was Ser Osmund.

The knight was already cold and drained of life. Ivy dropped down to the blood-soaked ground next to him and screamed. Helvarr sat laughing at her from his place atop the stump while Ivy sobbed down in the dirt. Rayner's voice came sailing in on a breeze; she lifted her head and wiped the tears from her eyes, trying to follow the voice. As she stood up, she saw Rayner standing off to the side, bloodied and bruised. His armor was dented and smashed. He spoke, and Ivy felt a shiver. "We will return home. I promise." Over and over, he repeated the same words, but they meant nothing to her. Ivy screamed at him to stop, but he only grew louder. She forced her palms over her ears, but still, her brother's voice haunted her, and Ser Osmund's corpse grew colder.

Ivy woke to Finn shaking her violently—her hands were covering her ears, muffling his voice. Finn looked scared as Ivy sat up, letting the furs fall away from her shoulders. "You were screaming," Finn said in a quiet voice as if he didn't want to frighten her. Ronin sat on a nearby rock, sharpening his sword, and Ivy realized it was still dark out.

"How long was I asleep?" Ivy asked in a raspy voice.

"Only an hour." He reached out to touch her cheek, but Ivy turned away. "Ivy, you need to sleep. It's been days."

Worry and pain hung in his voice as he looked at Ivy. She had black circles under her eyes, which were red and puffy from tears. "We'll be in Port Tsue tomorrow," Ronin said. "Finn's right. You need to sleep."

Ivy scowled at him and pushed herself to her feet, going to sit by the fire that still raged against the chilly spring night. Ivy hadn't said a word to Ronin since he stopped her from killing Helvarr. Finn tried to comfort her, but she didn't let him. She wanted to feel the pain that she caused. She needed to remember this feeling when she got her chance again.

Finn came and sat next to Ivy, leaving space between them. He poked at the fire with a stick, staring deep into the dancing flames. Finn hadn't said much to Ronin in the past few days either; they spent their days pushing their horses farther north and camping only when the sun was gone and the world black.

Ronin sat across from the two and put his sword back in the scabbard. He closed his eyes and took in a breath before speaking. "I'm sorry, Ivy. This wasn't supposed to happen."

"Well, it did," she said through her teeth.

Ronin held her gaze. "You're right. But if you have to blame someone, blame me. It's not your fault. I made the decision to follow you too late. If I'd arrived sooner—"

"I'm so glad you had a choice." Ivy interrupted. "Ser Osmund didn't. He didn't decide to die. He didn't decide to break his promise to my father to see me safely home. He had no choice but to fight." She leaned forward to glare at him. "But I'm glad you had time to ponder your decision while Ser Osmund's was made for him."

Ivy got to her feet, and Finn reached out and took her hand in his, but she snatched it away and stormed off into the dark field. Ivy sat under a maple tree and brought her knees up to her face and let the tears come again. They burned her eyes, but she reminded herself that she needed the pain.

It was fueling her.

The wind scratched the branches together and blew the soft dirt beneath her boots. Ivy picked up a handful and let it fall between her fingers; it felt cold and soft, the way the sand felt the night Finn kissed her. She wanted to tell him to leave...to go back to Kame Island because if he stayed, he would only be killed.

After a while, Finn came looking for her, and this time she didn't brush him off. It hurt Ivy to make him this way; she knew he was worried about her, and it showed on his face every time he looked at her. He sat down without saying a word and leaned his head back against the bark of the maple tree. The wind blew his brown hair out from behind his ears to swirl across his forehead. Ivy reached for his hand and brought it up to her chest, holding it tight against her. He turned and placed his other hand over her heart, staring into her eyes for something.

"You should go back," Ivy whispered.

Finn only shook his head and leaned in closer. "We belong together, Ivy. Your fate was forged by the gods to meet with mine, and I'll never leave you. Do you hear me?" He brushed her hair behind her ear. "You belong to me as much as I belong to you."

Perhaps Finn was right, and the gods had brought them together for a reason. No matter how dangerous the war got, Ivy knew that Finn was sincere. He'd never leave. Ivy sniffed and forced her tears back as Finn placed a gentle kiss on her cheek.

"Ronin wants to talk to you," he said. She looked at him for a long moment before a thin smile spread across his lips, and Ivy agreed to go back.

Ronin was still sitting by the fire, leaning his elbows on his knees as the flames lit up his face. Finn wrapped Ivy's cloak around her shoulders and sat with an arm around her waist as Ronin began. He took a deep, steady breath and looked at Ivy before casting his glance down to the dirt.

He told them the story of his wife and the life he had before going to Godstone. He didn't look up to see their faces or how they reacted to the story, only pushing through it to the next part.

"I was living in Volantar at the time, taking small jobs as a sellsword. A young knight came looking for me in the city. He was from Godstone. I remember thinking I should just walk away, that I was done being a sellsword. But the knight told me he wasn't looking for a sellsword; he was looking for a trainer. He said King Erwin sent him to find me--that he'd heard of my fighting skills and wished to have me train his son. I said no and told the knight to go away, that I wouldn't teach a young boy how to fight. But he persisted and followed me for days until I finally gave in, and we set off for Godstone that day.

"When I arrived, the knight brought me to meet King Erwin and his son. The king praised me for my skills and asked again if I would teach his son and heir to fight. Magnus came out and ran to his father, who was seated on the dais. He couldn't have been but five years old with a shaggy head of auburn hair bouncing as he ran. He was shy at first and hid behind his father's throne while we talked. King Erwin confessed that Magnus wasn't the only boy who needed training. He told me of a young boy of the same age who just lost his father in battle. He explained how close he and Magnus were and that if I agreed to train Magnus, then I would also need to train this other boy. I reluctantly agreed, and a knight escorted the boy in and introduced him as Helvarr.

"I knew the minute I laid eyes on him who he was. His hair was black like mine, but his eyes… His eyes were the same shade of bright copper as Yacira's, and I knew then that this was my son." Ronin's voice grew distant as he continued. "Cold sweat poured over my body as I looked at the ghost of my dead wife. His eyes shimmered in the light just as hers did, only something was different, but I didn't know what. I debated for a long time whether I should tell Helvarr that I was his father, but in the end, I decided against it.

"I'd left him in the woods to die, and never looked back. He seemed to have a good life in Godstone with Magnus, and I didn't want to take that from him. I asked around about Helvarr's father. Turns out, he was from the South and came upon a baby crying in the woods, surrounded by horned eagles. He took Helvarr north with him where he planned to swear loyalty to House Blackbourne, and there he stayed until a battle with the raiders cost him his life. Helvarr lost the only father he'd ever known, but I still couldn't bear to tell him the truth.

"I vowed to stay by his side, to train him and teach him how to be a man. But as he got older, I started to see the darkness within him. He became cruel and cold his anger consumed him, and my best efforts did little to lead him down a different path. Ser Osmund saw it too and confronted me about Helvarr, saying that he needed to learn to control his anger if he was to become a knight. I tried to help him, to teach him what my trainer had taught me, but he was stubborn and only wished to learn how to wield a sword. Helvarr was too far gone, and when Magnus came back that day without him, I knew what happened. He'd pushed your father for years, and Magnus finally pushed back. Helvarr's banishment was the reason I left. I had nothing left in Godstone, and I'd failed my only son."

Ivy sat in silence after Ronin finished his story. She didn't know what he wanted her to say, or the reaction that he was looking for. Ivy was still angry with him, and no story would change her mind.

"Why did you never tell me?" Finn asked Ronin.

"You didn't need to know. No one did."

Ivy pulled her cloak tighter around her shoulders and shifted closer to Finn. "Why did you follow us?" Ivy finally asked. She'd wanted to know for days now, but her head was fogged with too many thoughts.

"When I went to Xanheim with King Mashu's Shadows,

I was to find the leader of the raiders and kill him. Helvarr was in the central market when we spotted one another. He ran, so I followed him. I wasn't sure what I'd do if I caught him, only that I needed to try. It became clear to me that Helvarr was their leader after he sent raiders back into the city to kill me. I can't say why he ran from me. Perhaps seeing me was like seeing a ghost. A bad memory from a past life that he no longer had."

Ivy ran her hands over one another and considered what Ronin said. She decided that he must be telling the truth, but some things still didn't make sense to her. "I'm truly sorry for your loss, young Ivy. If I could change what happened, I would."

"Stop telling me that you're sorry." Ivy looked past the flames to where Ronin sat. "You can tell my father when we arrive in Godstone. You can tell King Magnus how sorry you are. How do you think he'll react, knowing you watched Helvarr grow into the monster he is and knowing all along that he was your son, an evil man that you helped create? Do you think my father will blame you for not killing Helvarr when you had the chance? You were a coward who deserted a baby you didn't want. Anything that happens in this war from now on is your fault." Ronin didn't move or blink, and Ivy got up to leave again, letting her anger wash over her in a wave.

Finn made no move to grab her this time.

They arrived in Port Tsue the next day, and Ivy felt a sudden stab of guilt, knowing she had to face Ser Caster and explain why Ser

Osmund wasn't with them. As they rode their horses down to the docks, Ivy spotted the ship that would take her home. Her father's banner of a Blackwood tree with its dark purple leaves snapped against the winds of the sea. Her heart began to race, and she kicked Cassius into a gallop, leaving Finn and Ronin behind.

Ivy heard someone shout her name and quickly yanked up on the reins, searching the faces around her. She spotted Ser Caster in his shiny armor, waving to her from a vendor's booth. Ivy swung down from Cass and ran to him, a lump forming in her throat. Still, she was happy to see someone from home.

Ivy jumped into his arms and let the tears fall as the knight embraced her.

"Lady Ivy." He pulled away from her. "Why are you crying?" She opened her mouth, but no words came out. She thought she might be sick when Ser Caster started scanning the people behind her. Ivy knew who he was looking for, but he wouldn't find Ser Osmund's face. "He's dead," she blurted out before he could even ask.

"What are you talking about, Ivy?" Worry starting to cover his face like a thick fog.

"Ser Osmund…" she said between sobs. "He's dead. He was killed on the road."

"By whose hand, Ivy? What happened?"

Finn and Ronin came trotting up before she could answer, and Ser Caster let his eyes fall on Ronin.

"What are you doing here?" Ser Caster demanded of Ronin. "What's going on? And who's that?" He gestured toward Finn.

"Come," Ronin began. "We have much to talk about."

They sailed for days, the swift spring wind pulling Ivy closer to home with every breath. Ser Caster took the news as expected, but Ivy was grateful that she didn't have to tell him. As soon as they set off from Port Tsue, Ronin took Ser Caster below decks to tell him all that happened. They were down there for hours, and Ivy was beginning to feel panicked. She sat in silence with Finn on the upper deck, keeping a watchful eye on the door and nervously twisting her golden scarf in her hands. Ivy didn't know what to expect, but her dark thoughts told her that Ser Caster would barge through that door and scream at her, blaming her for everything that happened. She had to trust that Ronin would tell the truth.

When they finally came back up, Ser Caster walked swiftly toward Ivy, and she instinctively stood, ready for anything. He wrapped her in a hug and kept whispering in Ivy's ear that he was sorry. Ivy mourned Ser Osmund's death with Ser Caster, and they drank to him that night after supper. Ivy felt some relief, but she knew she had to be the one to tell her father tomorrow when she arrived home. Ser Caster got drunk and passed out, mumbling Rayner's name and things like "sorry," and "gone." Ivy shrugged it off as ale filled dreams.

Ivy walked down the hall, swaying with the rocking boat and the ale that sloshed in her belly. She knocked on Finn's door, but when he didn't answer, she let herself in. The room was dark, and Finn appeared to be asleep in his bed. Ivy knew he hadn't slept much in the past week because he was always keeping an eye on her, making sure that she was alright. She climbed into bed next to him and wrapped herself in his arms that were heavy with sleep.

Finn stirred and pressed a kiss against her temple, squeezing her tighter. "It will be alright, Ivy," Finn spoke softly, his voice raspy from sleep. "I'll be by your side the whole time."

Ivy turned to face him, letting a tight smile spread across her lips. His hair was messy, but his eyes were fully alert and locked on her. "I'm glad you came, and I'm sorry for how—"

Finn hushed her. "Don't apologize for your grief." He kissed her cheek, allowing his lips to linger for a moment. "We'll be in Godstone tomorrow," Ivy whispered. "You'll get to see the place that I hope you'll call home."

Finn gave her a warm smile. "You're my home, Ivy. No matter where we are or what happens in the future, as long as I'm with you, I'll be home." Ivy brushed his hair from his forehead and kissed him, long and soft.

Finn fell asleep with Ivy in his arms, and Ivy thought of Godstone. Its black beaches that she loved so much, her maple tree and her family. Though she was arriving without Ser Osmund and that hole in her heart couldn't be filled, Ivy had also gained something. Finn was an unexpected part of her journey, though now she accepted that they were always fated to meet. Their lives had been woven together since before they ever met.

Tomorrow she would see her family again, her father, her mother's warm smile, and her brother. She drifted off to sleep, thinking of all she had to tell Rayner, all that had happened to her while away. Ivy had been beaten, broken, bruised, and filled with more fear than she'd ever experienced. But she'd also been forged into something new, no longer the young girl that never left the North. Ivy had changed in so many ways over the past few months, but one thing always stayed the same. Ivy would never give up, and she was willing to fight to protect her home and the people she loved, no matter the cost.

# EPILOGUE

Helvarr stomped his way down the stone path that led up to the king's castle. Arne's dark shadow circled the stone ground around Helvarr; his horned eagle was never far away. As Helvarr reached the steps to King Caato's castle, he paused and drew in a deep breath before pushing through the doors.

King Caato eyed Helvarr from his throne as he approached. His pale purple eyes filled Helvarr with a particular rage as they reminded him of his old friend. King Caato wore a crown of iron, twisting in and out of his wavy blond hair.

"What are you doing here?" the king demanded as Helvarr stopped before the dais.

Just over two weeks ago, Helvarr had been in Hideaway Harbor after giving over the command of his raiders to Ser Marion. Not two days later, his raiders brought back word of Ser Marion's beheading at the hands of King Magnus the Mighty. Helvarr twisted his mouth at the name "Mighty." He'd never thought Magnus to be a powerful nor demanding king. That was until the day Magnus banished him and years later tracked him to make sure Helvarr wasn't staying in the North. Most of the northern houses had pledged loyalty to Magnus, forcing Helvarr over the border that separated the North from the South.

"I have news from Hideaway Harbor," Helvarr started. "It seems King Magnus has beheaded Ser Marion and pushed our army out of Temple City."

King Caato tapped his fingers on the armrest of his throne, taking in the news. "I entrusted Ser Marion with leading the raiders against—"

"You entrusted him?" King Caato interrupted, his tone mocking. "Some good that did., The man has no head thanks to you." Helvarr balled his fists but tried to calm himself. King Caato was known to have a temper worse than Helvarr, and he wasn't in the mood to listen to the king talk down to him.

"This isn't the first time you've failed to lead my raiders against King Magnus. I fear you're becoming a disappointment to me, Helvarr." The king eyed him with a wry smile, waiting for him to grow angry. "Nothing to say?"

"I have some good news as well," Helvarr stated through gritted teeth. "My informant has given me the whereabouts of Magnus's daughter. That's why I left Ser Marion in charge of Temple City. I've come south to capture her."

"And where is she?" King Caato asked suspiciously.

"She's been on Kame Island for a few weeks now. A knight from Godstone is accompanying her, but he shouldn't be a problem."

"Shouldn't?" King Caato lifted his eyebrow.

"Won't. He won't be a problem. He's an old man now, and he can easily be killed."

The king sat back in his chair and continued to tap his fingers on the armrest, considering Helvarr's plan. "Very well," he agreed. "Gather some raiders from around Lamira and set off for Kame Island tomorrow." Helvarr nodded to the king and turned away to leave.

"And Helvarr," the king called to him, "do not let me down again."

The following week, Helvarr marched into the city of Xanheim with an army of raiders ready to attack the island. He told the raiders to take control of the harbor and steal some boats to get across Serpent's Pass. Helvarr pulled one raider to the side, a man named Ekert, and briefed him on a solo mission. They found an inn and ordered a flagon of ale while the other raiders prepared the boats. "I have a special mission for you, Ekert." Helvarr began after the ale had been brought over. "King Mashu's island is full of Shadows, and we can expect much resistance from them at the docks. I want you to go off on your own."

Ekert looked at him curiously and smiled at the thought of being chosen for this mission. "What do you need of me, Helvarr?"

"Our men will keep the Shadows busy down at the docks. You'll sail to the western side of the island. There's a dock there that isn't in use anymore, so it should be easy for you to get on the island without being spotted. You'll then find a place to hide until sundown. Then, I want you to find a Shadow and give him a clean death, making sure you don't bloody his uniform. Once you're disguised as one of the king's Shadows, you'll be free to roam the island and find the girl and bring her to me. Do you understand?"

"How will I know who to look for?" Ekert asked.

"That island is full of black-haired people. Find the girl with auburn hair and purple eyes. It shouldn't be too difficult for you, I hope?" Helvarr glared at him over the rim of his cup and waited for an answer.

"No, Ser. I'll find her."

"Good. Set off from the western dock and make sure no one follows you. Try not to kill anyone. We don't need a trail of bodies left behind to be discovered before you've even made it out of their waters."

"I understand. I'll bring you the girl." The two raised their cups and drank the ale before setting off toward the docks where the raiders were preparing to leave.

Helvarr stayed in Xanheim while the raiders went and did his work for him. He watched them push off in the middle of the night and counted the hours until they returned. He strolled through the streets of Xanheim, thinking about what his next move would be after he had Magnus's daughter. The king's son had proved challenging to capture or kill as he was always with his father. But Helvarr had been playing the odds and instructed his informant to kill the Blackbourne boy at the next available opportunity.

Helvarr was tired of waiting. He wanted nothing more than to be back in the North, ruling Godstone the way Magnus never could, though he had a more important reason to be back north. It had been his home too, and Magnus had cast him out, away from everyone he knew and cared about. When Helvarr lost his father in a battle, he had no family left. Magnus filled that hole and became his brother and best friend.

Arne called out from above, and Helvarr turned his head

toward the sky, watching his horned eagle soar above the streets of the city. His raiders came back later that day with fewer boats than they started with. Helvarr stormed down to the docks as the boats were anchoring. His men looked bloody and beaten, but Helvarr had sent them off, knowing they had no chance against the Shadows. Of course, they didn't know that, and Helvarr moved his eyes over the horizon, looking for the small boat that would bring him his only chance to go home.

"What happened?" he asked the nearest raider, trying to sound sincere. Ser Harken was a sworn knight to King Caato, and Helvarr knew the man would willingly die for his king, making him an excellent puppet to do Helvarr's bidding.

"The Shadows," he started, out of breath as he jumped into the knee-high water. "There were too many; they came down on us like a storm. They must've seen us coming and warned the others. Half of us didn't even make it off the boats before the Shadows started shooting flaming arrows at us. We returned fire and managed to burn a few of theirs, but there were too many."

"That man killed more of our men than the Shadows did!" a raider called out from the boat. "He moved like no knight I've ever seen!" another raider yelled.

Helvarr called them over and demanded that they explain themselves.

"He wasn't a Shadow," the first raider said.

"Had no armor either," the second one continued. "He fought three of our men at once with little effort."

Helvarr asked what the man looked like, and they described his small black bun and narrow eyes, the way his face never seemed to change while he was killing their men. Helvarr felt a sudden chill but quickly shook it away.

"You say he fought alone?" he questioned the raiders.

"That's right. A lone knight. I watched him cut one of ours in half like he was slicing through the air."

Helvarr turned away from them and started back toward the city. His mind was racing; he didn't understand how it was possible. He never knew what happened to his former trainer after his own banishment from Godstone. He always assumed Ronin would've stayed to train Magnus's son when he grew of age. He let a smile spread across his lips as he thought about Ronin cutting a man in half. His trainer was always hard on Helvarr, but somewhere inside him, he felt a connection to the man. Ronin was the only man to guide Helvarr after his father was killed, but he'd been hard on Helvarr from a young age.

Helvarr spent a few days sitting at the docks of Xanheim, waiting for Ekert to return with Magnus's daughter. His raiders had been drinking themselves into comas for days after their failure on Kame Island, and Helvarr knew they couldn't stay here much longer. He'd expected Ekert to return the night after the raiders attacked, but the seas remained empty. He commanded his raiders to set up posts along the docks to make sure no boats went out while they remained in the city. He grew furious, sitting there day after day, waiting for a boat that would never come.

On the third day of sitting at the docks, Helvarr spotted something on the horizon. Boats were sailing toward Xanheim, flying the red turtle flag of King Mashu. Helvarr knew it was the king's Shadows, likely coming to flush out his raiders to eliminate the threat that they posed. Helvarr ran toward the city to find his raiders and warn them, Arne sailing high above and casting his long shadow over Helvarr.

Helvarr instructed his raiders to move deeper into the city and kill any Shadows that came their way. He needed to capture one of the Shadows and complete the mission that Ekert had failed. He wondered what happened to Ekert and how far he managed to get before he was captured or killed. King Mashu had never taken part in the war until now and likely would have stayed out of it entirely if he wasn't harboring King Magnus's daughter. He balled his fists in anger at the thought of this girl he'd never met. Without her, he had little chance of taking Godstone from Magnus, but there was still a small hope that his informant could manage to kill his son.

He walked through the streets and came to the central market. Helvarr scanned the rooftops for Shadows but saw no one and decided to stroll through the vendor's booths. He moved through the booths and stopped at one where an older woman was selling metal bowls.

Helvarr picked up a silver bowl and looked at his reflection. His black hair fell to the nape of his neck, and his cold copper eyes ran over his crooked nose. He let himself smile as he remembered how it got that way before the older woman asked if he was buying anything. Helvarr scowled at the woman and moved on, setting the bowl back on top of its stack. He made his way to the back of the market and started to walk up a cobblestone street to find his raiders when a loud crash turned his attention.

Helvarr whipped his head back and scanned the crowd before spotting the old woman picking up her metal bowls and yelling at a man who stood over her. Helvarr's eyes widened as Ronin spotted him from across the market, and he took off running. Arne took off in flight ahead of Helvarr, leading him around a corner and down an empty street. He couldn't understand why his former trainer was working with the Shadows. Ronin had never helped Magnus fight off raiders when he still resided in Godstone. It was almost as if Ronin was looking for Helvarr. When they locked eyes, Helvarr noticed the sword in Ronin's hand.

Helvarr had no desire to hurt his former trainer, let alone kill him, but he would if he had to. Helvarr turned into an alley and climbed a set of stairs that wound their way up to the roof. He peered over the ledge as Ronin ran by and watched him stop at a fork in the road. Helvarr ducked down as Ronin turned his head, scanning the rooftops. His heart was pounding against his ribs as he thought about facing Ronin, but even he knew that fighting him would be risky. Ronin was the best fighter Helvarr had ever seen, and if Ronin was pursuing him for some reason, Helvarr decided it was wiser to stay hidden.

He poked his head up over the ledge again and saw Ronin sitting in the middle of the street, eyes focused on something Helvarr couldn't see. Arne called out from above, but Helvarr didn't call his eagle to him. Instead, he sat quietly and watched Arne circle Ronin before flying off. Helvarr watched Ronin sit in the street for a long time before he finally got to his feet and made his way back to the market. Once he was out of sight, Helvarr took off running through the streets of Xanheim to find his raiders.

He came upon them gathered in the back of the city, fighting off a group of Shadows. Helvarr drew his sword and smiled before slicing his way through the crowd. A Shadow dropped down from a roof behind him, and Helvarr quickly twisted on the balls of his feet and brought his sword around to meet the Shadow's neck. His sword was a beautiful piece of metalwork. The blade was black with markings like running water. Helvarr had a new sword made when he left the North, spending the rest of his money on it and giving it the name Revenge.

Another Shadow ran his way, and Helvarr slid on his knees under the man's blade and turned, driving Revenge through the Shadow's back and out through his chest. His raiders were being pushed back, and Helvarr looked around to see more Shadows making their way down from the rooftops. He yelled over the sound of metal and screams and ordered his men to retreat farther back, out of city limits. The Shadows didn't chase them once Helvarr and his men were outside the city. He watched them move into the shadows of buildings and disappear over rooftops.

Helvarr made his way through the raiders, pushing past them until he found Torkel. The man stood taller than Helvarr and fought in the style of the northern clans, carrying both an ax and a sword.

"Torkel!" Helvarr roared and grabbed the man by the collar of his leather armor, pulling him away from the others. "I need you to find someone and kill him."

Torkel only nodded his head and waited for instructions. Helvarr described Ronin and which way he went and told Torkel to hunt him down and tell him their leader sends his regards. Helvarr couldn't justify killing his old trainer himself but knew he would continue to be a problem so long as he was still breathing. He concluded that Ronin meant to kill him, likely sent by King Mashu to find the leader of the raiders, which happened to be him. Ronin couldn't have known he would find Helvarr, but it didn't matter. Now that they had seen each other, he doubted that Ronin would stand aside and let him take Magnus's daughter.

He sent Torkel off, along with a handful of raiders to kill

Ronin, something tugging at his heart as he watched them tear back through the trees in search of the lone knight. Helvarr pushed that feeling down, knowing it had to be done and glad that he didn't have to do it himself.

Helvarr waited in the tree line behind Xanheim for Torkel to return with news of Ronin's fall. When none of the raiders came back, Helvarr grew furious. He'd put his trust in too many people only to be let down. He decided that he would do things himself. Helvarr ordered the raiders to go back to Lamira and tell King Caato of their failure.

He knew the king would be angry and likely send a group to bring Helvarr back, but by then, it would be too late.

The raiders gathered themselves up and headed west through the woods, making their way back home. Helvarr went back through the city to find his horse when he came upon the bodies of the men who failed him. Torkel lay in a heap with many raiders surrounding him inside the central market where Ronin had spotted Helvarr earlier that day. He strolled past them, not feeling anything for the men, and made his way to the stables near the docks. He mounted his white mare and turned back to the city, weaving his way through the streets.

Arne flew overhead, staying just above the rooftops until Helvarr broke into a gallop outside the city and made his way through the trees. He would meet up with the raiders he'd planted around the border and gather information from them. If he were lucky, his informant would be nearby and come to meet with him so that they could discuss a plan. Helvarr wasn't giving up on the idea of capturing Magnus's daughter, but he needed information about his son's whereabouts so that he could be eliminated.

Helvarr knew that Ser Osmund was with the girl and that he wouldn't allow her to leave so soon after an attack. Ser Osmund had always disliked Helvarr, ever since he was a young boy, training alongside Magnus. The knight would run to the future king anytime Helvarr knocked him down or hit him with their wooden swords. It made Helvarr angry that Magnus had all these grown men to care for him, and Helvarr had none. He'd started to think that Ronin cared for him until he made Helvarr and Magnus fight on the beaches of Godstone.

Helvarr remembered that day on the beach vividly. He remembered the proud look on Ronin's face any time Magnus managed to disarm Helvarr. But mostly, he remembered the look of shock, and disgust on Ronin's face after he beat up Magnus. All he wanted was to impress his trainer, to get some kind of recognition that he was strong—that he would make a great knight one day. But Ronin was cold toward Helvarr. As the years went on, Helvarr became a shell filled with anger, and sadness, so when Magnus banished him, Helvarr had immediately traveled to Lamira to serve King Caato. But Helvarr didn't care what the king believed or what he wanted—all he saw was an easy way back home, where he planned to take the throne from Magnus and crown himself king.

Helvarr came to a clearing and decided to camp for the night. He tied up his horse Hela; she'd been the only one to stick with him through his banishment. He stroked her soft white fur and fed her an apple. Hela was an older horse, but she could still charge into battle just as ferocious as any young colt. Arne came to find Helvarr some hours later, carrying a fish between his talons. The horned eagle landed before Helvarr and backed away from the fish, a gift to his master.

The eagle ruffled his feathers and sat down in Helvarr's cloak, forming a nest for himself. Helvarr sat back and cast his eyes north, where Godstone awaited him. Magnus could never have known what he'd done to Helvarr the day he banished him, but he'd make sure Magnus felt the same pain he did. Helvarr had always been a private person, never letting his personal life leak into his duties as a knight. Not even Magnus knew what had been going on in his life; otherwise, he might not have banished Helvarr.

He thought about telling Magnus that day but decided it would only hurt his pride, and he wasn't going to beg Magnus for something he already had. Helvarr swore he would get it back and take Godstone in the process, no matter what he had to do. Magnus would feel his wrath, and soon.

That night, Helvarr dreamed of Godstone rising before him, like a mirage too sweet to be real. He dreamed of ruling as king inside those very walls, knights swearing their loyalty to him, and his beautiful queen ruling alongside him.

# PROLOGUE

**Continue reading for a sneak peek at book 2 in
The Blackbourne Series.**

Magnus ran along the stone path of the western wall, glancing over his shoulder and losing his breath in belly laughs. The wind whipped his wavy hair back from his brow as he rounded the corner. His little legs ached from running, but he didn't stop. Magnus hopped up onto the wall and began to run along it, stretching his arms out from balance. He could hear him coming, his laugher clawed at the little prince's back. Magnus dared a look back and almost lost his balance.

"Magnus! Get down from there!" someone shouted. He froze and looked over the edge to see his father, frantically waving at him to get down. King Erwin stood tall and lean, his wavy auburn hair burned with the dying sun. His face was twisted with anger.

Magnus jumped down from the wall, unaware that Helvarr had caught up to him. He tackled Magnus to the ground, and laughter bubbled up from his core. Helvarr's black hair swept across his forehead and clung to his skin. He was soaking wet.

Moments ago, Magnus had caught Helvarr off guard, standing alone at the practice yard, watching the knights fight. His eyes were as big as saucers, and Magnus knew he'd be distracted. He'd taken a pail of water and dumped it on his friend's head. Helvarr turned around with a scowl on his face, but it brightened when he spotted Magnus. When Helvarr made to grab Magnus, the prince shrieked with laughter and took off running.

Now, Helvarr couldn't control his laughter as his shaking arms tried to pin Magnus to the ground. They laughed like fools, and Magnus already forgot about his father's scorn. Helvarr was his best friend and brother and always knew how to make Magnus laugh. Though they were only five years of age, Magnus knew in his little heart they would be brothers for life.

"Give up!" Helvarr's tiny voice roared.

Magnus tried to crawl away. "A king never gives up!" he yelled between chuckles.

"You aren't king yet, Magnus," Helvarr retorted.

"Yet." Magnus slipped through his hands and got to his feet. He looked back to see Helvarr scrambling to catch up when Magnus ran into a sheet of metal.

Magnus was knocked off his feet, and when he looked up. Ser Osmund stood over him, arms crossed, but a smile painted on his face. The knight was tall and broad, with a head of long, brown hair and a scruffy beard. Helvarr came running up, and

Ser Osmund's smile faded. Magnus got back to his feet and stood alongside his friend.

"Did you enjoy giving your father a heart attack?" Ser Osmund asked sarcastically.

Magnus lowered his head, and Ser Osmund crouched before him. "You can't do things like that, Magnus. You're the heir to Godstone. What if you would've fallen?" His voice was gentle.

"I wouldn't have let him fall." Helvarr stepped up.

Ser Osmund raised his eyes to Helvarr and gave him a faint smile, but there was something else in his gaze. He turned back to Magnus. "Go find your father. I need to speak with Helvarr."

Magnus glanced at Helvarr, but Ser Osmund assured him everything was alright. Helvarr stood still and watched Magnus run off, looking over his shoulder every few feet until he disappeared.

Ser Osmund turned back to Helvarr then got to his feet, motioning for him to follow. They walked silently along the wall until it ended just below the black cliffs that rose above the beaches.

"Helvarr." The knight's tone was quiet and careful. "There's something I need to tell you." He bent down to get eye level with Helvarr, his brow creased with concern. "You know that your father went off on a special mission." Helvarr nodded his head.

Ser Osmund had watched his father explain to Helvarr before he left that the king needed his help, and it was his duty to protect his home and the king's family. Helvarr was too young to fully understand, but he'd given his father a hug goodbye with tears in his eyes and his father had kissed his son, promising to be back soon.

"Helvarr," Ser Osmund repeated, clearing his throat. "Your father...I'm afraid he died."

Helvarr's face crumpled and tears shone in his copper eyes. "No." His little voice was raspy. "No, Father said he would be back soon. He promised!"

Ser Osmund pulled him in for a hug, wrapping his arms around the sobbing little boy. He stroked Helvarr's black hair as his tears plopped on the knight's metal armor. "I'm sorry, Helvarr. Your father was a brave man, and he wouldn't want you to be sad." Helvarr sobbed even louder, and Ser Osmund felt his eyes threatening to betray him. He pulled away and held Helvarr at arm's length. "King Erwin will take good care of you. You and Magnus will be like real brothers now." The knight tried to smile.

Helvarr wiped his nose. "Brothers?"

"That's right. Don't you want a brother?" Helvarr nodded and wiped his tears away. "We're your family now, Helvarr, and we'll always take care of you. Do you understand?" Ser Osmund was sure he didn't, but Helvarr nodded anyway.

"Good boy." Ser Osmund messed his hair. "Come on now, Magnus will be waiting for you in the Hall. I hear the cook made mutton stew." He crossed his eyes and pretended to gag. Helvarr giggled, and Ser Osmund stood up, offering his hand. "Maybe we can sneak some extra apple tarts after supper."

Helvarr grinned big and nodded his head. Ser Osmund squeezed his little hand in his as they made their way down the wall of Godstone. He looked into Helvarr's eyes that burned in the dying sun, but in that moment, he saw something else, too.

# ACKNOWLEDGMENTS

Is anyone actually here reading this? Bueller? Bueller? Okay, if you are reading this then, welcome, and please enjoy the rambling that follows. Let's begin and hope I don't leave anyone out.

To all my early readers, you guys are rockstars! To Maureen for helping me with the very first round of edits and my many (so many) mistakes. Thank you for being so supportive and a great and honest fan. To Amanda who blew through not only this book but the entire series and got so emotionally invested in these characters! Sorry I made you cry... but also not sorry. (Insert maniacal laughter).

To my family: Dad you aren't much of a reader and certainly wouldn't have picked up a fantasy book on your own but there you were, calling me every night after reading a chapter to discuss what happened. We had our own little book club going and those calls were always my favorite! I only had to threaten to cut you with a spoon a few times. To my mom who spent most of our vacation in Maine talking about the future of this book and letting me ramble on and on about characters, plot, worldbuilding, story arc, etc. I'm so glad that my book opened up the world of fantasy to you! To April for keeping a spoon handy when

Dad was slacking on reading! Thank you for falling in love with this book and supporting me. You all have been so supportive of my dream, and I can't thank you enough.

Crystal. Oh, Crystal, yes you get your own section. #1 fan special treatment right here. You've become such a great friend over the years and though we have many miles separating us, we've grown close through our shared love of reading and writing. I can't thank you enough for the support you've shown- all the long talks about my fears of publishing, fangirling over my characters like I'm not the one who wrote them! You've easily become my first obsessed fan and I couldn't be happier and I hope to have more fans like you as Ivy's story continues.

Okay, publishing team, you're up next. To Coco for creating the amazing cover art and capturing my characters perfectly! To Franzi who did the book design, formatting, and those beautiful chapter page designs! To Sarah for your meticulous editing and patience when I edited my entire book in the wrong file (sorry). To Eris for your keen eye and talent. I can't thank all of you enough for your patience and support and hope to work with you all again in the future!

I'd also like to thank all the writers and authors who have helped me along the way. Thank you Liz for guiding me through how self-publishing works and not giving up when I asked way too many questions! To Corbin who got me out of a writing slump and spent many long nights discussing our books and futures. To every single person on Instagram who supported this book from the start and helped me promote it when you didn't have to, you are all amazing!

To my readers: It's still surreal to me that I'm an author and actually have people buying my book. Whether it was recommended, or an impulse buy or you just had nothing better to read (I hope not) thank you! I hope you all will continue on this journey with me. There are so many great stories and authors out there and I'm humbled that you chose my book to spend time with. Thank you so much!

For my husband Vaughan who not only helped me come up with the title but many aspects of the book. The biggest one being my character Ronin. If not for you and your (healthy?) obsession with anime, and storytelling I'm not sure that this character would have been fully rounded and I'm so thankful for all your help. You listened to my ideas, picked me up when I got rejected time and time again, and supported this dream when I decided to go off and publish this story myself. You made sure that I had time to write and kept my wine glass full as we sat and had long discussions about this book. You believed in me, made me laugh when I wanted to cry or rip my hair out, and kept me (mostly) sane through the entire process. Thank you pie for everything. I love you and hope you'll continue to help me with my future books. I'll bring the ideas, you bring the wine.

From the depths of my cold, black heart, thank you all so much!

## BRITTANY CZARNECKI

# ABOUT THE AUTHOR

Brittany Czarnecki is a first-time author from a small town in Massachusetts. She's a book nerd and only just started writing two years prior to publication and has since completed eight manuscripts. When she's not writing, she's earning her degree as an English major at MCLA. You can find her most nights with a glass of wine in hand, and her nose in a good book.